T0080060

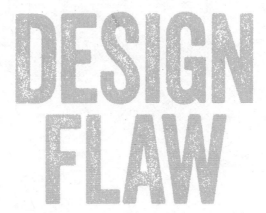

DESIGN
FLAW

HUGH SHEEHY

stories

ACRE
CINCINNATI 2022

Acre Books is made possible by the support of the Robert and Adele Schiff Foundation and the Department of English at the University of Cincinnati.

Designed by Barbara Neely Bourgoyne
Cover art: *Pico canicularis,* watercolor on paper by Daniel Bahena, reproduced with permission of the artist

ISBN-13 (pbk): 978-1-946724-55-7
ISBN-13 (ebook): 978-1-946724-56-4

The press is based at the University of Cincinnati, Department of English and Comparative Literature, Arts and Sciences Hall, Room 248, PO Box 210069, Cincinnati, OH, 45221–0069.
www.acre-books.com

Acre Books books may be purchased at a discount for educational use. For information please email business@acre-books.com.

For my parents,
Michael Sheehy and Sandra Barron Sheehy.

Fat monitored his own mind and found it defective. He then, by use of that mind, monitored outer reality, that which is called the macrocosm. He found it defective as well.

—PHILIP K. DICK, *VALIS*

CONTENTS

DESIGN FLAW

ESCHATOLOGY LTD.

HI THERE. Are you tired of death? Dying? Irrecoverable loss? Insurmountable grief? The rending of garments and the tearing of hair, the gnashing of teeth, etc.? Waking at night to ponder your own utterly inconceivable yet entirely imminent demise?

Well, we at Eschatology Ltd. hear you—you and people like you. We want to help, and that's why we're here today to talk to you about something we call the Spirit World.

What is the Spirit World? you ask.

It's simple: the Spirit World is the place we go when our bodies die, and it turns out that it's located right here, on top of this physical world.

What's that? You find that hard to imagine? That's because you can't see into the Spirit World—unless you're a spirit reading this, haha!—but the spirits there sure can see into this one. And wow, do they ever keep their eyes on us. Watching over us is their biggest pastime. That's right: there are no mysteries or secrets waiting for you on the other side of existence, only all the loved ones who've been missing you as much as you've missed them since the moment they let go of that last whistling breath. So cheer up, and don't sweat the death thing. However much life you have remaining, there's a big reunion party waiting at the end. Do us a favor: tell Uncle Howie we say *Hey*.

. . . .

HELLO AGAIN. Are you tired of hearing about the Spirit World? All that hocus pocus about immaterial beings hemming you in wherever you go? Have you had it with considering the possibility that your great-grandparents are looking on each time you notice a sexy stranger or use the toilet? Do you have doubts that Earth is destined to eventually become home to countless ghosts with nothing to do and no source of entertainment? Are you sick of shamans who spend all week getting high in the woods insisting that you listen to their drug stories? Are you disturbed by the apparent lack of justice for all that happens in the world you *can* see, feel, hear, taste, and smell?

If so, we at Eschatology Ltd. get it. We really do. The Spirit World ain't what it's cracked up to be, and if we're being completely transparent (figuratively speaking), it was just a prototype, a kind of rough draft we decided to run with while we came up with a better product. And we'd be lying if we said a few heads hadn't rolled since the Spirit World went live. Okay, more than a few. Our current team wants you to know we're grateful for your patience, and we're just as upset about all your ancestors who had to be put to death because they broke a rule some shaman made up after eating a fistful of datura seeds. That said, we are happy to report those people are now in Heaven.

That's right, Heaven! Heaven is a new development, one that has everyone here at Eschatology Ltd. over the moon, in a manner of speaking. Think of Heaven as a destination for all the good people. All the well-behaved, morally upright, heroic, generous, popular, wealthy, and physically attractive people go there once they die, and when they arrive, they have their bodies back and can do whatever they want to. Plus the experience of dying leaves all the Heaven-worthy people even more conscientious, charitable, and grateful than they were on Earth. Consequently, everyone in Heaven is extremely chilled out. It's basically a big resort, extremely live-and-let-live. Do a few people sleep around or occasionally snort a little cocaine? Probably, but what's the harm? Isn't it great to be alive? It goes without saying that the location of this place is top secret.

What happens to the people who don't get into Heaven? you ask.

As it turns out, there is a destination for them. It's called Hell. Also remotely located, the physical geography there consists of a flat, fiery plain stretching as far as the eye can see under a permanent night rent by crackling bolts of lightning. People who go to Hell find that their nerves are continuously regenerated, so that they experience the pain of burning to death without ever getting any relief. As to whether an individual's stay in Hell is permanent, the jury's out on that. But don't worry—sentencing is our job. You probably wouldn't know anybody there, anyhow. The place is full of murderers and thieves, people who worship the wrong gods or spend beyond their means or both, the acne-scarred, relatives you'd rather not think about, the weak-personal-hygiene crowd, and the folks who always say the wrong thing. You won't even notice they're missing.

. . . .

HI. THAT'S RIGHT, it's us again. Nice to see you. So, yeah. Heaven and Hell, not plausible. We should have seen this coming. What did we expect, that you'd buy the idea that all the good people go to live in a country club in the sky? While the impoverished, ugly, or psychologically disordered were sent to burn in a giant bonfire? Did we truly think you'd imagine separate worlds like this could exist in the absence of other alternatives? That you'd be comfortable with everyone born into a different religion being consigned to eternal suffering? That you'd fail to grasp that Heaven and Hell were basically the Spirit World all over again, only divided into a pair of dissimilar and noncontiguous continents? That you'd miss the emerging ideas in cognitive science and physics indicating human perceptions of the universe are delusions at every level? That you wouldn't catch the increasing evidence suggesting we're totally alone, existentially speaking, in our cluttered corner of space?

Yikes. You're right. Not a great look for us here at Eschatology Ltd. We are more than a little embarrassed. But maybe you'll let us explain.

When we came up with Heaven and Hell, we were under tremendous pressure. There was this whole set of revolutions taking place—agricultural, industrial, scientific, cultural. To say this made for fierce competition would be an understatement. Things were changing so quickly that, for a while, we thought we'd better sit back, let Heaven and Hell ride, and see how it all played out. Surely things will slow down, we thought. Well, no, you're right. Took the words right out of our mouths. They sure didn't slow down, and we've only recently started to think they never will.

We'll be honest with you. Some of us wanted to sell you the new Big Idea, the one where we solve the fear-of-death problem once and for all by taking death out of the equation. Let's call the proponents of this brave concept the Apotheosis Camp. They're a rowdy bunch. The only thing they agree on is what they want: immortality. How to achieve it, not so much. Some suggest gene splicing holds the key. Others argue we could all upload our consciousnesses into a big computer and simulate everlasting life—that's right, a kind of electronic, online Spirit World. Still others favor a middle-ground reincarnation program, engineered using a combination of advanced data applications and genetic manipulation. A few think organ replacements will do the trick, that we could just keep swapping out old parts until we're working with total rebuilds. We'll see. The various factions are still workshopping their ideas, and right now there's more speculation and imagination than cohesion and coherence. Truth be told, we at Eschatology Ltd. simply aren't comfortable bringing you Apotheosis on such shaky ground.

All this is to say: we were wrong. And we don't know. This leaves us in an awkward position with respect to fear-of-mortality mitigation. Not an easy thing to admit, mind you, considering we're in the fear-of-mortality-mitigation business. But we want you to know that we value your patronage. We'd like to keep you as a customer. We'd like to do better. It's with this in mind that we're bringing you this message: we've combed through the archives and sifted the data. We've test-run models based on concepts from other religions, ideas like samsara and immanent consciousness, and a few secular ones, including some frankly creepy Hegelian shit we'd rather not revisit. We've consulted all the latest science, and we've had long and painfully mathematical conversations about quantum mechanics that would make you regret ever wondering about the afterlife at all (though we are grateful you do, and always will be [we hope—haha!]).

What we've come up with, after much soul-searching (figuratively speaking, of course) and banging our heads against the wall (ditto), is this: Maybe.

That's right. *Maybe*. We can offer you Maybe.

Hold on. Don't go. Hear us out. We know it's not much, but it's not nothing, either. It might even be more than you think. Give Maybe a whirl. Take it for a test drive. Shape the word with your mouth. Say it. Out loud. *Maybe*. Maybe we don't die. See? Doesn't that feel good? Now repeat after me: Maybe there is no death. Maybe it only appears so. Maybe there is more beyond this Earthly life, and maybe the deceased subject discovers it upon the moment of expiration. Maybe they see something is there instead of nothing. Something like or unlike the world they left behind.

DESIGN FLAW

THAT MORNING, two police cars pulled up in front of the baby-blue colonial with the impressive flower garden. The name above the door, CHAMBERS, was familiar, though vaguely. David and I had lived on the block for years without ever becoming part of the neighborhood. The house and yard looked peaceful enough, and everybody was inside. Not my business and probably a faulty burglar alarm besides, so I jogged on through the fog. The worst I imagined was some aging homeowner had died in the night.

An hour later I was in the kitchen, eating a kind of health muffin while listening to news radio and answering emails on my phone. I was multitasking, as the business people say, which was probably, as the mindfulness people will tell you, a symptom of my problem. Possibly this state of diffuse, distributed consciousness was by design on my part. Or maybe it was how Bay Area people lived.

While I multitasked, I eavesdropped on David.

He was downstairs, feeding Alfie, and their voices drifted up through the open door.

Alfie was quoting Ecclesiastes in his warbling growl. Though he'd lived with us for more than a decade, there was still something uncanny about hearing an animal speak, and it caught me slightly off-guard. "Of making books there is no end," he was saying, "and much study wearies the body."

"Making books is what pays the bills," David said. There was a splatting sound of raw meat hitting the floor. "You should see the new

6

books. Books without pages. Books that read books. Books that write them. You believe that?"

"Belief," Alfie replied through a mouthful of beef, "is wanting not to know what is true."

"Always got to have the last word, don't you?"

I concentrated on my husband's voice, trying to gauge frequency and timbre, preparing myself for the sight of him, for while I'd grown weary of his cynicism, I continued to love the man and wanted our relationship to revert to a healthier state. David's depression had gotten severe, and things he used to say in sincere jest now came out performed and hollow, or worse, mordant and contemptuous, as if he hated the mind thinking his thoughts. Today he sounded a little better, I told myself. I was glad he planned to go in to the office. I was confident he'd feel better once he was out in the world, showered and shaved and smartly dressed.

Our neighbor Chuck rapped on the outer door, and I jumped.

Behind the screen, he was grinning. "Sorry, Natalie, didn't mean to startle you," he said, though he smirked like he had meant to, and I wondered how long he'd been watching me through the mesh.

"Hi there," I said, setting my phone down on the counter, keeping the gesture casual, neither raising nor lowering my voice. I maintained eye contact with Chuck, who had no way of seeing my palms sweating or detecting any of my other anatomical reactions to his presence. Downstairs, David was responding to the Kierkegaard Alfie had quoted. Seeing Chuck's eyes go to my chest, I put my hands on my hips and lowered my head. "What can we do for you?"

He let himself in, looking around at the '50s-style kitchen David and I had never bothered to update as if he were entering some pharaoh's tomb sealed for the last two thousand years. Chuck appeared to be headed to the gym, and his sleeveless shirt and running shorts showed his pumped-up arms and thighs. His hair, trimmed to a flattop, looked like a continuation of his short beard, and his richly tanned skin shone faintly, as if he'd oiled it. He was divorced, with a thirteen-year-old bully of son who biked around the neighborhood terrorizing animals. He made his money designing custom cars for tech millionaires. Parts of me couldn't believe I'd had sex with Chuck, and parts of me knew exactly why I had.

"You hear about the cat?"

I must have looked as confused as I felt.

"The Chambers's cat? Freckles?" he said. "They found his head on the front of their car. Stuck on the bonnet."

The image was so unexpected that I cursed. I supposed this explained the police presence.

Chuck squeezed his face into an expression of sympathetic disgust. "I know. Right?" He came further into the kitchen and stopped on the other side of the island, crossing his arms like some kind of gearhead genie. "Who does that?"

Your kid, probably, I thought, though I didn't say this. To hear Chuck tell it, Charles Jr. was as blameless in puberty as he'd been the day he was born. I'd seen the kid out back with his pellet gun, felling birds and taking potshots at squirrels and cats, and I might have said so if I hadn't learned from regrettable experience that Chuck interpreted pushback from me as flirtation.

Alfie stepped through the basement doorway, his unblinking eyes staring everywhere, it seemed, at once. He was dressed in a baggy black long-tailed suit that hung loosely on his forty-inch frame. With his large, black-furred, quasi-feline head protruding from the collar and his hairy monkey hands hanging from the sleeves, he resembled nothing so much as a tiny Mr. Hyde. "Send not to know for whom the bell tolls," he mewled. "It tolls for thee."

It was Chuck's turn to be surprised. David had probably set it up that way. He always knew more than he let on. I could see no other reason he'd send Alfie upstairs dressed like that. He'd picked up the outfit at a Goodwill eight years ago, in happier times, for a house party we were throwing. He hadn't put it on Alfie since, and I'd forgotten we had it. Usually we let the grot run naked.

Chuck backed away a few steps. "It wears clothes?"

I couldn't stop myself from letting out a laugh.

The designer animal continued on past Chuck, used to humans and unthreatened by them even when they were startled. He headed up the hall to the front room, where he would assume his usual perch in the bay window that looked out on our tree-shaded front lawn, to pass the rest of the morning watching the birds he instinctively wished to hunt and mumbling a random mixture of the quotations David had taught him.

"Fuck me." Chuck watched the little biped shuffle away. "I don't know how the fuck you live with that thing."

I shrugged. He'd said this to me before. "What did you need again?"

Chuck looked toward the basement steps. My husband was there now, tall and silent and full of gloom. He was dressed for work in his usual programmer's clothes, a loose button-down and jeans, and the glasses he wore when he didn't feel up to dealing with contacts. He put his large soft hands in his pockets and stood there, elbows sticking out shyly, as if by not moving he might blend in with the background.

"Hey, David," Chuck said quickly, blushing hard, intimidated by something in my gentle husband, height or intellect or some other quality that stood out to men. "I just stopped over to tell you guys about Freckles. You know, the cat?"

David blinked and said nothing. He had not looked at me since coming upstairs.

He knows about Chuck, I thought, not for the first time. I was feeling confident in this theory. The question now was whether he'd tried to arrange it. "Somebody killed it and dismembered the body," I said. "Put the head on their car."

"Like some kind of Mad Max hood ornament," Chuck said, excited to have someone new to tell.

David faced me, his brows lifting ever so slightly as he took this in. As usual, he avoided more than momentary eye contact. "Oh," he said, unable to hide how much he didn't care. "Well, nothing to do about it now."

Chuck glanced around uneasily. "Thing is, Chambers thinks it was Alfie."

"What?" I said, stiffening.

He was staring at the floor. "It's not just them. A lot of people think that."

In a flash, I went from feeling alarmed to burning with righteous anger. "Why would they blame us?"

He explained that eight or nine neighborhood pets had been killed

9

in the past few weeks, cats and small dogs alike. They turned up in swimming pools and on front steps, still leashed in backyards, their bodies broken and ripped apart.

"It couldn't be Alfie." I'd never wanted the grot, or any pet, but that didn't mean I'd fork him over to an angry mob. "He stays in the house. He spends most of the time in his cage downstairs. They can come and see for themselves."

Chuck held out his hands. "Hey, I'm just the messenger. I thought you knew about the other pets."

David narrowed his eyes. "Why would we?"

Chuck scowled at both of us and shook his head. Once again, we were the flaky, self-involved couple next door. "Everybody's talking about it. There's a neighborhood watch forming. Charles Jr.'s even patrolling with one with his buddies."

"Neighborhood watch?" I said, remembering certain details of the sex I'd had with this moron, things he'd shouted, encouragement I'd given. I shuddered with self-disgust. I needed to get out of the suburbs. "What are they watching for, exactly?"

"I don't know," Chuck said. "Anything suspicious. Somebody. Or some*thing.*"

. . . .

WHEN DAVID had brought Alfie home, he was still a grotlet.

It was a different time for us. We had bought a three-bedroom house for next to nothing and were planning our wedding. I had joined a consulting firm in the burgeoning reputation-management industry. My job, which I had invented and pitched to my employer, involved anticipating how emerging cultural trends might alter public perceptions of social media profiles and brands. Somehow, my firm thought it was a real thing to do. They paid me a lot to do it. It was like I was living in a happy dream where I said things and they became real, and I traveled up and down the coast, helping high-level managers and companies head off potential PR crises. David was busy, too, having launched an educational software company on the strength of a program he designed that could increase an average user's Spanish vocabulary by five hundred percent in three one-hour sittings. The program involved a video game in which players learned vocabulary words to get weapons and fight monsters. Children loved it so much, they didn't realize they were learning. David was good at tricking people like that.

One evening, just after our move, I came in a little drunk from happy hour with colleagues. It was early, and I was thinking we should go out and drink more. We were in the process of unpacking, and open boxes lay everywhere. I found David sitting in the middle of the kitchen with his legs spread wide. He was drinking a beer and rubbing the furry belly of what I took to be a black cat.

"What did you do?" I said, playfully but also seriously. I wasn't ready for a cat. I hated taking care of things and wasn't about to let anybody, not even David, spoil my freedom with some needy new responsibility.

At the sound of my voice, the animal flipped over onto all fours, rose to a squat like a spider monkey, and clambered up David's torso onto his shoulders. It clung to his head with slender primate fingers and watched me with yellow-green cat's eyes. Its face was like a cat's, too, but slightly longer, and with longer teeth. As David reached up, laughing, and tried to pry the thing off, I realized it was wearing a disposable diaper.

"What the fuck is that?" I asked, though I knew. We had talked about grots on multiple occasions, though always, I thought, in passing, agreeing the methods used to create them were ethically questionable at best. "When is it going home?"

"You get one chance to answer that question," he said. "And zero points for guessing correctly."

It took him a while to convince me to let it stay. He swore he'd take care of it and ensure it had everything it needed, including the proper cage and gym he'd planned to put in the finished basement. Since we'd decided against having kids, we had too much space, he argued, and the basement was likely to be the most neglected room in the house.

"Consider him a rescue, Nat," he said.

We were still in the kitchen. Enough time had gone by for us to cover the island with empty beer bottles. All the while, the grot was on David's shoulders or head, except for the few moments he put the little thing down on the counter where we chopped vegetables and, to my horror, changed its dirty diaper. Both of them remained calm throughout this process, as though they were on the same wavelength.

"They were going to euthanize him. He's sterile, so he can't reproduce. We're not supporting the company."

"They tanked last month," I reminded him. "For good reason. The world doesn't need designer animals."

"And yet here this one is," he said, pulling the grotlet out of his hair and cuddling it. It grabbed his fingers with its tiny agile hands and bit into his knuckle. He forced a smile, though he was bleeding a little. "What are we supposed to do with this little dude? Put him out on the street? Have him put down?"

Yes, I was thinking, maybe a little coldly. *He shouldn't exist in the first place.*

"In the whole history of the universe, there has never been a being like this one," he said. "I'm not ready to put that light out."

I could understand that. Just not why we had to be the ones to keep it on.

In the past, David had always deferred to my preferences when we disagreed about a big decision, but now he was insistent. He was telling me that he had made a choice to nurture this thing, and he hoped I would be willing to put up with them both. It was a new rhetorical approach from him, one I could not have predicted, and I both respected and despised him for it. I wondered if he'd been saving it for a moment like this.

"Whatever," I said finally. "I don't want him in our bed. And I'm not picking up any poop. Also, if he's part monkey, won't he masturbate?"

David started to remove the diaper, but I stopped him with a hand. "The previous owner took care of that," he said. "And he's already accustomed to sleeping alone. Just think: in a year or so, he'll start talking to us. Not like a parrot, either. He'll engage in full-blown discourse. It's going to be like having a live muppet."

"Great," I said. "Just what every girl wants. Oscar the Grouch downstairs. What are we going to call this little freak of nature?"

"Alfie," he said. "He's just like in the old TV show, but more perfect."

. . . .

I FORGOT about the neighbors' pets shortly after Chuck left and didn't think of them again until a few evenings later, when two police officers rang the doorbell. A tall, heavyset man and a short, tough-looking woman asked if they could have a word with David and me about the grot we allegedly owned.

"Allegedly?" I said.

The police both stared at me.

"Does this have something to do with the dead cat? Freckles?"

I was a little out of breath and sweaty. I had been on the treadmill in the bedroom we'd converted into an exercise space. David was in his office with Guided by Voices turned way up on his speakers, working on an update for the AI he'd designed for a social media giant to recognize images that violated their terms of use policies and block them with baby animal GIFs. Alfie was downstairs in his cell, probably swinging around on the bars David had installed so the grot could indulge his climbing instincts.

"No cat, ma'am," the woman cop said. "We're here about a dog that lived a couple of houses down. A cocker spaniel named Elizabeth."

I was familiar with this one, having seen its owners walk it on the street in the evening. It was also the same animal I'd seen Charles Jr. teasing and harassing on a few occasions. I wondered if the police had met Chuck and his son. "What happened?"

The male cop frowned and said, "The owners left her out by accident last night. When the wife remembered they hadn't brought her in, she found her in the backyard. It looked like something pretty big or strong got hold of her. Broke her neck and took a big chunk out of her belly."

"We don't know anything about that," I said, hoping to nip this in the bud. "Our grot hasn't left the house since the last time my husband took him to the vet. It's been months."

Out on the street, Charles Jr. rolled by on his stunt bike, studying first the police cruiser parked at the curb and then the pair of officers on my front porch. His dark little eyes found mine, and he started to smile, as if he knew a nasty secret about me.

I might have said something then, pointed at the boy and suggested the cops question him, but I wanted to avoid any further entanglement with Chuck. "Sorry we can't help," I said.

"We understand, miss," the big guy said, making his eyes large and sympathetic. "We don't want you to think we're jumping to conclusions. But these pet killings have been excessively gruesome, and people around here are pretty bent out of shape. You and your husband are the only ones in the neighborhood registered as owning an alpha predator—"

I laughed. "An *alpha predator*?" It came out more condescendingly than I'd intended.

The cop resumed where he'd left off. "The only ones who own an alpha predator, and we'd prefer to set your neighbors' minds at ease by paying a visit and making sure everything is in order."

David joined me at the door, towering and demure looking in his glasses, hesitating before he offered to shake hands. He looked like shit, in need of a shave and wearing week-old clothes. Somehow his presence still had a calming effect on our guests. It was annoying.

"I have all the paperwork from when I adopted him," he said. "You're welcome to come in and take a look at Alfie. He's usually exercising at this hour."

Down in the basement, the officers stood rapt at the spectacle of Alfie bounding around in his cage like some kind furry gymnast. David had paid big money to install a wall of steel bars, effectively turning the basement into a jail cell. Twelve hundred square feet and fifteen feet high, the cage contained a dozen gymnastics bars of varying heights, an exposed bathroom, and the large pet bed where Alfie slept each night. Excited to have an audience, the grot leapt up and grasped a bar and swung all the way around it, then dropped to his feet and came to the locked cage door. "Talk of the devil," he said, "and see his horns."

The woman cop looked at me. "He understands English?"

"The man who is born into existence deals first with language," Alfie said. "This is a given. He is even caught in it before his birth."

The big policeman shook his head. "This thing sounds smarter than me."

"It doesn't mean anything to him," I said.

14

David leaned on the cage, his forehead resting on a horizontal bar. "Or we think it doesn't."

"So it's like a parrot?" the woman said.

"Not really." I sighed, preparing to explain what took so many words, most listeners lost interest before you were halfway through. "It's complicated. Parrots can actually sort of learn human language. Grots are better mimics, but they quote by sound association. To them, it's like saying 'blah blah blah,' only more nuanced. Anyway, that's what we think is going on."

The police were looking at David for confirmation, which was typical and infuriating.

He stared back blankly, still leaning against the cage. "She's right," he said. "There's a seeming randomness to it, but it's almost algorithmic."

"Huh," said the woman. "I'm guessing you guys are in tech."

David smiled joylessly.

"Pretty creepy if you ask me," the big guy said. "So you don't know what this thing is thinking."

"No more than you know what your cat or dog is thinking," I said. "You know, in reality."

The officers both focused on me for a moment.

"Fair point," the big one said.

At the door, the woman asked if we were sure Alfie had no way of escaping his cage, though she asked in an uninspired way, like a high school student instructed to read aloud in English class. When we told her we were sure, she nodded, then looked at her partner, who shrugged.

"Could be a mountain lion," David told them as they turned to go.

They paused and looked back, making skeptical faces.

"They're indigenous," he observed.

Beyond the police, in the semi-darkness, Charles Jr. and two other boys his age straddled their bikes, watching us.

"That's true," the big cop said. "But nobody's seen one here in decades. Not likely."

"But possible," I said.

The policeman seemed about to say something more, then lowered his eyes, as if to look into the basement where Alfie was still locked up. "But possible," he conceded.

. . . .

IT'S DIFFICULT to say what went wrong in our marriage. There wasn't one big event. Our careers seemed headed one way, then turned and went another. Not a single trajectory proved predictable, with the exception of the money, which kept spilling in. We had stumbled into success early, but oddly, as our wealth increased, David abandoned his own projects for corporate ones. I, meanwhile, relinquished my role as a trend-predicting guru so that I could oversee the younger people who were better at it than I was. Alfie never quite became the companion David had predicted, but rather grew into an adult animal without a peer, a singular eccentric consciousness persisting under our roof without ever connecting with us the way a dog or a cat might have. He'd look up at you puppyishly, or close his eyes when you scratched behind his ears, but then he would speak in his detached way, clearly not understanding the words that issued from his cat's mouth, and you'd know there was something foreign in his mind, something unrecognizable. It would have been interesting to get him together with another of his species, but when we looked online, the closest we could find was hundreds of miles away, and the owner seemed a little bonkers, wearing a *Grot Mom* t-shirt in her profile pic, hugging a terribly obese grot dressed like a cowboy. Most of the other grots were dead by then, though sometimes one turned up in the news, usually for something bad, like attacking a mail carrier or a Jehovah's Witness. There were stories from Florida and Louisiana about sightings in the wild, but these were never substantiated.

David became disappointed, and then unhappy, growing ever more distant. It had been a few years now since he started having spells of prolonged depression. He would put on weight, stop taking care of himself and cleaning up his own messes, and he ignored me when I tried to get him to talk. He would let Alfie out of his cage and hang out in the front room, wearing the same dowdy sweatpants for days, laptop open on his thighs, the screen gone dark, while the grot randomly quoted from famous books.

He never completely recovered from these low periods, and he had little to say about them after he did get his act back together. He went to therapy and tried different drugs, but in the end he rejected these treatments. He decided there was nothing to be done. "Something is wrong with the world," he told me. "A design flaw. It's so thoroughly corrupted, I'm not sure how to fix it."

I agreed with him. Something was wrong, but it was impossible to say what. By all indicators, we should have been happy. We were wealthy and privileged, surrounded by interesting people. We lived in a city with outstanding property values and amenities. We were relatively young—and healthy, too, according to the vital statistics we tracked with our devices. Though it wasn't my personal thing, we owned an exceptional pet. But something was off.

Maybe it was us, our marriage. Maybe we were too familiar to each other. David thought so, anyway. He confessed this one evening, out of the blue, while standing in the basement and lobbing little cubes of steak through Alfie's bars. He'd teased the grot into a frenzy and had Alfie bouncing on all fours, leaping up to catch each scrap as it flew through the air. David's face registered no feeling as he flung each piece and watched Alfie go up and down. "You're not as excited about me as you used to be," he said. "You know me too well. It's not a solvable issue. We can't become strangers to each other again. We can't get that excitement back."

"We're not the first couple to face this problem," I said, a little drily.

But he wouldn't talk to me after that, not that night or the next week, during which he holed up in his office, emerging only to get something from the refrigerator or to go downstairs to Alfie.

I never planned to have sex with Chuck. I can't say I ever even wished to, though of course I was aware of how he looked at me. He was everything I despised in men: vain, tacky, simpleminded, and coarse. But he was available, just outside my door the morning I reached my breaking point. I'd woken up to find David gone, and when I called him in a panic, terrified that he might have done something to himself, he didn't answer the phone, and let an hour pass before texting that he was on his way to Seattle to meet a potential client and would see me in a few days. *Besos*, he signed off, as if everything between us were normal.

When I stopped shouting and crying, I looked out the window and saw Chuck kneeling in his driveway, his stupid muscles shining in the sun as he fitted a wheel onto an aerodynamic-looking car, and I knew what I was going to do. As for the seduction itself, there was nothing to it. He was more than willing when I asked if he would help me out with something. The sex was more exciting than any I'd had with David, who represented every quality I found appealing in a man. It had nothing to do with either man's performance or body or any of the other things to which Chuck would surely have attributed my excitement. It was excitement with taking a risk, feeling alive in a way I hadn't in years.

Afterward I made Chuck leave and then washed everything, the bedclothes and my own clothes, and took a long shower. I felt a bewildering combination of pride and vindication and guilt, and I was desperate to clean the house and run errands and check my work email, to do the things I knew were constructive and ordinary and to keep at them until the bad feeling abated. I went downstairs to feed Alfie, who promptly told me, "Where id is, there shall ego be."

"Thanks, Alfie," I said, tossing an unopened package of steak through the bars.

It wasn't until evening that it occurred to me David might know what I'd do in his absence, under a certain amount of duress—that he might attempt to change our lives in this way without telling me. I knew couples who slept with other people. Some of the women talked about the awkward double dates, the eccentric strangers, the odd rules and coded language, all the discomfort they tolerated in the pursuit of fresh erotic thrills. I didn't want to live like that, and I doubted David did. Maybe, I thought, he wanted something else, an excuse to leave because he didn't have the nerve to dump me.

I went upstairs and had a drink, supposing I would remember this as the moment I started distrusting my husband. I couldn't be sure he'd set me up, but he was always setting people up, and I had difficulty believing the chain of events leading to my infidelity was any different.

. . . .

THE POLICE didn't come back, and our days and nights resumed their usual hectic character. I woke early and went to my office and had dinner and drinks with colleagues. David stayed up all night, working on his latest projects, coming and going without bothering to tell me what he was up to. Of course, he took care of Alfie, and when I checked in on the grot, he was his usual self, part body and part dream. One moment he'd be lounging by the bay window, hungrily watching magpies in the branches of the oak in our front yard, the next down in the basement, exercising vigorously in his locked cell.

I began going for runs in the evening, getting out of the house to clear my mind. I wanted to confront David about the state of our relationship and his behavior over the past few years, but I needed to muster the courage to tell him about Chuck. When I imagined this scenario, I had a visceral reaction, breaking into a walk and putting my hands on my side as I panted, "God, why?" or "Oh, fuck you."

On one such occasion, I became aware as I was muttering obscenities that I had company. I had reached the place where one street ended at an intersection. The streetlamps had come on, and all down the block, the windows of the houses were bright. I heard a whirring sound and looked back to see Charles Jr. behind me, coasting along on his bike. His soft little face was grinning proudly, and he wore a black tank top featuring an image of some manly, shining pickup truck framed by jagged red words. It struck me that when he finished growing, he would look just like his father.

"Who are you talking to?" he asked.

"I don't know what you mean," I said. I owed no explanations to this horrible boy.

"I just heard you cuss." He smiled up with the smug confidence of a child who has never questioned his perceptions, for whom the world remained a simple place. "You're not wearing earbuds, so you're not on the phone. Who were you talking to?"

"I think you're hearing things," I said. "Maybe you should get that checked out. Anyway, I've got to finish this run."

He snorted, pedaling a couple of times to keep pace with me. "Your pet killed the Mitchells' chihuahua, you know."

"There's another dead dog?" I said, then cursed myself for rising to the bait.

His grin widened, as if I'd just confirmed something he'd heard about me. It was easy to imagine Chuck bad-mouthing me to his son without ever revealing his motivation for doing so. "Maybe if you thought about someone other than yourself, you'd know what was going on around here. Everybody thinks you guys are way up your own asses."

The fact that he was clearly quoting his father made me laugh, and in response he frowned, looking frustrated, which only made me laugh harder. I slowed and gave him a skeptical look. "And how do I know you aren't the one who's been killing these animals? I've seen you shooting your stupid little gun at birds."

He skidded to a sideways stop and squished his face up. "It's totally normal for boys to shoot birds in their yards. Who are you, the feds?"

I gave him my best fuck-you smile. "I remember at least one occasion when I saw you shoot a cat. It was a gray Himalayan, and it ran right out of your yard. This was last summer."

Charles Jr.'s face drained of color. "You saw that?" he said, suddenly looking as though he would cry. "I didn't think I would hit her. She's the only one. You won't tell, will you?"

I was unconvinced by his emotional display. "Why would I?" I said. "It's not like I have proof. Just like there's no proof Alfie did anything wrong."

He reached into the pocket of his baggy denim shorts and pulled out a smartphone. "I have a video to show you," he said softly. When he looked up, his eyes were shining. "You know, that cat I shot is dead, too. I'm pretty sure Alfie got her."

. . . .

THE TV SHOW *ALF* ran in the late 1980s. It was about a furry orange alien who briefly lived with a human family, the Tanners. While ALF had relationships with each of them, the show was really about his connection with Willie, the father, for whom ALF acted as a kind of alter ego, a living demonstration of why the head of a household must control his or her most destructive impulses. The show was interesting conceptually, but it wasn't very fun to watch. Not that Alfie would have understood that, even if he had liked watching TV. On the occasions that David streamed it for him, supposedly for the animal to see the alien, it was David who became happy each time the puppet appeared onscreen.

"See?" he said once. "His name is ALF, a lot like yours."

"What's in a name?" Alfie said, indifferent to the moving images on the screen a few feet away.

"It was worth a try," David would tell him. "Wouldn't you agree?"

"Ever tried," Alfie said. "Ever failed."

Not long before I left David, I asked why he let Alfie out all those nights, knowing what the grot would likely do when loose in the neighborhood. "You're the one who's always talking about flawed design," I said. "Why would you set up something to go terribly wrong?"

"I wanted to give things a chance to run their course. Without interference," he said. "You ever think that might be how it's supposed to go? That we're all just holding back from what we could be, and maybe that's the source of our trouble?"

Saying no more, he turned and went into the next room to be alone. That was fine, though. I'd heard enough.

. . . .

THE LAWS governing the ownership of a grot were vague, and in the end, the police charged David with reckless endangerment and revoked the license he'd purchased years earlier when he adopted Alfie. Some of the neighbors sued him for various things. I'm not sure how those actions all played out, though I imagine David had to cough up some money. It was a minor detail. Money was the least of his problems. Everyone appeared to believe me about not knowing my husband had been setting Alfie free at night to wreak havoc, and it probably helped that I moved out around the same time the police saw the video of the grot leaving through our back door, crossing Chuck's yard to climb a tree, and disappearing into the dark upper branches.

Alfie was put down, of course. Because of all the dead pets and the furious neighbors, the police forbade David to leave the premises with him, and he had to pay the veterinarian to come to the house. I agreed to be present when it happened, concerned that my soon-to-be-ex-husband would react poorly to having indirectly caused the death of this animal that he'd once felt so strongly about caring for.

To my surprise, David was nowhere to be seen when I arrived. Chuck was out in his driveway, talking to the police officer who had come to witness the grot's death. It was the big guy who had paid a visit some weeks before, and the two men were talking about the sea-green hot rod Chuck was polishing with a soft rag. The vet, a woman in her sixties with a long gray ponytail, was waiting by the front door in a pale green scrub shirt and jeans. She carried a black medical case that contained, I assumed, everything she'd need to kill Alfie.

"This is a little awkward," I said as I unlocked the front door. "I moved out two weeks ago, and I haven't been back, so I don't know what's been going on in here."

Her smile said she'd seen it all before, had saved and put down animals for every possible configuration of human family. "I'm sorry," she offered. "Sometimes animals bring out the worst in people."

I nodded at the officer and ignored Chuck, who was moving his head back and forth, trying to catch my eye. Opening the door, I worried we'd find something terrible inside, like Alfie shot to death or poisoned or David hanging from a rope. Or that neither of them would be there, that David had spirited the grot away to the wildlands and set him free to wander the coastal forest for the rest of his days. For a moment, anything seemed possible.

"Hello," I called into the dark house, doing my best to appear calm in front of the policeman and vet, though both of them were looking around anxiously. When there was no reply, I shrugged and gestured for them to follow me inside.

The place was trashed, but no more so than it would have been after I'd been out of town for a couple of weeks on a job. Empty takeout containers littered the kitchen, and there were flies and garbage all over, but I could see David was keeping himself going. The fact that he was out of the house told me he wasn't done living yet. That was a small relief, knowing I was not the cause of whatever harm he did to himself in the future.

In the basement, we found Alfie sitting on his bed, clearly waiting for someone to come down and let him out. He was dressed in his little suit, the long-tailed jacket and baggy pants, and it was tempting to imagine him donning them before he committed his crimes against the pets of the neighborhood, cleaning himself afterward in birdbaths and swimming pools, as if he were a misguided soul and not just some botched creation summoned to life by human tinkering. I knew, though, that the suit was David's doing. It was petty of him to humanize the grot further, a last swipe at those of us he'd left to clean up his mess.

The veterinarian reached into her bag to withdraw a kit of hypodermic needles. As I opened the cage, Alfie sprang to his feet, and the others grew tense, preparing to defend themselves in the event the so-called alpha predator became hostile. Alfie took no notice of their alarm, hurrying to me with the expectation I'd brought him breakfast, which I had—a clutch of meat sticks I'd picked up from a gas station on the way over.

He crouched at my feet, artfully peeling back greasy cellophane and stuffing the long cylinders into his mouth. The doctor and the cop stood back patiently, waiting for him to finish. The whole time I was talking, saying what people say to soothe a pet in a stressful stretch. Alfie appeared unaware as he ate, and I took comfort in this, though later I realized I was looking at us the wrong way. The truth is, he probably did hear my jumbled words, the way he always had, and knew all along they weren't for him.

REST AREA

AROUND 1:00 A.M., Jeremy completed the walkthroughs and hung the clipboard on the screw threaded incompletely into the cinderblock wall. The snow was melting as it fell, sleeting out of the sky in globs that streaked slowly down the windows. No one had been in since the woman with the stumbling, half-awake boy complaining loudly that he had to pee. She waited at the counter, mixing creamer into a cup of complimentary coffee and digging suggestively in her purse without ever touching the donations can. Not that Jeremy cared. She had been kind—a surprise given her gaudy makeup and elaborate hair, her slinky leather jacket with fake fur trim. People who worked so hard on their appearances rarely acknowledged him, but she had, peering over the carafe to say it was nice, this practice of serving fresh coffee on cold nights, and he'd said to tell the Department of Transportation; heck, they probably saved money, keeping drivers sharp. She'd smiled at the pop song issuing from his small red radio and said this seemed like a nice state, much nicer than the one she was from, where the few troopers on salary cared more about giving out tickets than keeping people safe. That moved Jeremy to nod, for he believed this state was one of the country's last bastions of civility, and he was primed to warn her the roads would freeze by dawn, but then her boy wandered out drying his hands on his coat, and she became a mother again and forgot Jeremy, not so much as saying goodbye as she herded the child into the falling snow, toward the red minivan with a screen of translucent slush already covering its windshield. Moments later, the headlights flashed on, the wipers heaved off the accumulation, and then they were gone.

He missed them a little, the way he missed all late-night guests once they left, no matter how rude and noisy they might have been, though most were courteous, even chummy, glad to see a gentle face after hours of driving in the dark woods. He hoped the woman and her son would quickly reach their destination, though his gut told him they were in for an all-nighter. Families who came through at night were usually in trouble, running from something or to someplace. This route was lightly traveled after sunset, and apart from truckers and state police, the people who stopped during the small hours seemed adrift.

Beside his personal red radio, the black police walkie-talkie stood in its dock, silent and charged. The station's night DJ reached the end of the rotation—they played about forty songs—and started from the top. The lamps along the long, narrow parking area showed mounds of frozen mush on the sidewalks. Jeremy pulled on his parka, reluctant to go out but also grateful for the chore. He trudged into the weather, blinking at the wet particles blowing into his eyes and nose and thawing and refreezing in his beard. At the end of the sidewalk, the salt hut loomed, dark and bullet-shaped on the white hill.

At this time of night not two years ago, Ashley would have been back at home, nodding off in front of the TV, waking hours later when he walked in to take her to breakfast. He thought of Patrick Maloney, probably asleep and somehow gloating, as if even incarcerated he'd gotten one over on Jeremy. Jeremy knew it wasn't like that, and that most likely Maloney, a confused young dishwasher, had stupidly made a series of bad choices one night, starting with the decision to follow a cute older waitress home. Most likely, Jeremy had never entered the shifty-eyed boy's thoughts until they saw each other under the courtroom's fluorescent lights. The boy had looked away immediately, rarely glancing at Jeremy afterward.

It had been a strange trial, and at times jurors and even the judge appeared sympathetic to Maloney, as if he were the heartbroken boyfriend and Jeremy, sitting out in the gallery among the spectators, were the monster. Maloney wept often during the proceedings, and he had declined to speak before the judge passed sentence. Jeremy knew Maloney must regret what he had done, that the kid probably suffered from depression and suicidal thoughts. In the year or so following the trial, Jeremy had read a lot of books about victims and violence. *It becomes necessary to kill the figure of the past self*, one book said. *Only once the former identity is imagined purged is "rebirth" possible. Many subjects adopt a "born again" narrative, though the memory of the crime remains close. As many as three-fifths of murderers do not progress from this state of affairs.*

He'd thought studying this stuff would help, and for a while it seemed to. It was a little relieving to imagine Maloney feeling guilt. Recently, though, Jeremy found himself wishing the worst on the guy, not just the standard rape-and-beatdown prison clichés, but other things, torture scenes he would never admit to dreaming up. He blinked away a burning in his eyes, took a breath of the bracing air, then picked up his pace, pulling boots from sucking slush.

· · · ·

HE'D SEEN a therapist that whole first year, under what amounted to threat of termination if he didn't, something he understood later, when he was clearheaded enough to see how the incident with Ashley had frightened his boss. After the murder, the fidgety gray-haired man never lingered at the rest area past sundown, as if some lycanthropic transformation might come over Jeremy once darkness fell over the surrounding woods and mountains. Jeremy had inwardly laughed at the man's anxiety, fought the impulse to smirk at the monthly meetings, where his boss changed the subject when he came in—switching from traffic fatalities to the state's initiative to seed wildflowers in the medians, as if he'd trigger Jeremy by talking about death.

Therapy had been effective. He'd learned some things, like *victims' families report higher levels of well-being once they have come to see the transgressions against their loved ones as impersonal events, incidental in spacetime.* He had stopped wishing so hard for revenge, not just because it was impossible, blocked off by a prison filled with guards, but because those fantasies ate up time he could spend remembering Ashley. When he told the therapist he felt out of place in her waiting room, that the neatly dressed children sitting out there with their mom looked at him like a fairy-tale woodcutter who'd taken a wrong turn,

26

she had risen to her feet, crossed the room and, smelling of musky and probably expensive perfume, gathered him in her long, hard arms. He was stunned by the gesture, but more so by how welcome he found it, by how easily he had surrendered to the urge to weep.

. . . .

HE CAME IN, hair and beard wet, and grinned at the tall, lanky figure standing by the coffee carafe. The man pinched a packet of sugar between stained fingers and shook grains into his styrofoam cup, careful to not spill on his stretched-out longjohn shirt. He turned a bland face and looked at Jeremy with dull intensity.

Jeremy let out a low chuckle, as if there were a joke between them. "Hey there, Damon. Where you headed tonight?"

The trucker reached for the can of nondairy creamer, saying, "All the way up. Land of ice and snow."

"Anything interesting out there, man?"

Damon shrugged his high, narrow shoulders and poured more powder. He had dropped the empty sugar packet on the table where someone else—Jeremy, probably—would have to clean it up later. As if oblivious to this fact, Damon plucked a red straw from the wicker basket beside the sugar and sweetener packets and stirred his cup. "Televisions. Flatscreen." He blinked, appearing thoughtful. "Guess they all are now."

Jeremy stamped his feet and wrung softly electrified sensations back into his hands. He'd been intending to make a fresh pot of coffee until Damon dropped his trash. Now he would wait until the guy left. In the years Jeremy had known the trucker, Damon was always doing little things like that, tracking in mud or leaving crumpled paper on the floor, and while Jeremy had accepted this was garden-variety negligence, he nursed the tiniest suspicion that Damon was flaunting how little he cared about Jeremy's opinion of him. Now, as ever, Jeremy went past the trucker, around the shelves of ads for area attractions, and pulled off his coat. He turned down the squawking radio. "Come on, man. Can't be that dead out there. What's the word?"

"Just fixing to take a nap. Accident up the way, maybe a hundred miles. Got the road closed. Might as well use the time."

Before he could ask if Damon always drank coffee before going to sleep, the thought of the woman and the boy from earlier leapt into his mind. "You know the vehicles involved?"

"Minivan and a rig."

He held his breath and then sighed, feeling slightly sick to his stomach. "Any fatalities?"

"At least one, from the sound of it." Damon looked into his coffee as he stirred. He nodded toward the walkie-talkie on the battered wooden desk. "One of the drivers."

Jeremy turned off the radio and cranked up the volume on the police unit, making himself still as he listened to the voices forming out of the static, speaking codes and other jargon. He picked up the words *female, early thirties* and *male, age ten* and *ambulance is en route*, then *adult male, deceased*. When he glanced up, Damon had turned to watch the snow falling on his truck, which was parked down at the end of the lot. It was his habit to park there, far out of the way, which would have made sense at a crowded stop, but not here, and especially not tonight. He seemed to be studying his rig as though concerned, and Jeremy wondered if he had a woman out there, one of the prostitutes truckers called *lot lizards*, or maybe some hitchhiker he'd picked up. Strange things happened on the road, and Jeremy had heard about them from drivers and cops. None of it was his concern, but it was horribly tantalizing and disturbing listening to the descriptions of some atrocity or thrill, not to mention seeing the MISSING posters of mostly girls' faces inside the glass case on the wall.

But Damon's air of preoccupation tonight was probably all in Jeremy's head. The trucker had been stopping in for more than a decade. He was eccentric, but so were most guys who spent their conscious hours driving enormous vehicles back and forth at high speeds. It would have been more suspicious if Damon seemed normal. And in the months following Ashley's death, he'd proven himself to be a good guy overall, doing things for Jeremy like bringing bottles of Canadian whiskey and sitting here, keeping Jeremy company when he should have been back on the road. Small gestures like that made a world of difference. He remembered that *the bereaved show improvement when exposed to a community.*

He spoke to Damon's back. "They were in here earlier, I'm pretty sure. The lady and her son."

The trucker nodded slowly, then raised his coffee and drained it in a single gulp. "Guess I better get out there." He looked back at Jeremy, then said in his monotonous voice, "It's good seeing you."

"You, too, man."

"It's like I always know when you'll be here."

"Probably because I'm always here," Jeremy said, laughing.

"Not always," Damon said. "You think the ground will freeze tonight?"

Listening to the chatter on the radio, hoping to hear something about the conditions of the survivors, Jeremy recalled the details of the weather forecast automatically, saying, "Not till tomorrow. That's when the real cold's coming. It's going to blow through and turn all of this to ice."

"That's what I'm afraid of."

Jeremy watched Damon drift through the wintry mix, shrinking as he approached the dark truck until he was no more than a tiny silhouette making its way around the enormous tractor trailer. Yeah, Damon was a funny bird, but he'd been there when no one else was, had borne witness while Jeremy drank himself into a burbling stupor, had been a friend when Jeremy needed one.

. . . .

HE HAD NOT known he could forget her until the process set in. At first, he thought about her constantly, often crying, it seemed, for whole days. And then it was like he ran out of material. Like the old memories lost their shine. Coming in with the mail one day, he stared at a model on a lingerie catalog, aware he'd gone all morning without envisioning Ashley's face. It occurred to him that if he lived long enough, there might come a time when he stopped thinking of her altogether. He looked through his books and read, *At the end of the grieving process, patients report a feeling of reconciliation, which signifies an unconscious acceptance of loss. The bereaved may now begin to successfully adapt to life without the deceased.* He closed the book. He was sitting at the kitchen table. The house was silent. Beside him, his lab mix, Buddy, watched him attentively. He thought of Patrick Maloney, lifting weights in the prison yard or eating cheap cafeteria food among his fellow convicts. He wondered again what the boy had seen in Ashley, why he had chosen her to follow. He went upstairs and got his rifle, then went out with Buddy to shoot any creatures that seemed to be asking for it.

. . . .

HE WAS STILL listening to the police radio, waiting on news about the mother and child, when the door opened and in came a pink ski-jacketed young woman whose tight blue toboggan pressed her dread-locks against her bold cheekbones. Marta. It had been a while, and he smiled despite his reservations about her line of work. He even blushed slightly. He couldn't help it; she was so pretty in her sunburnt farmer's way. Behind her, the familiar white container truck idled, its exhaust steaming in the precipitation that was now becoming a mist. She raised two fingers in a peace sign and glanced around the empty lobby, at the glowing windows of the candy machines and the framed maps of the state's highway system. She pulled a fistful of change from her pocket and dropped it in the donations can.

"Hello, Jeremy," she said. "Ça va?"

"Hey," he said, refraining from saying her name. He was unsure whether it was *Martha* or *Marta*, having heard only her boyfriend call her the latter and somehow imagining that French Canadians all said the name wrong. That was stupid, maybe even offensive, but Jeremy's prejudice persisted alongside his vague awe of anyone with the temer-ity to smuggle drugs across the border. Not that Marta admitted this directly—she claimed to move Christmas trees, never saying why she delivered them year-round—but she had a tendency to smile slyly when she talked about her work. It was as though the police no longer cared about marijuana traffickers so long as they put some effort into hiding it.

"Isn't it late to be out driving cross country?" he asked, stepping closer as she reached the coffee station.

She grinned, filling her cup hastily, pressing the flap on the carafe so that hot liquid sloshed out. Her eyes had a glazed look, and when she laughed, the alcohol on her breath stung his nostrils. "Leonard and I got delayed in the city," she said. She sipped and wiped coffee from the faint blonde hairs of her upper lip. "We made the mistake of sitting down at the bar."

"Whoops," he said, feeling a twinge of jealousy. To have work take you someplace, he thought. To have the leisure of stopping at a bar there. To be there with Marta smiling at you. He knew what was happening: *manifestations of resurgent libido commonly take the form of ostensibly non-erotic fantasies.*

Pouring a second cup, she tipped her chin over her shoulder. "He's out there, waiting. Some husband, eh? Send the woman in while he wait in the car." She paused, smiling around as if the lobby had an atmosphere worth soaking up. "Quiet tonight. You alone?"

"Yeah, mostly." He nodded toward the shape of Damon's truck at the end of the lot. Someone was out there, a figure moving slowly in the darkness, away from the trailer, carrying what looked like a suitcase. He wondered if the trucker was cleaning out the back, or if the hitchhiker or whoever he had in the cab with him was getting out to wait for a ride. "I mean, there's Damon."

She shrugged. "Who is Damon?"

His neck grew hot. Of course she wouldn't know. It was easy to forget that people who passed through routinely had no reason to notice each other. "Never mind," he said. "Just another friend."

"Well, then, bonne nuit. See you next time." Marta smiled pleasantly, despite carrying a coffee for a husband who had not come in to serve himself, as Jeremy would have done in the man's place. Maybe she hadn't minded the lack of courtesy. One of the perks, he supposed, of living your life stoned.

. . . .

HE HAD BEEN a good boyfriend, he felt—not perfect, but good. This seemed clear when he compared himself to other men, and yet afterward, he wondered what people thought. Ashley's parents behaved coldly toward him at the trial. At first he thought he was misreading them, but then her mother had tried to hide from him at the grocery store. As he was pushing his cart through the produce section, past long beds of freshly harvested apples, he'd caught a glimpse of her by the pale heads of lettuce. She'd looked in his direction, then backed away and ducked around the corner, leaving her half-full cart behind.

That hurt—enough that he could have gone down to his knees right there—but he forced himself to keep pushing his cart idly, as if he had not noticed the sudden flight of his once future mother-in-law, the once future grandmother to the children he would now never have.

It had come to him later that he and Ashley were fighting in those last few weeks, that she must have told her parents, as she always did when things were tense—opening up to them and anyone else who would listen in ways that struck him as unseemly, as if the world were her confessional. He had forgotten, or tried to forget. He wondered what she'd said to make her mother fear him. He wondered at the stupid tragedy of it all. That fact that they'd been fighting was beside the point, a minor detail in the bigger story of their love. There had been many chapters, and to dwell on this one was to disgrace Ashley's memory, to distort the truth of what had been. Even so, he'd begun to doubt himself. He remembered the grocery store incident whenever he read that *subjects exhibited changes in their memory of loved ones throughout the grieving period. Memories most prone to revision served a distinctly etiological function in the subject's narrative of the past.* Those lines came from a study he read more than any of the others. They terrified him. If he had changed his memories, how could he ever know?

. . . .

HE LEFT through the side door, where Damon and any passenger would be unable to see him. As he prepared to go around behind the building and sneak up on the truck, a Crown Vic's unmistakable profile and lights came racing up the entry ramp. Jeremy stuck his hands in his pockets, drumming up an excuse to be outside. He didn't want to draw police attention to Damon when the guy was probably just helping someone. He wondered with amusement if this was *employing a delusion as a coping mechanism.* The trooper sped through the falling sleet and put the cruiser in park in one of the diagonal spots, then climbed out, leaving the engine running. He wore a green waterproof coat and, seeing Jeremy, raised a hand in greeting. After looking around the lot once, showing no interest in Damon's truck, he walked across the glittering pavement and up the sidewalk.

It was Edwards, one of the younger guys. He was usually upbeat when he came in, as if he weren't policing one of the state's main heroin corridors. "Bitch of a night, huh, James?"

"You could say that," Jeremy said. "Any word on that lady and kid who were in a wreck north of here? Know what kind of shape they're in?"

"Kid's stable," Edwards said without hesitation. "The mom not so much. She was in the ICU, last I heard. Why, they friends of yours?"

Jeremy shook his head, dismayed. He wondered if anyone was expecting them to arrive somewhere, whether those people knew what had happened. "I think they were in earlier. Seemed nice."

"You know what I would do if I had a family? Move someplace where nobody drives."

"I hear you," Jeremy said.

Edwards moved to the coffee station. "Say, you see anything strange up around here tonight? We've been looking for these heroin dealers out of Quebec."

Jeremy shook his head. Apart from the mother and son and Damon, there had only been Marta and her husband, people he knew. Before, at dusk, the usual rush of truckers had come through, some gnarlier-looking than others. One thing they'd shared was a soiled look eventually imparted by life on the road. A few families, too. Most likely, these dealers hadn't stopped. Though there had been one young man, a Lexus driver who strutted around as if he owned the place. He'd looked at Jeremy without smiling, poured himself a coffee, and left without acknowledging the pay can's existence. He was long gone, but maybe he and Edwards could laugh about the guy. He was conjuring an image of the man's round face to describe to the officer when Damon switched on his truck's headlamps and rumbled down the ramp to the freeway.

The trooper's gaze followed the departing vehicle. "Hope it's nothing I did," Edwards said.

Jeremy wondered if there were some young woman now shivering at the far end of the lot. If so, he hoped she had the sense to hide herself.

33

"Traffic must have finally cleared up," he said, hearing the nervousness in his voice.

Trooper Edwards winked and lifted coffee to his lips. "A joke."

. . . .

"IF I DIE before you," she said. "I don't want you to wait around. You should move on."

They were drinking beer from the old *Star Wars* glasses from her childhood. He had Boba Fett, she had Princess Leia. It was early summer, the evenings still free of mosquitoes. They sat in the yard watching lightning bugs flash overhead. Sensing she required some kind of reply, he turned and stared, hoping to make her laugh it off.

"I mean it," she said. Leaning forward, she held Buddy's head between her knees, frowning as she scratched behind his ears. She was drunk enough to feel bad about something. "I mean it. I hate the thought of you grieving. I hope you'd move on."

"All right," he said, trying to hide his irritation. He hated these conversations, which she seemed to think were necessary from time to time, like checkups at a doctor's office. They were thirty-two, for Christ's sake. He only had so many days off, and this was a waste of his free time. "I hear funerals are good places to meet women."

She let go of the dog's head and went in. She slammed the door, though he already knew. From the instant the words had left his mouth, he'd known they were a mistake, that now she would go and cry, and he would have to follow and tell her he was sorry. Put on a show, play the part of the concerned boyfriend. Then she would confess what was really bothering her.

He didn't go in right away. Something in him wouldn't allow it. He sat in the thickening dusk and drank his cold beer and told himself he might as well enjoy this quiet moment at home, such a rare thing since the end of his bachelor days.

. . . .

AFTER THE TROOPER drove away, Jeremy waited a few minutes to ensure he wasn't looping back. When Edwards spoke over the radio, identifying his position eleven miles north, Jeremy went out the main doors, heading toward the dark end of the lot. He took the long flashlight from inside his coat and switched it on, moving its beam over the landscaped picnic area just below the wooded mountain slope. The air was growing warmer, and the snow had turned completely to rain, making streaks in the snowy hillside and causing little streams to pour down into the picnic area. Trickling water burbled all around him. He didn't want to know what it looked like on the knoll above, where more tables had been overturned for the season. It would probably be one large, slushy pool by morning.

He made slow progress toward the lot's edge, not wanting to surprise the hitchhiker if she was hiding there. For his own sake, he hoped she was a teenager, not a lot lizard. Someone young and mostly innocent, someone salvageable and not entirely unpleasant to be around. He would help her regardless, invite her to come inside the facility, where she would be warm and safe. He would buy her something to eat from the vending machines, get her to tell him her story, maybe try to convince her to go home to her parents. At the very least, he could help arrange her next ride, when a trucker he trusted came in. Maybe he would be *transferring qualities of the idealized loved one to a new object*, but in the larger, more objective reality that had nothing to do with his mind, he would be helping somebody.

Seeing no one in the lot or on the sidewalk, he flashed the light up the hill, supposing the person could be crouching in the trees where he couldn't see her. "Come on in," he shouted. "You're not in any trouble, hon. Police are gone."

He stood waiting for a reply, listening to the drizzle on pavement and grass. He began to feel spooked. The back of his neck crawled, as if someone were standing directly behind him, and he wheeled quickly, stepping back as he did.

The lot sprawled out, shimmering black, rippling with tiny rivulets. The lights inside the building suggested the warmth of a bed where he could hide under the covers, pretend to be safe against the larger forces of the night, but of course it would provide no real protection. He began to climb to the picnic area, muttering and sweeping his light over glinting slush and dark puddles. Up on the hill, a set of footprints led into the forest's pines and bare black hardwoods.

It was hard to gauge the size of the prints in the melting snow, but Jeremy was now almost sure it was a kid, likely a young one, too—running scared. Goddamn it, he thought. There was no way he was going very far in. He wasn't going to get wet feet and a case of chills just to save some idiot runaway. Even so, his legs were carrying him into the woods, and soon the picnic benches on the knoll lay behind him, out of sight. He kept his flashlight pointed ahead, trying to avoid any surprises, and held a hand out to protect his face from branches and who knew what else. There was no telling what a runaway girl might carry these days. It was easy to imagine a handgun, and that was not the way he wanted to go, shot down by some freaked-out minor he was trying to help. He remembered that *In the aftermath of a loss, the bereaved may suffer, and act on, heroic delusions*. He wondered what Damon had been doing with a kid in his cab. Maybe Jeremy had misjudged him, given him too much credit, though Jeremy knew he shouldn't make assumptions. Or judgments. He was lonely at the rest area, but not as lonely as a truck driver, and you never knew how an experience might change you until you passed through to the other side.

When the footsteps disappeared in a puddle of icy mud, Jeremy scanned the surroundings with the flashlight beam, looking for signs that the kid had turned one way or another, then brought his light back to the puddle at his feet. The water and snow pooled around mounded earth. He grew very still, listening, then shined the light around once more.

Water dripped from the trees, forming runnels on the soil, moving downward, making its way to the rivers underground. He squatted and shuffled closer to the puddle and the hummock of mud, trying to judge if the mound was manmade, and if so, what it might conceal.

A strange excitement came over him as he went down to his knees, the wet earth packing under his weight. For a moment he hesitated, then reminded himself he was alone in the woods. He need not fear humiliation in any discovery. Not this time. Reaching both hands into the frigid slop, he pulled back water and mud in a pile, then scooped another layer of slurry, and another. When his fingers froze, he dug with numb claws, heaping the earth up in front of him. It was raining softly. The trees were alive but oblivious. The numbness worked up into his brain, but he kept going until he hit something solid, then sat back and aimed his flashlight at it. Fabric. A patch of jeans filled out by a leg, too small to be a man's, too big to be a child's. He raised his head, holding his breath, and swept his light in a slow semicircle. Melting snow ringed the shapes of other mounds, seven or eight, maybe more.

. . . .

SHE WAS LYING facedown on the bed when he finally went in to talk to her. He sat on the edge of the mattress, placing his hand on the back of her thigh.

She slapped out randomly. "Don't," she said. "Don't touch me. I don't deserve it."

Jeremy sighed, then turned and took his beer from the dresser, where it had left a ring on the wood. He could tell she was no longer angry and wondered what it was he needed to say to make her feel better. "Whatever it is," he said. "It's no big deal."

She spoke into her pillow, which distorted her words. "You don't know everything," she said. "There are things I haven't told you."

Sobered by the sharpness of her muffled tone, he thought of the woman at the blues show last summer, the one who'd kissed him on the mouth, her thick tongue bitter from smoke. She'd been younger than Jeremy but had the bewildered eyes of someone older, a longtime drinker. Her plaid shirt was unbuttoned, and she hadn't been wearing a bra. "I could use a good fucking," she said, and a moment spooled out between them before a friend came and dragged her away. He'd never told Ashley about it. That long moment. The possibility that sprang into his head. He wasn't about to tell her now. There were things he could live with, a reasonable burden of guilt. "It's fine," he told her in the darkening room. He put his hand back on her thigh, and this time she let it stay there. "Whatever it is, it doesn't change a thing."

She sniffed and looked at him, her eyes lined and sad. She shook her head and tried to smile. "I don't deserve you."

"Sure you do," he said.

"I'm going to do better," she said. "I promise."

. . . .

37

BACK INSIDE, having peeled off his soaked clothes in the small locker room, Jeremy slipped into a pair of Carhartt overalls from the utility closet. They were tight, but they covered him. He was barefoot but didn't care. The doors were locked, the lights bright and screaming. Edwards had radioed saying he was fifteen minutes out. In the silence, Jeremy gradually noticed the top forty station playing on the radio. They were on a commercial break, and a man was speaking enthusiastically about a local skiing resort that offered *special discounts for family fun*.

The air carried the rank odor of his wet socks. He paced by the big maps beside the door, the windows reflecting his moving figure. He could just make out the parking lot beyond the glass. There was no one out there, no Damon come back to get him. In all likelihood, Jeremy would never see the man again. The thought agitated him, though he told himself that what he should feel, what a reasonable person would feel, was relief. He grew angry and began to say things that had no intended meaning or even shape, a gibberish of halfwords and curses. All those hours Damon had sat with him, keeping secrets while Jeremy revealed his own. He must have enjoyed sitting there, watching Jeremy squirm like a bug on the end of a pin. Jeremy wondered how many others had seen him that way, remembered standing at the window of the morgue when they'd let him see Ashley.

He got on the radio and interrupted the frenzy of voices. "Can someone tell me about the woman?" he said loudly.

After a silence, the dispatcher responded, sounding annoyed. "This channel is for official use only, sir."

"It's me," he said. "I just called this whole thing in. I have a question. Can you please tell me what happened to that woman tonight? The one in the wreck? Is she going to survive?"

It was an impossible request. The dispatcher couldn't know, had had even less contact with the woman than he. The absurdity of his demand was clear to him, and yet he bent toward the radio, holding the transmitter his ear, as if he could draw answers from it. You could find out, he thought. You could do that for me. I'd do it for you.

Other voices came on now, sharing what they knew. Jeremy closed his eyes and waited for answers. The police were on their way. Then would come the news vans carrying people and cameras. There would be other officials, too, and then his boss, his boss's boss, and so on up the chain. There would be his face on the TV and in the papers, the dumbstruck expression he knew all too well. Later, grieving parents, brothers and sisters, friends and boys who'd hoped to be more than friends. Patrick Maloneys. They would be sorry. They would apologize and weep. This place would close. He would lose this job. That was not important. What was important was to make peace with what he did not want to know. Jeremy almost believed he could. Starting tomorrow morning, mere hours from now, when a bigger storm arrived, and everything froze again.

AMONTILLADO

I WOULD NEVER have known Bobby Bell died had I not been at my mother's the morning his obituary ran in the newspaper she still got—though she only did the crossword and the Quizzer and read the obits, complaining she knew fewer names than she used to, the deaths of what she called *her people* having come like a wave that peaked and passed, leaving her alone in its wake. The edition in my hands was thinner than the ones I had delivered as a boy, the newspaper itself gradually diminishing along with the people old enough to consider it an essential daily connection to an outside world, people like my mother, who was smaller and frailer and mentally feebler than she'd been only last year.

Her speech trailed off now as she wandered the kitchen, supposedly making tea but rummaging suspiciously in drawers and cupboards unrelated to teamaking, as if she'd lost track of what she was doing and hoped opening the right storage compartment would jog her memory. She was grumbling about the women who appeared twice a week to clean her house, assigning them offenses that ranged from putting things where they didn't go to theft, though she could not name a single possession taken by the two short, polite women who came in a station wagon with a rosary hanging from the rearview and gray rubber tubs of cleaning supplies in the back. It was more likely that my mother's accusations against these women—conversing in cheerful Spanish as they worked energetically through each dusty room—was due to the disappearance of the world my mother had known, which is to say that my mother felt lost in time and space and lashed out at the incomprehensible strangers who entered her home every few days. This was unfair and petty of her but ultimately harmless, because the slander began and ended with me, her son, who absorbed her dark imaginings without any change in attitude toward the cleaning ladies. In other words, it was a routine Saturday morning with my mother, her lamenting and cursing and me reading the newspaper I'd actually never subscribed to, both of us performing without interacting and quietly cherishing the companionship we knew would not last, and it was in this mundane moment, with sunlight shining warmly on my hands and my mother recalling *Ah, yes,* she was making tea, that I read Bobby Bell was dead.

My mother had not mentioned Bobby, though the pages were wrinkled where she'd held them, and I supposed enough years had gone by that she might see his name and make no connection to her own little piece of the past, despite what he'd done to her only child. This was likely, I decided, the more I thought about it, because I had turned out okay, or I had as far as anyone could tell, and I'd never told my mother that I still thought about Bobby, even though decades had passed, or that I sometimes dreamed he was hurting me all over again, violating me in ways my mind invented and against which I was helpless to defend myself.

Bobby was my age almost exactly—my age plus twenty-three days and several hours and minutes—that being one of the details about him which had proved impossible to dislodge, a piece of useless information like my first phone number and the name but not the face of the first girl I liked, detritus of a vanished, more solid world that created the foundation of the more elusive and complicated one I inhabited now.

I was not shocked to learn Bobby had died, because I was old enough to feel accustomed to thoughts about mortality, my own and that of everybody I knew and did not know. A number of relatives and some acquaintances from my so-called generation had died, and I'd responded to their deaths with more resistance and sorrow than I experienced as I read and reread and read yet again the short column of about a hundred words, my mother's talking becoming all but inaudible as I looked at each letter and the typo (*their* where it should have been *there*), as though the print could reveal something other than the barest facts about who Bobby had been in life, the names of family members who had survived him, where his body would be displayed and where buried. After a while I had to admit to myself that parsing the letters and words would yield no more understanding of what had happened to him or to me. Bobby Bell was dead, and dead was dead forever, yet as the morning wore on, my mind replayed scenes of the last time I'd seen him.

. . . .

I HAD RUN into him a few years earlier, and it had been an interesting encounter, not only in the ways Bobby and I each responded to this unplanned meeting, but because of who we'd been as teenagers, and as children before that.

It was winter, around the holidays, just before or between or just after. The sky was blue, and the sunlight, a limited resource that time of year, was pale and harsh, with a frigid wind striking randomly, blasting everyone into their coats. The parking lot at the electronics store in the part of the city devoted to malls and chain restaurants was vast and crowded, the blacktop fouled with rock salt and oil. A major sale was in progress, as always seemed the case, and I'd come to purchase a new television, something I'd never done, having been the recipient of several second- and third-hand sets.

Inside, the store had the feel of an international airport during a time of government collapse, with disorder in the checkout lines and the aisles, the shoppers turned in every direction as if nobody knew which way to face, the grimacing cashiers and baggers in red polo shirts, beige aprons, and navy-blue pants looking harried and disheveled. The ceiling was high, with a number of errant holiday-colored balloons hovering against the corrugated metal, and looking into that space above the aisles and people's heads, I hustled into the chaos, toward the large television displays mounted on the back wall.

The many brands on sale appeared more or less identical, all of them flatter and with much larger screens than the televisions of my childhood, and the primary differences boiling down to types of display and technicalities that were quantified on white placards and meant nothing to me. The sets all showed the same nature program about the Great Barrier Reef, presenting dozens of moray eels varying only in size and shade of green.

An employee whose blue vest distinguished him from the workers in the front of the store rounded the corner, smiling confidently to himself. He was on the short side, with a balding head and prescription sunglasses and a belly that pushed his button-down shirt out through his vest's opening.

"Is it possible I could be of some assistance?" he said, which struck me as an unnecessarily formal iteration of *Can I help you?* I glanced at the name tag identifying this stranger as a Purchasing Consultant as I said the words, "I guess I need a television." Then the name below the title registered, and I lifted my gaze to look through shaded lenses at eyes that had already been averted.

Immediately the old feelings seized me, the resentment and fear and the urgent need to defend myself, but something new rose as well, because he had seen who I was half a second before I had made the connection between his name—Robert Bell—and his altered appearance, and his pitted cheeks were darkening fiercely.

I was taller, more athletic, and pleased by the feeling that I remained his physical superior. He was not only losing his hair but gaining a slouch, and several long black hairs grew from his ears like antennae. It took me a moment to comprehend he would not admit that he knew me, and I saw, as heat flashed through my own face and left a trace of sweat at my hairline, that I could not only play this game but possibly win it.

Strange, I thought. It was a marker of how old we had become. A few years earlier, Bobby might have said my name, beating me to the punch in this mutual ambush, brushing off the implications of our respective roles by saying the electronics store was a stepping stone to some other career. But things were different now, as if we had passed through an invisible phase, one dividing successes from failures, all of us shaped by the last flickers of youthful energy into people who would be known and people who would languish in the realm of the forgotten, and there was no mistaking which of us was which as we stood in the TV section of the electronics store where I was the customer and he was the so-called Purchasing Consultant, both of us surely thinking about the night Carl Parsons and I nearly murdered him.

. . . .

THIS WAS senior year, and Carl and I had invited Bobby to join us on one of our Friday evening excursions out onto Lake Erie, where we motored around in Carl's father's large power boat, drinking beer and smoking cheap pot we rarely bothered to fully clean, despite the fact that smoking the seeds was rumored to cause sterility. Eventually returning to the marina to dock among the darkened sailboats and yachts, we'd get fucked up until we puked over the side of the boat and passed out and woke up shivering and hungover and drove to a nearby diner to eat eggs and bacon and smoke cigarettes among surly truckers before we gave up our freedom and went home. Sometimes we had girls along, Carl being then, as now, large and brawny but with a child-like face women trusted. Puberty had made me long and rangy, trans-forming me the way it had transformed my father, who said we had *the same time-release genes*, and while I never possessed Carl's charm, I always knew one or two girls willing to spend time alone with me.

Carl's access to his father's boat made females easier to interest, and until he'd taken a serious girlfriend, he and I had made a regular practice of inviting girls to hang out with us on the thirty-foot vessel, which had separate enclosures where we could pair off, one couple be-low deck and one up in the cockpit, a name that took on a euphemistic meaning hilarious to us. After Carl got a serious girlfriend and a job in his uncle's auto shop, a position worth holding onto after graduation, he and I went out on the boat less often, and when we did make these expeditions, we did so in a nostalgic spirit, like two aging bank robbers in the Old West, reunited for one last heist before we split up to retire in separate South American countries.

Ordinarily, we would never have invited Bobby. He'd moved back to town just before our senior year, after seven years in coastal Cal-ifornia, where his father's job had taken him when he and I were middle-school classmates. Their leaving had been a big deal in my neighborhood, a signal of the family's ascent to the next American level. This departure for a place where few of us had vacationed, let

44

alone owned property, left my parents and the other grownups in my orbit second-guessing their evaluations of the tightlipped little man and aloof, willowy woman who had occupied the big Victorian that predated all the brick-and-mortar structures in our neighborhood by half a century.

Now Bobby was back among us, his father's career having disintegrated somehow, and his parents had taken typical jobs—him managing a tire shop and her answering phones for my family's dentist. They could no longer afford a house like their old Victorian, where different rich people dwelled now, and instead occupied a rusty-looking shack in a cluster of mostly prefabricated homes across the road from the oil refinery. Both parents appeared at peace with the reversal of their fortunes, smiling when they saw me from their new places of employment as if they had not previously been the ones served, but Bobby carried himself like a tragic figure.

His family could no longer afford the quality clothes they'd bought him out west, and he went on wearing those brand name shirts and pants as they grew too small and frayed at the collars and cuffs. When the soles of his pricey sneakers finally detached, they revealed socks that had holes of their own.

While he'd once been conspicuous, exhibiting an air of natural pride that had intimidated me, now Bobby kept to himself, avoided social situations, and he might have escaped my notice had not Carl's increasing seriousness about his girlfriend left me with more free time, and had not Bobby and I been scheduled for the same study hall during our final quarter of high school.

When I'd first walked into the cafeteria where we held study hall, I saw him glance away. As always, he'd seen me first, but now he could not hide from me or stop me from taking the seat directly across the table. I towered over him, and the way he glanced at my large veiny hands and thick wrists and grunted when he moved his books told me how much stronger I'd become. He lowered his eyes to his chemistry reading, reluctant to look into my face, which was understandable, given what he had done to me when we were younger.

"Hey Bobby," I said, affecting an innocent smile and pushing the false enthusiasm I'd perfected. I had become a well-liked person, someone expected to appear at parties and say something entertaining, and everyone called me *a nice guy*, though my smiling attention masked a vast indifference to most people and the things they did and cared about. "I didn't know you were in here."

Bobby nodded and lifted his head, though he continued to avoid my eyes. "It appears I am," he said, which struck me as exactly the sort of thing he would say, and which confirmed my suspicion he was still the boy who believed he was my better, despite all the changes to our persons and our portions in life. "It appears we need credits to graduate, even if we're not actually in class and engaged in learning. This whole education thing is fraudulent."

I let out a low chuckle, as if he'd said something smart. "I guess so." I glanced down the table toward a few junior girls, one of whom smiled and blushed. "There are some hot girls in here," I whispered, knowing he'd both noticed and was thinking the kinds of dirty things he'd always thought.

He reddened and focused again on his book. "I should study."

"Cool, dude," I said, starting in on homework of my own and pretending I didn't see all the times he peeked across the table, aware I would have his confidence within the month.

It took less than that, though, and by the second week he'd entrusted to me his opinions that the girls in our study hall were *stuck-up bitches who only gave it up for jocks,* and the bored teacher charged with seeing to it that the students never became too rowdy was *a fucking cunt,* in addition to a host of other horribly unfair judgments he'd formed about people at our school in his brief time back. Many of these people I considered friends, but I never contradicted Bobby, preferring to giggle behind my fist when he said something cruel, which inspired him to regard me as if I were stupid, and I delighted in having duped him. I invited him over a few times when my parents were out, and I got him stoned and drunk and let him tell me more terrible things he thought of our classmates. One night he got to Carl's girlfriend.

"She's kind of meretricious." He was sitting on a swivel chair in my parents' garage. We were smoking a joint by the open back door, and now and then I turned on a flashlight and shined it out on the bats flying

46

around the yard. Bobby shook his head, sure I didn't understand. "You know, slutty? Still, I'd put my erection in her. I'd do her better than Carl. He's probably got a big dingus, but he's slow. I'd know what to do with her."

I let out a big dopey laugh, one that was partially sincere because of the words he'd used to articulate something I deemed unspeakable. I waited five minutes and said I had to piss. Inside the house, I called Carl and told him what Bobby had said, then suggested we meet up at the marina.

An hour later, Bobby occupied a seat near the back of Carl's father's boat, drinking beer and talking more and more as we plowed out into the dark water. The higher he got and the farther we traveled from shore, the more confident he became that I'd forgotten what he had done to me when we were ten.

. . . .

I THOUGHT OF their house as *the castle*. Its Victorian tower rose out of the treetops and attracted crows, and in the years before Bobby and became friends, I would play in the woods around their property, listening to the cries of the black birds perched high above, pretending the place was in Transylvania and the dark-haired, thick-bodied boy I occasionally glimpsed was one of the vampires who lived there. One day he spoke to me without turning his head to look.

"I can see you, you know," he said, stabbing a stick into a heap of dead leaves. "I always do."

There being no other children our age in the neighborhood, we soon were together each day. Bobby was openly critical of how small my house was, and how poor we were, making my mother blush and compelling my father to send us outside. As a result, we played only at his house. I didn't mind this arrangement. Bobby's father was always away at work, and his mother was indulgent, feeding us Twinkies and cupcakes until our stomachs ached, letting us do as we pleased in the many rooms of their vast home. Most of the time, we occupied ourselves with video games and watched cable, but sometimes Bobby became bored with these things he considered everyday luxuries and suggested we play pretend.

Pretend involved going into the basement—which consisted of multiple chambers itself and was twice the size of the house I lived in—and becoming people we were not. Bobby oversaw these games, always designating himself king or prince or hero, while I was the thing that needed killing or saving. Around that time, he discovered the stories of Edgar Allan Poe and became so enamored of them that he incorporated them into our play. He insisted that I read them as well, so I would know my role in the game without needing to have it explained. Bobby would choose the story, decide which character each of us was and what the rules were, the result being that I was frequently dismembered or tortured or buried alive by him. The moment I objected to his slightest whim, he would begin to whine, and this was the one noise he made that his mother seemed capable of hearing, at which point she would descend to wherever we were and ask if it wasn't time for me to go home. Once I figured this out, I tended to go along with whatever he wanted, because I was ten and lonely and there was nothing worse than being home without a friend.

"You're nobody, you know," Bobby reminded me one day, leading me to the slatted wooden door in the floor of the wine cellar. None of this was different from any other day, and I had no reason to suspect that he had grown bored with our game and wanted to take it to another level of intensity and risk. "You're my slave, and you'll do as I say."

I wasn't sure where this was going, but I guessed he was imagining something medieval. "Yes, my lord."

"Have you done your homework?" he said, meaning *had I been reading Poe?*

"Yes, my lord."

He pulled on the rope that lifted what looked like a trapdoor in movies. "Get into the hole."

I looked into the dark opening, imagining spiders and snakes, multitudes of biting insects hiding in a pool of slime. I knew the alternative: going back my house, where my mother would be doing household chores or watching soap operas, and where my room and old toys waited, devoid of anything surprising. I took a deep breath, held it, and slipped into the blackness feet first.

· · · ·

THIS UNDERGROUND storage space was short enough that I had to squat so Bobby could close the trapdoor. The hole was damp and packed with clinging cobwebs, and I imagined the surrounding air swarming with mortal threats. I held my body still, doing my best to avoid contact with anything more than I'd already touched, thinking it would be only seconds before Bobby opened the door and the game changed back to something more familiar.

I heard a dragging sound directly overhead, and a fine dust rained onto my hair and the back of my neck, spilling down inside my shirt. When I pushed against cold, dirty planks above me, the door didn't budge, and I squeezed my eyes and mouth shut as the cold soil that had accumulated on the wood sifted into my face. I spat and called to Bobby to let me out.

"Fortunato," he said. "You know my name. Call me by it, or I will not respond."

I tried to stand, using my leg strength to topple whatever he'd placed on top, but succeeded only in scraping my shoulders. "Come on, Bobby," I yelled between the dull thuds of my beating fists. I was already beginning to panic. "Open the door."

He did not reply, and I continued to shout until I was crying hysterically, a state that lasted until I comprehended he might have abandoned me down there. I'd recognized the Poe story he had tricked me into playing, and now the name and lines came to me from somewhere, and I said, in a voice now hoarse, "Please, Montresor, please let me out! For the love of God!"

A moment of silence passed, and then something shuffled above. Bobby laughed a pretend laugh and spoke in a theatrically antiquated voice. "Yes," he said. "For the love of God."

I heard his footsteps, loud at first and then softer, moving away, diminishing until I could no longer detect them. Then another sound, a clunk: he'd left the wine cellar and closed the door behind him. I was alone, shivering and filthy and crying, in a hole underneath Bobby Bell's house, and only he knew I was there.

There is an objective measure of how long he left me down there—a period of several hours—yet the duration was beyond my powers to quantify. It was a span in which I hoped to escape and gave myself up for dead and rediscovered hope and gave up again, and I hallucinated myself freed so many times I stopped believing it could happen; the divide between my fantasy and my reality broke so irrevocably that there are times, even now, when I am with my wife or my colleagues or outside and a crow makes its sound, I am distracted by the fleeting thought that I never escaped, that I'm still there, lost in the dark, imagining this life in which I find myself.

Eventually my mother came looking for me, of course. When she rang the doorbell a third time and insisted, Bobby's mother took her through the house, going through each room and calling my name. Eventually both women came downstairs, entered the wine cellar, and seeing crates stacked on the storage door where they were not supposed to be, Bobby's mother moved them, pulled the rope, and looked on where I lay curled, my clothes soiled and my lips blue. Though I don't remember this part of it, I'm told I refused to speak for a full day, as if I thought I had not been rescued and was simply dreaming.

. . . .

"YOU EVER THINK different times coexist?" Bobby said. "That each moment is a world in itself? It would make a single life an infinite number of worlds. When you look at this way, you can get a hint of how complex the universe is."

He was talking in a way that made it clear he wasn't asking for answers, going too quickly to let Carl or me get a word in. He wanted us to sit and listen. He was the same person he'd been when we were ten.

We were anchored more than a mile offshore, and the lights were off, but the moon was bright enough for me to see Carl roll his eyes. "Like if you said some shit earlier," he said. "You'd still be talking the same shit now?"

Bobby did a doubletake and studied Carl, his mouth hanging open slightly. "You know, you might be smarter than you realize."

"Is that right?" said Carl. He glanced at me as if to confirm that this little dweeb was in fact saying these things to him. He raised the joint he had been holding, took a sharp hit, and exhaled swiftly. "Would you talk to some of my teachers?"

Bobby frowned sourly. "I don't know what good it would do."

I ripped the tab on a beer and swilled it, crushing the aluminum to force the liquid into my mouth more quickly, and when it was gone I pitched the can into the lake, because that was the kind of thing I did when I was young. "Let's go swimming," I said.

Carl was already undressing. Soon he and I were both in the lake, which was bracingly cold and smelled vaguely of fish. We floated on our backs under the moon and stars, laughing and splashing and making too much noise to hold a conversation, though we kept an eye on Bobby, and when he'd gotten in and swum out into his own space, we stroked quickly back to the boat ladder, climbed in, and drove away as he paddled after us, begging us to wait.

. . . .

AFTER PAYING FOR the television in cash, I made a point of walking behind Bobby as he carted the large cardboard box out to my car, watching his head drop slightly each time I gave directions to turn or to head up a particular row. I was pleased that I had driven my wife's black Mercedes, which was new and more impressive than the car I usually drove. As we approached it, I pressed the button on my fob, which popped the trunk, drawing Bobby's attention. His ears were red from the cold, and his teeth chattered slightly when he nodded at the vehicle, saying, "This is yours, I take it?"

I didn't answer, just opened the trunk and let him do the work of hoisting the box from the flat red cart and easing it into the Merc. He stepped back and rubbed his palms together, exhaling a visible breath. "It's a decent car," I said. "I'm thinking of upgrading."

He was shivering now like he had on Carl's boat when, after twenty minutes, we'd sobered enough to be scared by what we'd done. Turning on the lights, we circled back and, luckily, found him still treading water. He didn't protest or complain on the ride back to land, only sitting in the corner trembling until we reached the dock and Carl said he could go, then disappearing into the night and later from study hall, too, so that I only glimpsed him in the halls a few times before the graduation he did not attend.

He waited now for the same permission to go. "All right," he said. "I suppose I have fulfilled my obligations here."

"I guess so," I said, staring as he ducked eye contact and turned, presumably taking satisfaction in my failure to tip, as it would give him cause to judge me as cheap. I waited until he was halfway across the lot to call him back. "Oh, hey," I shouted through my hands. "Excuse me! Robert?"

He stopped, shoulders tensed against the freezing wind, and spun around. I held up a bill, a larger one than it was customary to give. He scowled and came striding toward me.

"Happy holidays," I said. "Sorry, must have slipped my mind."

"Thanks," he grunted, concise for once.

"You're welcome." I took care to infuse my voice with cheer, completing the image of the perfectly happy, successful man I'd tried to create.

. . . .

THE SERVICE was small. His parents were dead, I learned from eavesdropping, and he'd had no siblings. The cause of death had been a congenital heart defect, which someone muttered had taken his father, too. A few elderly people I thought must be uncles and aunts sat in the front near Bobby's son, who resembled his father strongly, short and thick-waisted, miserable-looking behind his glasses. This younger man was going bald, and he had come alone, in a suit that was too small and without a ring on any finger. Whoever his mother was, she was dead, too, or else she had not deigned to pay his father any final respects.

It was a nice day, blue-skied and loud with cicadas, and butterflies made their wandering ways past the gravesite while the priest said his words, the usual bit about the forgiveness and redemption none of the bored mourners appeared to believe were waiting in some afterlife. After the funeral home workers lowered the casket, the small group began to move away, returning to their cars.

As I stood motionless, held at the lip of the grave by a feeling I could not name, Bobby's son came over and introduced himself. He was an awkward young man, curious about me and how I'd come to be at his father's burial.

"My dad didn't really have friends," he said. "Only a couple people from his work came. He got to where he didn't like humans a whole lot."

"I knew him when we were kids," I said, feeling inexplicably anxious. "He ever mention any friends from childhood?"

Bobby's son stood mulling this question, teething a lower lip, and for a terrible moment it seemed he might conjure the story of a small boy in a hole in the ground, crying so long he'd lost his voice and given himself up for dead. This replica would begin to laugh, and the world I knew would fall away.

Finally he shook his head, looking fretful. Perhaps he worried the flaw in his father's heart was built into his own. "No," he said. "He almost never talked about his childhood."

I nodded, and though I could see he wanted me to tell him more, I said it had been nice to meet him and turned away. It was a cold thing to do, the sort of action my wife would have scolded me for, but she was not there and in fact did not know that I was. I had never told her about Bobby Bell and never would, and no accounts of this day I gave in the future would include this event. As I walked off, I heard the sharp intake of breath that comes with tears, and I did not look back.

I followed the winding paths among the old stones and shade trees that gave the cemetery a tranquil and idyllic appearance, though I never lost sight of the tent where Bobby had been put in the ground, and when one workman had taken down the canopy down and another rumbled up in a yellow frontloader, I went back. I had decided I didn't care if his son were there, but by then the kid had gone, driving off in a small blue car with a loud muffler. The man in the front loader looked down at me and nodded, and I gave him a wave, indicating I wished to stay and see him fill the hole. I turned my eyes back to the open grave and waited until the machine's steel bucket was spilling dirt down onto the coffin, down onto Bobby. Then came a second bucketload, a third, a fourth. The operator pulled levers casually and expertly, carefully watching the earth he scooped and dumped, doing as he had done for countless graves before this one, and before long we both seemed to forget we were not alone.

THE HELP LINE

AFTERWARD, DAVE couldn't say how many times Gordon called the help line, asking to speak to him. A few hundred, at least. Maybe a thousand, though that number seemed high when he thought about it. Had he, Dave, ever called anyone that many times? He imagined his index finger, in the days before cell phones, punching a familiar pattern of buttons over and over. He'd probably called his parents a thousand times. Maybe the friend who'd lived down the block when he was a boy. And yet a thousand seemed too small a figure to measure Gordon's calls. The sum total felt bigger than ten thousand or even a hundred thousand. Something absurdly large, approaching infinity. Gordon had phoned so many times it was like he'd been doing it since Dave started taking calls, and Dave had been taking calls so long he hardly remembered doing anything else.

There had been other jobs, of course, a long series of positions before this one, menial gigs that lasted anywhere from a few weeks to a year. The more Dave thought of jobs he'd had, the longer the list grew. It was amazing, really, how many things you could do, how many bosses you could have, in the inertial stretch between turning sixteen and finishing college. He had mowed a golf course, shoveled stone with a road crew, fried things in a diner, recited specials from memory for hungry yuppies. He'd hawked expensive sunglasses at the mall, had cold-called the elderly, selling bad deals on energy. (Now those jobs felt remote, abstract, the labors of a near stranger, someone about whom he knew only a few facts, like Torquemada or the guy who'd played Freddy Krueger.) Then, after completing his degree in computer science, he'd provided technical support for a hospital, helping doctors with their email and upgrading the pharmacy's inventory software. When Mystic Games called to offer him a place, he'd jumped at the chance. *Lunged* was more like it. He'd lunged, and he hadn't looked back.

He had been working the help line for a decade, a fact so unfathomable that each time he recalled it, he counted the years on his hands. Maybe Gordon *had* called a thousand times. To arrive at that figure, he'd needed only to call a hundred times per year, or about twice a week, and sometimes Gordon phoned several times in a few hours, ever willing to pay two dollars and ninety-five cents for each minute of personal game assistance. It had taken the man a few calls to recognize Dave's voice. And then he had begun to ask for Dave. Gordon said they *really clicked*, and as he called more and more, he talked to Dave with increasing frequency about things that had nothing to do with games, things that troubled or baffled him, like how computer people were taken for granted by noncomputer people, who seemed to think that computers and telecommunications devices grew on trees, which they assuredly did not. Like the women who didn't give him a chance, even though he had a lot to offer them, especially in the way of personal loyalty, which in Gordon's experience was an extremely limited human resource. Like the kids who worked at the Burrito Shack near Gordon's house, who stood behind the counter in their purple polo shirts, smirking as they took his usual order. So cocky, so vain. They probably thought they could do what he did! (Gordon never mentioned what it was he did.)

Dave had been good to Gordon, reminding him what the help line cost each time Gordon went off on his tangents. Other team members would not have been so kind. Callers with tendencies to go off-topic were fairly common, and when one of these Chatty Cathies (as the office dubbed them) started talking about his personal problems (this type of caller was rarely a woman, though Dave had noted the fact didn't diminish the merciless sexism of his fellow operators, who tended to be pale, sluggish men with bad eyesight and an aversion to confrontation, men much like Dave himself), many an operator would grow quiet, would sit and watch the clock as the money rolled in. Dave did not like laughing at fellow gamers, nor did he care for the chilly silences his colleagues cultivated in the breakroom at Mystic Games, and he made a point of being cheerful and candid with the people he encountered over the course of each day, be they colleagues he met in the halls or foreign voices speaking through the earphones of his headset. He knew he couldn't make a dent in the culture of his work-place, but being kind had its own rewards, such as when he found he no longer remembered his last fantasy of hurting someone. Such as when callers started to ask for him by name.

He could tell it was Gordon calling by the pause that came after Dave said, "Mystic Games. This is Dave. What are we playing today?" It was a long pause, pure digital silence, pregnant with possibilities, as if Gordon were considering saying nothing right up to the instant he spoke. Gordon had a distinct voice, deep and stupid-sounding, and pronounced his words awkwardly, as if he were reading aloud unfamil-iar terms. Gordon said he appreciated Dave's honesty about going off topic and added that he didn't mind paying a little extra.

"That's not part of the scheme here, I hope," Gordon said once. "Reverse psychology or something." He'd been going on about how annoying it was to have to stop playing games to eat, sleep, and use the bathroom. In Gordon's opinion, the human body was a very flawed vehicle for consciousness. He was constantly crashing up against its limits. He'd been thinking about switching to a high-protein liquid diet, which would save time usually devoted to sustenance, but he seemed to need a hard six hours of sleep no matter how he chopped it up throughout the day. He sounded flustered. He made no further mention of defecation.

Dave was hurt by the suggestion that he would lie. "I'm a little confused," he said, though he understood, "by what you mean when you say *scheme*."

"You know what I mean. I hope you're not being all nice and pretend-concerned to keep me jabbering. Stretch out the call and run up the bill. I hope they don't teach you that in training. Be a terrible thing if they did. Not cool at all, man."

"No, no," Dave said quickly. He had enough gamer community ex-perience to know how delicate these guys could be. Though when he spoke of this he used the word *hypersensitive*, sometimes he thought the word *babies* when considering their level of vulnerability, and sometimes he caught himself muttering "Fucking babies," but he did his best to hide this sentiment. He hid it from the callers and from his colleagues, who also struck him as fragile males. He didn't want to hurt anyone's feelings. And he liked his job. "I say what I think and what I mean," he assured Gordon, "I'm a simple person when all is said and done. Duplicity's never worked for me."

Gordon was silent for the better part of a minute. He seemed to be mulling over Dave's words at first, and then his breathing had grown faster and heavier, as if he were crying or exerting himself physically. Soon he was panting, and Dave began to feel uncomfortable, to wonder whether he should sever the connection. This wasn't a line for phone sex. Then Gordon had let out a long sigh, followed by a truncated moan. "I appreciate you being straight with me," he said. "You seem like a nice person. I like that about you, Dave. I really mean it."

. . . .

HE WAS WORKING the night shift, six in the evening until six in the morning. It had been a terribly hot day, one of those scorchers where getting into your car was intolerable, as olfactory in nature as it was tactile, the smell of scorched vinyl coating your nostrils down to your stomach as your skin burned in the light. He'd stopped for an iced coffee on his way to the office and was so intent on keeping his arm in the air-conditioned interior that he'd pulled away from the drive-through before realizing he could identify neither the age group nor ethnicity of the woman who'd prepared his drink. She had simply been a voice, and then a hand offering him a cup, the drink so important in his estimation that he'd not bothered to register skin color. He wanted to think this was a good thing, a sign he was moving away from the racist views he'd inherited as an upper-middle-class white male, but he knew it wasn't that at all, was in fact something worse, a sign of his willingness to look past the existence of others to get what he wanted. Sometimes he hated the person discomfort brought out in him.

Things were easier once he was seated in his cubicle, surrounded by the voices of colleagues offering game-related instructions. He scrolled through familiar game maps and talked callers through the problems they were unable to solve. He helped a preadolescent boy defeat a golem using a vorpal sword, led a middle-aged man through a forest teeming with blood-vomiting ghouls. Dave was good at this stuff and only kept the game maps open in case he misremembered a minor detail, of which there were so, so many, and so many of which barely differed from game to game. His specialty was Mystic Games's roleplaying features, and he'd worked through them all multiple times, won using multiple strategies. Receiving games from Mystic months in advance of their release, he stayed awake at home, playing them during his off hours while having takeout delivered to his front door. Dave loved learning each game, even the ones that were obviously derivative or involved elements he found uninteresting or corny, such as extraterrestrials or fairies, because each game's story revealed something about its designer. Some designers were smarter than others, some more imaginative and daring, some noticeably sexist or possibly even racist. Dave had played so many role-playing games that he'd come to recognize certain designers in game details, just as he had, as a teenager, been able to discern familiar patterns in novels written by certain authors. Gaming really was communing with others, he thought, not only when you could play interactively with other users, but because each game *was* an interface. In the end, you were always with someone else. Other people populated your imagination, gave you things to talk about, and in a sense supplied all the tiny pieces that made up your own mind. You were never truly alone. "There is no I," he said aloud sometimes as he played alone in his apartment with the shades drawn and the lights off. "There is only *we*."

On the phone, he talked slowly and clearly, sitting patiently when callers cursed because their avatars had been killed or when they couldn't get his instructions to work. When a teen accused him of misunderstanding a question, he gently explained he'd said to attack using the Atlas Wand and not the Atlas Sword, even though the latter seemed more intuitive, and when the boy then felled the golden giant, he told him, "It's okay you lost your temper. Gaming can be incredibly stressful."

He was still sipping the watery dregs of the iced coffee when Gordon came on the line. By then it was past eight. He thought it might be

Gordon even before he answered, because the caller remained on hold for more than ten minutes, an orange light blinking steadily while he told two kids who had him on speakerphone how to beat the skeleton chessmaster in Deathtrap. It was either Gordon, he supposed, or one of five or six other men, Chatty Cathies all, who had latched onto him recently.

"Mystic Games. This is Dave. What are we playing today?"

The caller was silent against a silent background.

Gordon, Dave mouthed soundlessly, trying to remember the last game the man had needed help with. Devil's Tree, he thought. In one of the late stages, Gordon had been unable to find the secret underground entrance in the abandoned YMCA. He wondered if Gordon had gotten around to Terminal Labyrinth yet. He felt supremely confident Gordon would love Terminal Labyrinth. He raised his drink to his lips and sucked from the corner of the bottom, filling his mouth with cold liquid that tasted faintly like sweetened coffee but also of something mushroomy, which he supposed came from inside the coffee shop ice machine.

"We're playing Family Secrets, Dave."

Gordon sounded congested. He lived in Kentucky or Missouri or Illinois or Ohio, one of those miserable midwestern places where the humid summers brought a flood of molds and pollen. Dave pictured a rolling landscape of farm animals, barns, and fat white people with bland expressions. "Hey, Gordon. It's good to hear your voice. How are things in your part of the world?"

"They've been better, Dave. Things have been much, much better. I'm having some real difficulties here."

Dave smiled and moused the tiny white hand on his computer screen to the map of the game Gordon was playing, selected the map, and opened an overview of hundreds of different screenshots each of which could be pulled up and expanded to display a different feature the gamer had the option of employing. The day had started out poorly, but now it was going well. He'd quickly resolved the problems of his previous callers and was certain he could help Gordon. Family Secrets was not one of his favorite games—it was too grisly for his taste, too morbid in its outlook—but he had the possible storylines memorized. He leaned back in his swivel chair and cracked the knuck-les of both hands. "Let's hear it, Gordon. I know all about Family Se-crets."

Some twenty seconds passed in which Gordon did nothing but breathe heavily.

Not for the first time, Dave tried to imagine the man. He knew the profile of the average adult caller. Age eighteen to thirty-four, though in Gordon's case, he thought, a little older. Maybe forty to forty-five. Overweight, deficient in vitamin D, possibly didn't bathe for long stretches. He either lived alone in a rented apartment or with his parents. Was unemployed or only partially employed. If he worked, he did so remotely. There was a good chance he was a virgin, and he was probably very poor, spending whatever disposable income he had on gaming. Dave did not feel guilty or especially sad anymore to think these thoughts. He knew what these callers wanted, knew firsthand the thrills of their chosen passion. He had been struck by that partic-ular lightning himself long ago, at age eleven, and he was resigned to the world being the peculiar way it was.

"I'm having some difficulty with the mother's corpse," Gordon said. "I've put her in the barrel in the basement, but there's an issue with the odor. The police detective keeps knocking on the door. I'm not sure how long I can keep him away. I'm not sure what other lies I can tell him. I've told him so many already."

"Hold on. Are you the father?"

"No," Gordon said, sounding irritable. "Of course not. Are you in-sane? I'm the son."

"Okay, okay, okay." Dave scrolled through various pages of his game map until he found the son's taller perspective peering down at a large black barrel on the dirt floor of an unfinished basement. God, Family Secrets really was a sordid story, the product of a perverse mind. Not surprisingly, it had been wildly popular. In the game, the player chose the avatar of one member of a nuclear family in an abusive household. The most disturbing choice was the role of the sexually abusive fa-ther, whose goal it was to fend off attempts at revenge by his wife and children while continuing to dupe the police detective and the social worker about what was going on in his home. You could also opt to be the detective or social worker, but the most popular options were the youngest daughter, who was still a virgin and oblivious to her father's budding interest, or the oldest son, who had recovered repressed memories while fighting in Afghanistan and then come home to get even. Dave had played through all the options, and he was knowledgeable of the game's hidden functions, nasty things like the potential to dismember one's victims and make clothes out of their body parts, all of which he kept to himself unless a caller asked how to unlock them.

"Okay, Gordon. Have you killed the father yet?"

"He's in the panic room and won't come out. But I've disabled the landline."

"Good. That's important. That's key."

"We have to hurry. The detective on the street, talking on his cell phone. I can see him from the upstairs window. I know he's going to come back and search the house. He's going to find the bodies. Dad's going to get away with it."

Dave frowned at the use of the word *Dad*. Some players got a little too involved in these games. "You need to move the body, but that's a long-term solution. You can't move a body while the detective's watching you."

"You got that right. So what?"

"You need a short-term solution."

"Like what?"

"The most effective way to mask the smell is to start a fire," Dave said.

"Start a fire?"

"Go into the backyard."

"Okay. Okay, I'm there."

"See how there's a shed in the back corner? It's leaning, with a hole in the roof?"

"Yeah. Looks old. Rotted out."

"That's right, Gordon. It's made of old hickory boards. That's an aromatic wood. You're going to chop that shed up, you're going to put that wood in the fireplace, and you're going to use the matches to start a fire. Got it?"

"How the hell am I supposed to chop up the shed?"

"To fit the mother in the barrel, you first had to—"

"The Eagle Scout hatchet," Gordon said, his voice cold with recognition.

"There it is," Dave said. "Now we're on the same page."

. . . .

HE MADE COFFEE in the breakroom, flipping through a recent issue of *RPG Magazine* while two team members drank energy drinks and peeled open chocolate bars. It was almost ten, and he'd have to get back to his station before long. The weekend had begun in earnest, meaning the help line had entered its busiest thirty-six-hour stretch. He kept thinking of Gordon's call. Something about it had been amiss. In part, he was surprised Gordon was playing Family Secrets, an old game that had been thoroughly mapped online. There were dozens of walkthroughs out there, maybe more. And he was sure Gordon had called about this game in the past, asking similar questions about how to do away with the body of a family member. Furthermore, there was the fact that Gordon had referred to the axe as an *Eagle Scout hatchet*. Normally this kind of mistake wouldn't have bothered Dave, but now he was remembering another conversation with Gordon, a Chatty Cathy call in which Gordon had described his troubled relationship with his father, who had been an Eagle Scout and showed disappointment in his son's hatred of camping.

The breakroom window looked out on the parking lot, where countless insects drifted in the lamplight like tiny mindless angels. Beyond, a wall of trees darkened the street. A few blocks away, the bars were getting full, people were sizing each other up, taking the pleasure immediately available to them and moving toward more. Dave could have used a night like that, of assaulting his senses with alcohol until he could no longer think clearly and had to call a taxi, some friendly stranger to take him home. It would have to wait until tomorrow.

"Probably nothing," he said, focusing on his own ghostly reflection in the glass. Its face was a hole, all darkness, and had been staring back at he looked outside. Gordon was probably replaying a game he'd enjoyed in the past. Gamers did that all the time. "It's probably the way his memory works."

. . . .

GORDON CALLED again after three. Dave was coming out of a stupor, entering one of the strange frames of mind he experienced when he stayed up all night. In such states, he felt wide awake but was capable of perceiving hallucinatory images, as if part of his mind were dreaming while the rest of its machinery attended to the business of conscious thought. Though not exactly pleasant, this unstable condition was preferable to the murky headspace that preceded it, and Dave hoped it would last through the final hours of urgent calls from sleepless kids and drug-fueled adults. He looked around in the fluorescent glow, immersed in the buzz of electronics and voices, stunned by the realization that the room had been exactly this dim since he came in.

"Mystic Games," he said. The light had been blinking during most of his last call. He thought it might be Gordon and felt both excited and afraid. He reminded himself he was safe in his cubicle, then realized how odd it was to be aware of feeling safe. These were the kinds of sensations brought on by working the help line all night. "This is Dave. What are we playing today?"

The caller was silent against a silent background.

"Gordon, is that you?" he said, then chastised himself when the caller made no reply. He didn't want to come off as disrespectful or flip. Callers were paying for his time, after all.

As the seconds passed, Dave moved the tiny white hand around his screen. He made letters with it, wrote his name, then Gordon's. *I see you*, he wrote.

"We're playing Family Secrets, Dave," Gordon said. "But I guess you knew that too. What, do you have me on caller ID there? Have you been tracking my internet activity?"

Dave sensed he had made a mistake. In trying to be affable, he had provoked the paranoia of a man who was likely a shut-in. He hurried to reply, trying to make his voice soothing, "No, no, not at all, Gordon. It's just that only a few people ask for me. You're one of my favorites. You're one of my . . . regulars." He had almost said *Chatty Cathies*.

Gordon laughed, catching Dave off guard. It was a strange, rough, breathless noise. "I knew you couldn't be tracking my browser activity," he said. "I have very good security. Very, very good security. State of the art."

"I am glad to hear that, Gordon. Very glad. We here at Mystic Games appreciate your business very much."

"I'm having trouble getting Pops to come out of the panic room," Gordon said. "I've tried negotiating, but he thinks I'm lying. I even threatened to kill little sis. She's his favorite and everything, the one he didn't assault. I held her in front of the closed-circuit camera so he could see me holding the knife to her throat, and I spoke into the intercom."

"Wow," Dave said. He had never tried to use a hostage to bring the father out, but he saw the possibilities of the approach immediately. He wasn't surprised that this game would allow such a feature. He shook his head, glad the motion was undetectable. "That's a new one to me. What happened when you threatened to kill her?"

"He told me to go ahead. Thought I was bluffing."

"What did you do?"

"I cut her throat. There was a lot of blood. Don't see the point in dissolving the mother now, but I guess that's acid under the bridge." Gordon gave a light snort, pleased with himself. "I'll have to cut and run. I didn't want to off little sis, but I did. Now she's propped up in the old rocking chair, right where Pops can see her."

Pops. Little sis. God, what a morbid game. Dave closed his eyes for a moment, wondering who designed this one, if they truly entertained such fantasies or if they were cynical enough to believe others did. He wasn't sure what was worse, designing such a game or getting excited playing it. Not that Dave believed in censorship, not beyond the kind that resulted from market forces. You had to give people what they wanted. You had to supply that old excitement, the thrill of those early games. It's what they all came back for. If you couldn't give it to them, you might as well quit, because someone out there would. "Yikes," he said. "So how is the father reacting to the sight of his murdered daughter?"

Gordon was silent. Then he began to chuckle. "You know, maybe you should be paying me."

"I can answer—"

"I'm kidding. Let me enjoy this, okay? I'll pay, sure. It's not every day I get to stump you, Dave. I'd love to do what you do. Pops was upset, to say the least. Oh boy, was he angry. He screamed a lot of things through the intercom. Some pretty obscene things, to be honest, things I shouldn't repeat. For a minute, I thought he might come out and try to fight me. But he stayed inside. I haven't heard anything for thirty minutes. He's probably crying. Or maybe he offed himself."

Dave hesitated. The game didn't end with the murders. You had to dispose of the bodies and either remain in the house undetected or escape. Didn't Gordon remember that? Maybe he never did call about Family Secrets, or maybe he never beat it. "He's probably still alive," Dave said. "You need to confirm."

"Thanks, Sherlock. Now how do I get in?"

"You can't. You need the father to open it."

"How? I can't cut off his air supply. The tanks are in there with him."

"That's true. You have some options. You could wait him out."

"I don't have time for that. I told you. That stupid detective suspects me."

"It does take a while to starve him out. And you need an exit strategy."

"Oh, I know where I'm going. I'm getting in the car and heading right to California. I'm coming out to your neck of the woods."

Dave swallowed drily, wondering why one fled west or south in these games, never east or north. "Okay. Here's what you could do. Pretend to leave. Drive his car out past the cameras. Let him see you go. Then walk back and wait in the blind spot for him to make a run for it."

"What blind spot? Is it behind the bush he's been asking me to trim? Is that why he was giving me such a hard time about it?"

Usually Dave was cheered when a caller put together an answer on the line, but hearing Gordon identify as the brother in Family Secrets, he felt only dismay and a desire for the call to end. "That's right," he said. "You want to wait out there with something that won't make a lot of noise."

"Like the hammer?"

It was a moment before he spoke. "Yeah. Like the hammer."

HE HAD TO GET out his calendar to count how many days had passed between Gordon's last call and the article. It was small and reproduced in only a few newspapers. He wasn't even sure how it made its way into his feed. A family murdered in a small town in Iowa, an old married couple and their twenty-four-year-old daughter. The police were looking for the son, Silas G. Wetzel. He was thirty-seven, unemployed, and described by people who knew him as *a hermit, eccentric, a shut-in. Addicted to video games.* There wasn't much information about the deaths, and the follow-up articles were still briefer before they stopped. Maybe they stopped because the crimes went unsolved, or because the people pictured were overweight and unattractive, dressed in dirty-looking clothes, and had died in a rural backwater. There were more sensational murders in the news that day, murders people cared about, like the woman who had stabbed her husband's new wife with a cleaver and kidnapped their toddler son, only to be shot dead by federal agents before she could harm the child. Or the high school boys who lured a classmate out on a boat at night on Lake Erie, only to leave him to drown when he jumped in to swim. There were so many stories like that, their numbers increasing, it seemed, the longer you looked.

It was as if nobody cared about the story of Silas G. Wetzel. Dave spent a lot of time online, searching for a photograph. He could only find one, a slightly out-of-date image that seemed to be from some kind of ID, a driver's license or an employee access badge. Wetzel was bald, round-faced, in need of a shave. He wore tinted prescription glasses and had faintly smiling, wet-looking lips. It was easy to imagine Gordon's voice coming out of that mouth.

It's not every day I get to stump you, Dave.

We're playing Family Secrets.

I'm coming out to your neck of the woods.

He considered phoning the police in Iowa, tracking down the detective who had the case. But the more he thought about it, the more stupid he sensed he would sound, calling out of the blue, trying to get involved in an investigation that had nothing to do with him. He imagined the detective growing impatient, finally interrupting him and ending their conversation. No, he wouldn't call until he knew something substantial. Online, he could find nothing about what the G in Silas Wetzel's name stood for. He began to think it might all be a strange coincidence, especially when you considered how many strangers he'd helped over the years, walking them through games that featured bloody violence. In the end, maybe this kind of thing was inevitable. Maybe it happened to other operators, too.

He went to work as scheduled and waited for Gordon to call and ask for him. After a week of nothing, he pestered an acquaintance in billing to look up the phone number. She identified Gordon's calls, but only the last five or six, because they'd been made with a prepaid calling card. Going back further was possible, she said, but not something she was willing to do without orders from higher up. Even then, she would probably only turn up more prepaid cards.

Her nostrils flared as she told him this. What she'd done could have cost her this job. She was mad enough that his apology might not smooth things over. She might look at him differently from now on. He said he was sorry anyway and went back to his cubicle.

An orange light blinked on his console. A caller was waiting. It might turn out to be Gordon, but probably not. The world in which Gordon called him had, in the passage of a single week, come to seem far away, a distant planet whose onetime proximity now felt like a product of his imagination. Something had passed through Dave's life, some connection he could not name. This caller was likely random, someone who, when he didn't answer, would be reassigned to another operator. It could be one of his Chatty Cathies, listening to upbeat electronic music and waiting for him to come on the line. There were still a few of them left, though he no longer addressed them by name and could not match their enthusiasm when they reacted to hearing his voice.

He tried to remember how he felt that morning after Gordon's last call, when he'd left his headset in his cubicle and stepped out into the crimson dawn and tasted bitter city air, heard the sounds of slow traffic and the voices of two women walking to work. He had been relieved, and then disappointed, to find no one waiting for him.

He'd pictured Gordon, a soft little man in a rusty car, speeding west through miles of corn, examining his fingernails for traces of blood, dreaming of a new life on the coast. Dave had laughed at himself uneasily, thinking he needed to get some sleep, though he had peered into the backseat before getting into his car and driving away.

He couldn't say exactly what had changed since that moment, except that he'd felt different upon awakening later and had felt different ever since. It was as though he had used up a life and moved on to another, become a new Dave in a series that would eventually reach its end—though not, he hoped, anytime soon. He moved the microphone over his lips and pressed the button beside the blinking orange light, then opened his mouth to ask a stranger what game they were playing today.

DEMONOLOGY, OR GRATITUDE

FOR A WHILE I lived with an older woman. Anyway, that's what I told people. It would be more accurate to say she stayed with me when she had nowhere else to go. The lease for the tiny house where she came and went as she pleased was in my name, and I was the one who stocked the refrigerator and cupboards and cleaned the place. I also covered her shivering body with an afghan after she passed out, and I turned her on her side when that's what was needed. I was generous when she asked for money, and I didn't mind that she never repaid loans or offered to help with chores or thanked me for feeding her cat when she wasn't around. Really, I felt lucky to have her in my life. I'd have put up with just about anything to make her stay.

Friends say I must have been naïve or suffering from low self-esteem, and it's easy to see why. I was in my early twenties then and had moved across the country to escape a fundamentalist community obsessed with the beady-eyed images of dismembered fetuses and cartoons depicting lakes of fire, and though my family still left daily voicemails proclaiming that Jesus awaited my return with open arms and angels watched over till then, I felt I had successfully broken with the beliefs that ruined my childhood. Finally, I could drink twelve beers or watch strangers fuck online or sleep late on Sunday without dreading social consequences. I felt like a new person, a blank slate, and with this came a certain blankness of character. I had a mild personality that matched my plain looks and my sweatshirt-and-jeans sense of style. I had a decent job, and my needs were so simple, my desires so unimaginative, that I found myself in the pleasant state of not worrying about money. I was happy, or thought I was, because my life was better than before.

I was in love with Nora. What I mean is· I wanted to be with her every moment, and if that were impossible, I wanted to marry her so I could trust her when we were apart. I thought about her when I was awake and dreamed of her while sleeping, especially when she was out God knows where, with God knows who, doing God knows what. She was in her late thirties, a former model and actress who liked to say she'd given up her career to search for *something real*. She was exceptionally beautiful, six feet of human magic with long hair and eyes that never stopped loving you. Strangers gawked at us in diners or at the park, and though their baffled smirks made me nervous, Nora was graciously oblivious. When we met, she was partying a lot, and her old activist friends had taken to calling her an unreliable addict. Some told me she needed professional help, as if I cared what they thought. To me, the environmentalists were as absurd as the Christians. Both groups had their sacred and unquestionable tenets. Both groups knew they were right, and everyone else was wrong. I kept their assessments to myself, hoping to guard Nora's feelings and also spare our relationship the distress such background noise can create.

Her drug habit bothered me less than how superstitious she was. Even during her sober stretches, she made the same insane pronouncements she foisted on me when she was loaded. Her ideas were all over the place, unlimited by traditional religious views or even the vaguest scientific framework. She believed in channeling spirits, past lives, and claimed she'd been a sex slave in some ancient Roman colony, a detail which seemed at first to explain why things between us were moving so slowly. To her, everything that happened was fated, from the person you fell in love with down to spider bites and the snowflakes that landed in your hair. Horoscopes were the newspapers' only truth.

I struggled to control my disappointment when she shared these beliefs. I'd learned young how to use others' convictions against them—that you could make someone weep by spelling a dead relative's message with a Ouija planchette, or make them scream by saying you'd seen a ghost behind them. I no longer believed in demons, gods, prophecy, or any of the other things Nora claimed were real, but because she was so damaged, from drugs and from things men (women, too, but mostly men) had done to her over the years, I told myself she'd eventually learn she could trust me, that she would then stop pretending and admit she and I were alone in the same godless world.

. . . .

TOWARD THE END, she disappeared for days at a time, turning up completely burned out, thin and skunky with secretions (her own and those of others), mumbling she'd protested in some march or demonstration. I knew she'd been in bars and strange apartments and houses and backseats, getting as high as possible and trying to stay that way. I stayed mum, reminding myself I was still young, growing and changing. That she could soon tire of being strung out. That, with a few slight modifications, an enduring romance might click into place.

One night while she was gone, I was in the living room, watching a trivia program until I could sleep, concentrating on each question to avoid thinking about what Nora was probably doing with some other male. I knew all the answers and said each one aloud in the lamplight, as if it were a meager little prayer.

Thunderstorms had come and gone all afternoon, flooding the alley and inspiring the neighbors' kids to paddle their inflatable raft around. The TV went to a commercial, and I heard rain lash the windows and remembered Nora's cat had asked to go out earlier. A happy-go-lucky tabby named Rasputin, he was probably crying at the door. Cursing over rain and TV, I got up to let him in.

The night was blustery and wet, and I covered my eyes as a dark shape streaked across the grass and up the steps, past my feet. As I turned, drying my chin on my sleeve, I heard the cat's distinct mewl behind me and looked out once more. Rasputin sat below, under a sheltering shrub.

My immediate thought was that I'd let in a feral cat, that now I needed to remove it before it ruined the furniture, and in rousting the animal I'd likely get bitten or scratched. I felt a pang of self-pity, then consoled myself with the thought that one day Nora and I would look back on this night and so many like it and laugh, that she would touch my face and convey an erotically charged mixture of contrition and gratitude.

I closed the door and searched the flickering shadows for a weapon or makeshift trap, bracing myself for the ambush of teeth and claws that would surely come at any moment. I settled on a cheap skillet and advanced into the living room, where the trivia show had returned. The studio audience was cheering the ancient, self-satisfied host.

That was when I saw the thing I've never been able to name. Filmy and insubstantial, it floated in the middle of the room and could only be described as a dark gray blob, a kind of unevenly round bubble. It hovered like a helium balloon, with no eyes or mouth or face or discernible front, and the front door showed, slightly distorted, through it, which made it appear more gelatinous than gaseous.

I stood there, caught up in frenzied thoughts. It went without saying that I was awake. The blob thing was real. Not *real* real. Someone was playing a trick, but how? The room was small and sparely furnished, with nowhere to conceal a projector.

"Okay," I said loudly. "Very clever. You had me going for a second."

The blob thing did not react in any perceptible manner, and I was tempted but afraid to touch it. It occurred to me that no one I knew in this part of the world would stage such an illusion for my benefit. The only person west of the Rockies aware of my background was Nora, and she was too respectful of spirits to ever counterfeit one for a laugh, that being more something *I* would have done in high school. I wanted to yell for backup, a witness, but my house sat a little apart from others on the block; no person would have heard. As I was sober, the only other explanation for it was that something had collapsed or ruptured in my brain, like a blood vessel, and affected the cognitive divide between dreaming and perceiving. Though the blob was noiseless and doing nothing I could identify, it gave off the sense of something—of *someone*—thinking.

My mind had definitely cracked. The best I could do, I decided, was wait until I recovered or someone came to take me away.

I might have remained there all night, staring at the blob thing, had not Nora chosen this moment to walk in the door.

It was immediately clear she was under the influence of some energizing compound, probably something she'd licked off a piece of foil. She also had someone with her. Convulsing with scratchy laughter, she dragged the creep inside and kicked the door shut, then staggered right through the blob thing, parting it like a hologram, leaving it intact behind her. She threw herself onto the couch and started in on the crazy talk.

"Thank Goddess for this weather!" she declared, shivering in the sodden shirt and tiny cutoffs that displayed the arcane tattoos covering her magnificent chest, arms, and thighs. "Pacha Mama's not going down without a fight. That's not just my feeling. This is where modern paganism and science agree."

I watched her with a feeling like she was drowning, but I couldn't help because I was drowning, too. Her face sagged under her eyes, the skin pale and slick like she was coming down with something. Somehow this had the effect of making her prettier.

"Eddie hates when I talk about my spiritual side," she told the guy she'd brought home. "Don't you, Eddie? Are you cooking? I'm starving."

I looked at the skillet in my hand, then at the gray blob that neither she nor her guest had acknowledged. Not waiting for an answer, she pulled the stranger down onto the couch.

Only now did I really look at him. Nora had a weakness for large macho eccentrics who wore trench coats and quoted occult texts, men who claimed to have vast and esoteric understandings of the forces behind matter. They tended to be long-haired and heavily bearded, to work in used bookstores and to play in terrible bands. They saw themselves as artists, philosophers, revolutionaries, and they didn't think twice about telling you so. They thought I was the wrong guy for Nora and it was their responsibility to take her from me. When they inevitably left, they habitually stole from us, or left turds drifting in the toilet, or both.

This man was another in that series. He groped Nora's thigh with an enormous hairy hand.

"Eddie, meet Charles," Nora said. "Charles, meet Eddie."

Sprawling over half the couch, Charles wore an old blue uniform shirt with a name patch that read *Manuel*. His dark hair and beard were shaggy, and he watched me with small, petulant eyes, radiating a smart-alecky malice I'd first come to know in the faces of ministers' children and their friends.

As his stare continued to burn into me, I realized he wanted me to say hi first, that, for him, withholding one's greeting was a power move. I pretended not to notice. It was my only weapon against him.

"Charles is an activist," Nora explained, looking around the room and scratching goosebumped arms. "He wants to blow up the lumber company. He used to fight for our country."

"Is that right?" I said, thinking, *Too bad he didn't die for it.*

"The group that kicked me out for bullshit reasons? They expelled him, too," she went on, smiling at me through the blob thing, apparently unable to see it. "They thought he was FBI or some kind of paramilitary infiltrator, all because he has the nerve to do what it takes to save the planet."

Charles's voice was deep and gruff. "I was in military intelligence, but I'd appreciate you keeping that under your hat," he said. "We don't want to attract the wrong attention."

"Sure, Scout's honor," I said, though I'd never joined.

"Where's Rasputin?" Nora said.

The cat! I had forgotten all about him. "He's outside," I confessed miserably.

"Eddie, he's probably soaked!" Nora rushed past me.

This left me alone with Charles and the blob thing. I looked at one and then the other.

I asked Charles, "Notice anything strange in here?"

He squinted fiercely, as if to ask what the hell I was talking about. He appeared to perceive me primarily as an obstacle to fucking.

"Never mind," I said.

Charles turned to the TV, blinked, and said, "The Alamo," spitting it out before the contestants on the trivia program could answer.

I watched as they hit their buzzers. When I looked back, the blob thing was gone, the middle of the room the empty space it usually was. I was flooded with relief and laughed involuntarily, peering into the hall to make sure it hadn't moved while I was distracted. Everything in the house looked normal again. Maybe, I thought with profound gratitude, my brain wasn't broken.

My eyes damp, I grinned at Charles in spite of the natural hatred I felt toward him.

He looked at me and said, "I have a body now."

"What?"

He twisted his head back toward the television.

Nora came back then, holding Rasputin wrapped in a bundle of dish towels. She and the cat snuggled under Charles's arm, both looking content. The trivia show was ending, and I pretended to watch the credits, waiting for my heartbeat to slow so I could walk back to my room, lock myself inside, and wait for something terrible to happen.

. . . .

BEFORE SHE MOVED IN, Nora would bring dead animals to the pet crematorium where I was the sole employee. My workdays were long and dull and consisted of incinerating the corpses of cats and dogs and depositing their ashes into boxes, so when Nora appeared one morning, rapping shyly on the door's latticed window and asking for help, it was a welcome break in the monotony.

She was then living on a commune where the members cared for chickens, goats, pigs, and lambs rescued from factory farms. Sometimes the animals did not recover from the abuse they'd suffered, and these Nora delivered to me. The bodies were pitiful sights, underdeveloped and bloated, mangy, missing eyes and limbs, stinking of shit and piss. I piled them onto the hearth gently, dutifully, pained by the evidence of their mistreatment. The big cremation chamber could destroy a thousand pounds in one go, and it never took long to burn them away. Nora hung around, waiting for the ashes, which she'd scatter in the river later, and soon we had a routine, making small talk while the oven hummed. Things were easygoing between us, and though I would never have admitted it, I began to think of her as my first real friend.

"Ever mix them up?" she asked one day. "Like, send ashes to the wrong house?"

I laughed in surprise and lied, said no, because naturally I had, first

76

by accident, and later, experimentally, on purpose. I'd surrendered to an impish desire to see if owners would somehow notice—sense—they had the wrong cremains. Of course, nobody ever did, because ashes were ashes. They were symbolic and nothing more. It was embarrassing to remember now.

"I hate the thought of mixing them up," Nora said, her soulful eyes searching my face. "Poor lost little ghosts."

Until this moment, I'd thought her just an aging hipster with a big heart. Unable to hide my disapproval, I shrugged and grumbled that it didn't matter. "It's just meat and bone," I said. "Everyone is forgotten in the end."

"So you're a Taurus *and* closed-minded."

"Whatever," I said, eager to talk about something else.

"You're a special person, Eddie." She gazed at me as if I'd made her sad. "But if you're not careful, you'll be a locked box, cut off from the universe."

It bothered me to think of myself that way, sealed away from everyone and everything, but I forgot it, and a few days later, when Nora came to the crematorium sobbing, saying the commune had forced her to leave, I instantly saw an opportunity. She claimed she'd been treated unfairly, and I accepted this explanation without hesitating.

"What I am I going to do?" she asked, her golden hair falling all over the perfect arms she'd inked with pentagrams and skulls. "I don't have anywhere to go."

"I've got an extra room," I said slowly, trying to appear nonchalant. "If you need a place to crash."

She grabbed my wrist. I let out a disgraceful little moan. She didn't seem to care or notice. Maybe everyone moaned when she touched them.

"I knew I was drawn to you for a reason," she said.

That evening she appeared in a rusty Hyundai packed with her belongings and Rasputin riding shotgun. I stood at the window and watched her unload, aware she would only see the reflection of the yard if she were to look up. In a moment I would go out and help, but first I wanted to stop and take note that a woman like Nora was entering my world.

. . . .

THE MORNING AFTER the blob thing appeared, I put Rasputin out and left while Charles snored and Nora mumbled in her sleep. I was dazed from a dozen startled wakeups and a seemingly endless dream in which gray blob things infested the entire house, blocking every path. Making my way across town, I looked at other drivers, wondering if any of them might be possessed by blob things, which part of my mind insisted Charles was. If this were possible, it seemed such entities could run the whole world, reading the news on the radio, making laws, directing capital flows, preaching, and starting wars. These were unsettling thoughts, and I was relieved to reach the crematorium, where I knew I would be alone.

When I returned that afternoon, the house was dark and empty. Rasputin was in the yard, meowing for food. The coffee table was cluttered with empties that had been used as ashtrays. The rooms were full of houseflies, the kitchen especially. Fast-food wrappers lay on the table, covered with bits of congealed American cheese and little puddles of beef fat. I stood in the mess, trying to identify a smell I could not account for, a sharp reek of raw onions and salami, until realizing it must be Charles's scent. It had seeped into every space, even my bedroom, and I shuddered remembering the night before, how he looked at me and said, *I have a body now.*

I told myself I was being ridiculous, that there were no gray blob things, there was no possession, it could all be chalked up to brain farts and lost sleep and hokum. I cleaned the common areas, trying to work off my anxiety, laughing emptily at the thought of someone being controlled by a spirit or demon or whatever you might call a see-through gray blob that came in out of the night. Nothing special had happened, I thought. Soon Charles would get bored and leave, and Nora and I would forget he'd ever been here. We'd be one step closer to the future I'd envisioned, planned for. I had finished straightening when I heard their voices outside.

They came in and removed muddy shoes and socks. Nora's face and arms were covered in scratches and bug bites. She looked radiant and strong, her cheeks flushed. Behind her, Charles loomed, larger and more fearsomely constructed than I recalled, his presence both intolerable and unmovable. His beard appeared to have leaf scraps in it; his factory shirt was smeared with dirt. He looked at me, and I lowered my eyes.

Nora was happy, oblivious or indifferent to my state of mind. "We've been in the old-growth woods, doing recon," she said, slowly and thickly, as she did when she had major dry mouth. "We're planning to spike the trees. It's time for action. The only proof of human free will at this point is our ability to counteract our species' worst effects on the world. Time is running out, and we have to, like, choose a side."

Feeling the weight of Charles's attention, I ventured a few peeks in his direction, unable to decide if he was a garden-variety psycho or an actual monster. I nodded and said, "I'm on the side of the nature, that's for sure."

Nora put her hands on Charles's arm, and I saw he held a small plastic bag that contained some kind of powder. "I told you we could trust him," she said, as if trying to assuage some fear in the enormous man. "I'm going to the loo. Meet you in back?"

Charles remained where he was until after the bathroom door closed behind her. He looked at me hard, eyes glinting, as if he could read my thoughts.

"I have a body now," he said.

Once more I had the distinct sense the blob thing was talking, and yet I had no proof. I searched for some indication, some confirmation. How would possession work, anyway? Was the real Charles still in there, helpless and watching while the blob thing puppeteered his body? Or did the blob thing control his perceptions, too? "Yeah," I said weakly. "I know."

For the first time, Charles smiled at me. Or the blob thing did. "No, you don't."

. . . .

IN THE WEEKS that followed, a pattern emerged in their daily activities. They would go out after lunch and buy drugs, then come home and take them over the course of the next several hours. Now and then they visited the living room and talked to me. Charles boasted of chaining himself to giant trees and sabotaging construction machines, pausing to smoke or inject or snort something, and Nora, nodding at whatever he'd just told her, would wait to take her turn.

Eventually they would run out of whatever they had, pass out in Nora's bed, sometimes after loud—and in my opinion, definitely performative—sex, and then do it all again the following day. When they'd spent all of Nora's money, they held a yard sale with a bunch of her stuff and a few appliances I told them I didn't want.

I was unsurprised when Nora came into the kitchen one evening and asked me to lend her a large sum of money. I leaned against the counter and crossed my arms. I'd seen this moment coming, and I'd imagined what I would say, how she would reply, and so forth.

I explained I didn't have the kind of money she thought she needed. She suggested various ways in which I might acquire it.

"The TV's not good for you," she said. "You could pawn it. You could do a cash advance on your credit card."

I looked at her for a long moment, saying nothing. It was dim in the kitchen, but I could see the expectation that I would say yes in the corner of her smile. Up until the past few days, I knew, I would have buckled and found a way to get the money for her. But something had shifted in me. I noticed changes within myself. At work I was like a different person, wondering, while I worked the incinerator, what happened to consciousness. Not a day went by that I didn't imagine the world mobbed with hungry, lonely ghosts. When my parents and siblings texted to say they prayed for me, I understood how religion targeted the weak.

I told Nora no, sorry, I couldn't give her any more money.

"Why not?" she said suspiciously.

"I don't think what's going on is good for either of us," I said.

She laughed in my face. She was high but sensed me hiding something. "It's because I'm fucking Charles, isn't it?" she said. "You're jealous. Such an ugly little feeling."

I shuddered, aware he was in the house. I didn't want him to overhear us and confront me. "Don't you think there's something off about him?" I said quietly.

"He's a pure soul," she said. "What would you know about it?"

"All he does is talk," I said. "He's a charlatan."

"We went tree-spiking," she said. "That one time."

"You just walked around in the woods," I said. "Remember?"

She pressed her lips together and glared.

"I'm worried about you," I said.

"Don't be." Her face was hard to read. "I'm part of the universe, Eddie. I can't be destroyed. Even if this body dies, I'm connected to something larger. Something you can't see. I've glimpsed things you couldn't imagine."

This, I knew, was my chance. If there was anyone who would believe a blob thing was in possession of her boyfriend, it was Nora. If there was ever a time to tell her, it was now. If I convinced her, I sensed she would see Charles in a new light. She would ask me to help her escape. We would leave this house and this city and go into the larger world. We would finally be together.

Even as I imagined it, this future felt wrong to me, diverging from the one I'd imagined. In this new future, we would never settle down. Nora would lead the way, making all the big decisions. She'd never stop reminding me I'd confessed to seeing a spirit. Sooner or later, she would resume screwing other men.

"I'm sorry," I said. I couldn't help trembling. On the other side of the house, Charles was moving around, shaking the floors. "I want him out."

"If he goes," she said. "I go."

Rasputin crept into the kitchen and wound between my ankles. I gathered him up and gave him to her. Nora held him close under her chin, heaved a little sigh, and passed him back to me.

· · · ·

A YEAR OR SO LATER, her sister emailed, hoping to collect whatever belongings Nora had not taken with her. The sister was going to be in the area on business and said she thought it best to *kill two birds with one rock*. I accepted readily, and we arranged a time for her to come by. I was eager to learn more of Nora, though I worried she'd want Rasputin.

Nora's sister bore a slight resemblance to her. There were family themes, the nose and teeth, the eye and hair color, but this woman looked more harried and uptight than Nora ever had, both less impressive and more relatable, more down to earth, the kind of woman who'd never look at me twice, and also the kind of woman for whom I felt no desire. When she introduced herself, I thought I saw a glimmer of recognition in her sad smile, as if she could tell what I'd gone through just by seeing my face.

I'd put Nora's belongings in the living room. She hadn't left much, and before long her sister and I had loaded everything into the rented SUV. The sister stood in the driveway a while, talking to me. She glanced down the road eagerly but went on saying things, wanting me to understand about herself and her family. She'd had a conventional upper-middle-class life, a husband and a couple of kids and a Great Dane. She had a career and passions for Asian cuisine, international travel, gardening. Her sister, she said, was the odd one.

Having stated this, she began to cry.

"She was difficult," she said. "But she wasn't always trash. The truth is she was very special. She could have been anything."

"I know," I said. I was choking up, too. I held Rasputin in my arms. We had agreed I should keep him, that this would be easiest for everybody. She reached out and scratched the cat behind the ears.

"It's his fault she'd dead, you know," she said. "The son of a bitch."

"I know," I said. I did not say I'd driven to the motel where a housekeeper had found their bodies, disregarding the privacy sign when the odor grew strong. A desolate string of rooms off the freeway, the place looked foreboding and shabby. Nora and Charles had been living there a while, the manager informed me. She didn't reveal how they'd paid for their room. She didn't need to. "Lot of couples like that around," she'd said flatly.

"She mentioned you took her in," Nora's sister said. "I'm grateful."

"I wish I'd done more." I'd allowed her to form a false impression of me, but there was something I wished her to know, a thing I'd never told anyone, something I felt vulnerable about, maybe the only real secret I'd ever had. My wanting to tell her had nothing to do with who she was. I thought Nora would want her to know. "I wish I—"

She put her hand on my shoulder and looked at me with a strange urgency. "I'm sure you did everything you could. I'm sure you said and did every possible thing."

"But," I said, "I—"

She blinked and said, "Every. Thing. Please don't say any more."

She climbed into the vehicle and waved from behind the glass. I watched her drive away, thinking of what I had not told her and wondering for the first time how many more times I would think of it. Because I had been thinking of it less and less frequently in those days, because I had begun thinking of other things. In a way, the thing I'd wanted to tell her had freed me to think other things. And time was moving forward, naturally. My life was taking on a new shape. Because you only lived for so long, and you never really knew all the possibilities, and by the time you understood that, you were too far along to waste time on regrets.

What I'd wanted to tell her was how I'd first understood Nora was dead, which I'd known before it was ever in the newspaper, or before a police detective came by to confirm that this was the house where she'd lived for a time, and that the dead man found with her had stayed here, too. I wanted to tell her how I'd come home from work and found the rooms in their typically ordered emptiness, how the sad vacancy left by Nora was still palpable, even though many weeks had passed. How I missed the sound of Nora's laughter and the crazy things she said and the smell of the lavender oil she wore, and how in that unbearable silence I sought the company of the cat she'd left, and how, reaching with my mind into the empty corners of every room, I went to the kitchen door to call him in. I wanted to tell Nora's sister how the cat was waiting at the bottom of the steps, as usual, looking up as if waiting for me to acknowledge him, and how in that instant I'd felt a rushing sensation pass through my body, a tremendous pressure that filled my chest and ears before releasing its hold on them, how my vision blurred and darkened briefly, and how, when I could see again, a familiar dark shape rushed out ahead of me—a gray not-quite-material thing that streaked across the yard, over the trees, and into the bright and cloudless afternoon sky, growing smaller and smaller until it vanished.

THE SEVERED HANDS

WORD OF THE discovery crackled over my radio in the convenience mart. I was at a low point. A few days earlier, a colleague at the precinct had confided he'd watched my wife leave a motel with a man who fit the description of her old boyfriend, the founder of a church Dolly had been attending for the past half year. Since then, I'd been watching her, but I couldn't make up my mind about whether she was fooling around or up to something else. I'd harbored vague suspicions for a while, but one person's report fell short of absolute proof, and I couldn't pinpoint the source of the bad feeling. All I saw was the same old Dolly, pleasant and happy in a remote, self-satisfied way, and as I'd prepared to leave the house that morning, she'd kissed me goodbye with the same sphinxlike smile I'd fallen for when we were juniors in high school.

It was around seven o'clock, breakfast time. Gimzer was blowing drunk, his face waxy as he hiked his pants and described screwing women from his dating app. He started out with last night and moved backward in time, detailing other conquests, his oily stare flitting between me and the store owner. He kept count and had recently passed two hundred. It didn't matter that I tuned him out, or that the nodding and smiling store owner had no idea what he was saying.

"I like them small and firm, so she was perfect," he informed the store's yellow glare. "More than a handful goes to waste, I say. Though sometimes you got to change it up—"

My radio barked, and I listened to the message coming through, watching rain drizzle across the blacktop. Another body part had appeared on the beach. I comprehended this, but my mind returned to Dolly's potential infidelity. I'd never thought her capable of cheating. It simply wasn't a component of the person I knew. "We have to go," I said. "Runner found something by the pier."

Gimzer winced. "Who runs in this?" he said, squinting miserably into the storm, too residually wasted to think about the implications of what I'd said. "They really need us?"

It wasn't a genuine question, and the door chimed as he walked out swearing. I paid the owner, whose country of origin I guessed was India, though I'd never found a natural way to ask. His English was heavily accented, and my grasp of his native tongue so nonexistent I had no name for what language he spoke to his son, who stood in the back, sleepily wrapping sandwiches for the hot case near the door. I felt a strong affection for this man and his family, and he and I mumbled pleasantries as money passed between us. His wife, an intense woman who rarely looked up from her novels when she worked the register, had come in moments earlier, spoken a few words, and walked out without looking at my partner or me, after which her husband grabbed a broom and swept behind the counter, smiling contentedly to himself. All seemed right with his world, and I suppose my envy showed when I wished him good day.

In the car, Gimzer slouched against his rainy window, chewing the rest of his bacon, egg, and cheese while thumbing through photos of various naked young women on the phone he rested on one thigh. He was only a few years younger, but watching him smirk over the images, I felt the difference between us was profound.

"Remember Shannon Daly, brother?" he said. "Head cheerleader at West? She's lucky number two oh one. I'm going to remember her."

I unwrapped the remains of my sandwich. Back home, Dolly and Timothy would be moving slowly, preparing for the day while the furnace hummed downstairs and a morning program chattered on TV. It was a good home, nicely furnished, clean, and warm, and it hurt to imagine it falling apart. "We talking about a high school girl?"

Gimzer gave a snort and angled his leg to show me an already playing video of a topless young woman with purple hair sitting astride someone filming her with his phone. She was bouncing and moaning, and Gimzer's voice rang out encouragingly from the background. "Eighteen years old. Dances at the Jade Jaguar."

"I guess you stumbled across her online."

He winked. "Met her on career day. She stopped by the table. She posts these pole-dancing videos."

I rubbed my head. I didn't want to think about Gimzer pursuing girls Timothy probably knew from school. A horrible scenario crossed my mind—of Dolly and me divorced, Gimzer taking her home from a singles bar. Once unthinkable, such a development now seemed possible. I wrapped up the last few bites of sandwich and breathed through a little wave of nausea.

My silence had the unintended effect of making Gimzer defensive.

"Is what I'm doing illegal?" he demanded. "Tell me one thing that's prosecutable. Girls nowadays want it. They want it like they never used to. You think I got this far into triple digits by some fluke? Shit's the Wild West. You're missing out. You should lose that wife."

I turned my head and glared through watery vision, searching for words, but he'd already raised his hands.

"Sorry man. Shouldn't have brought your lady into it."

I made myself smile. I couldn't tell him about Dolly. I'd never hear the end of it—how getting married in the first place was a mistake. Plus I couldn't say the words: *My wife is fucking her new preacher, who used to be her boyfriend.* The thought alone made my vision flash black and red. And maybe the colleague who'd seen her was wrong, had somehow misunderstood. If I did nothing, the whole problem might just go away, and the world I'd known would return. Maybe it would come back improved.

"So she let you make that movie?" I said, just to focus on something else. "Right in the middle of the action?"

Gimzer chuckled and put his phone away. "I don't show nobody. Just you."

. . . .

THOUGH I REFUSED to consciously dwell on it, I dreamed almost every night about the severed hands that washed up on the beach where I'd been going since I was little. In the dreams, I was down by the ocean, big gray waves crashing close by as I wandered otherwise deserted sand. Heavy fog obscured the coastline, but I continued on through the mist, and then I reached the stretch of the beach I had never before explored, though I knew in the dream the place was imaginary.

It was here that I met the man responsible for the severed hands. I could feel his presence before he appeared, could sometimes sense he was mocking me before he stepped out from the fog, impossibly close, tall and stark white and naked and curiously hairless, even his eyelids. At this point I would wake in my bed and see Dolly turned away in her usual sleeping position, her shoulders small under the blanket, and I would start wondering what she did when I was at work or on the nights she went out to the church for a special service or some other function.

After twenty-one years together and more than half of those married, we'd acquired some new kind of problem, one for which I had no words. Something had happened to our marriage, but there was nothing definitive I could point to—no harsh language or change in our sex life. Often when we made love she appeared to be concentrating on something else, and her orgasms had begun to seem mechanical. Not that we hadn't had hit romantic doldrums before, but this was something else, a sense of new absence, as if one of us had left the room, though we were both physically present. I'd get to thinking about Matt Morbina. I remembered him from high school, a poised joker who seemed to have an answer for every challenge the universe threw at him. After fifteen years in his dad's real estate business, he'd reportedly discovered his calling as a nondenominational preacher and founded White Sands Church, not an unsurprising move for a guy who'd always coasted along on slick personality. I didn't begrudge him his success, the world being full of hustlers, but I hated that Dolly had fallen back under his influence, driving out there two or three times a week to listen to his flimflam. Lying beside her there in the dark, recalling how she'd gone on and on about Morbina at dinner, I was consumed by rage and dread and a sickness in my gut, and the severed hands were the least of my concerns.

. . . .

87

SOMEONE ON THE scene before us had put the new hand into a plastic freezer bag. Like the last three, it had been severed above the carpus by what we speculated, because of the little chips and gouges in the bones that were visible, was some kind of saw. Also like the others, it was a left hand that had belonged to an adult white male and, once removed from the body, had been tied to a piece of driftwood and dropped or thrown into the water, where it floated for an indeterminate number of hours or days before washing up, shriveled and pale, fish-nibbled and partially decomposed, its fingerprints long gone. Once we had information from the medical examiner, we could make more educated guesses about what crime had actually been committed, but I doubted the findings would be any more helpful than those from the last three hands, all of which had left Gimzer and me mystified.

This one did have a distinct marking, part of a thorny tribal tattoo that climbed up the back toward the knuckles, but that seemed as random as the tat had likely been to its owner. I turned and trudged back across the sodden sand. There were six units with their lights on, plus a news van and cars belonging to the handful of reporters who'd somehow gotten wind of the story. They were all excited by the possibility that a serial killer was in the area.

One reporter blocked my way, a good-looking woman blonde under a golf umbrella. She flattered me with her attention as she asked a series of questions to which I could only answer, "No comment," and remind her that the police chief would make a public statement when the time came.

"Oh, come on," she said quietly, her sparkling eyes probing my face. "Give me something. You're one of the detectives on this case. What do you think? This has got to be the work of one person, doesn't it?"

I shook my head and told her I was sorry.

She stuck her card into my palm without breaking eye contact. "Give me a call," she said. "Maybe we could meet someplace quiet and talk about it."

Gimzer was waiting with his arms crossed when I climbed in the car. "You are going to fuck her, correct?" he said, but without his usual fervor. This told me he was upset about the new hand. Even so, the part of his mind that focused on sex went on functioning, though his voice sounded vaguely robotic. "Tell me you're going to fuck her. Because if you're not going to fuck her, I would like you to give me that card."

"Like you need help meeting women."

He looked at me and blinked. "You're right. I'll keep my distance. Consider this my donation to the Get Benny Laid Foundation."

I shrugged out of my wet jacket and tried to warm up. There was no point in engaging Gimzer, even to point out that the reporter wouldn't have looked at me twice if she didn't think I had confidential information. The truth was I didn't know more than her or anybody else. There were no bodies, only four left hands so sea-scrubbed and waterlogged that they no longer bore useful information. There was no rash of one-handed corpses or even missing individuals that could have been dismembered. Prone to hypothesizing, Gimzer speculated a spectrum of serial killer types and mobsters. A crazed Catholic priest bent on curbing self-pleasure. A sociopath with a yacht, marking his territory. Thick-bodied capo from Atlantic City, teaching lessons to card sharps.

I myself had no theories or even inklings. We couldn't prove a homicide had taken place, and I found no traction in any of Gimzer's notions. When he talked about his ideas, brainstorming as I drove us from one site to the next, I ignored him or quietly expressed a responsible degree of skepticism. I didn't mention my recurring dream about the naked killer with a hairless body. It would only have encouraged him.

Now Gimzer stared out the window, the reporter forgotten as he studied the distant uniforms standing by the water. "What are you thinking, Benny?" he said. "Something's on your mind."

"I honestly have no idea," I said.

He swiveled, and his eyes moved up and down my face until I was blushing. It was impossible, but it felt as if he could see what I'd been dreaming about, as well as what I was thinking right now. "You're working on something in there," he said. "I hope you're not withholding, just so you can be the hero."

"Trust me," I said, supposing that by now Dolly had heard the news. Once upon a time, she would have called for reassurance, just to hear the comforting sound of my voice. Now I guessed she saved her anxiety for Matt Morbina. The thought of her texting with him now caused me to groan, "I don't know a damn thing."

He narrowed his eyes. "Why the left hand?" he mused. "You know they call the left side of the body the 'sinister' side?"

"Who calls it that?" I said.

"I don't know." He shrugged. "I read about it online. People in the old days. That tattoo reminded me of it. I've always thought tattoos were a little sinister. You know?"

"It's one of those generic tribal things," I said. "Lots of people have them. I don't think they mean anything."

"Maybe," he said. He took out his phone and opened his browser to what appeared to be a message board. "Maybe not."

. . . .

BY THE END of my shift, there was no new information about the latest hand. Gimzer and I had spent the afternoon closing an unrelated street robbery case, and the next day I'd be tied up in court. If I hadn't been so suspicious of Dolly, so panicked she was going to leave me, it would have been a typical Wednesday evening. But I was suspicious and panicked, and as I drove home I was tense at the idea of seeing her, barely holding together behind a clenched jaw and blinky eyes. I'd been going over the details my detective colleague had told me—the most damning being that he'd run Dolly's license plate—and I'd spent the last hour at my desk trying to come up with an innocent explanation for why she'd been in a motel room with the one guy who'd always been able to make her laugh. Another man might have simply asked his wife flat out, but I felt I couldn't address the matter without upsetting her, especially since being wrong might create a problem if none actually existed.

When I pulled in the drive, her car was gone, and I felt like an idiot. She'd sent me a series of texts earlier, telling me there was a special service at the church tonight. They were honoring the memory of our old history teacher, Mrs. Cave, who had recently died at the age of eighty-six. This woman had seemed ancient even back when we were in school. She was famously absentminded, and I recalled Dolly and I sitting in adjacent desks in her American history class, stifling laughs on the days the poor lady forgot to draw on one or both of her eyebrows. Dolly hadn't spoken of the teacher to me in all the years since we graduated, yet her texts today suggested Mrs. Cave had occupied an important place in her adolescence. I'd been too cowardly and cautious to suggest she was lying to herself and to me, so when she conveyed there was lasagna in the fridge and she'd be home late, I'd sent her the usual smiley face.

Our house looked a lot like the other craftsman bungalows in the neighborhood, except all the lights were out. In the front room, Timothy lay on the couch under an afghan, sucking a chocolate milkshake and watching a horror film I remembered vaguely from my own teen years. When I switched on the lamp, he blinked, irritated, then refocused on the man in a rubber ghoul mask chasing a girl around a barn, trying to stab her with a track-and-field javelin. The remains of a sack of fast food items lay on the coffee table, and the room reeked of fryer oil.

Junk food, trash, gloom. This would be our world if Dolly were to leave. Rather, it would be my full-time world and Timothy's on the days he stayed with me. Dolly had a way of instinctively cheering up a space. Like me, Timothy lacked this quality. Also like me, he was on the short side and rail-thin, with a gaunt face that was sad until he grinned, revealing strong horselike teeth. Our resemblance was so great I sometimes felt he mocked me accidentally, and I loved him with an unrelenting grimness that, as he got older, became increasingly intolerable for us both.

"Mom's at church," he said unnecessarily. "There's lasagna in the fridge."

He was just as helpless as I was. I nodded at his fast-food mess. "Not feeling the lasagna, I take it."

He looked up blankly, as if to ask if I would really punish him for choosing a burger and fries over a dish neither of us cared for. It occurred to me that he might already know Dolly was seeing someone. He was around the house more often than I was, after all. He spent more time with his mother. Plus he was still partially a child, fresher in the brain, with a perspective he himself couldn't fully comprehend and that his mother and I could only guess at. For a moment, he appeared different to me, a potential secret-keeper, a person who'd long held me in contempt.

"Why don't we go out to the church?" I said, watching for a reaction.

Timothy sighed in disgust and made a pleading face. "Church?" he said. "Do we have to?"

My relief was instantaneous. He suspected nothing. I started to hope again. I had to give Dolly the benefit of the doubt. "Come on," I said, knowing he'd be excited to hear about the new severed hand. Like everybody else in our city, he loved stories about bloody psychopaths. "Guess what washed up on the beach today?"

He sat up. "Another hand?"

"Let's talk about it in the car," I said, squinting a little, as if to imply this hand was different from the others. "Ready?"

· · · ·

WHITE SANDS CHURCH was a new building north of town, a long low brick structure with a brown roof that rose and peaked over the nave. A large carport sheltered the main entrance, and if it weren't for the skinny cross in the lawn out front, the place would have been easy to mistake for a hotel.

It was full dark when Timothy and I arrived, and cars were streaming out, their headlights illuminating the woods across the street before veering right, toward where most people lived. My son sat quietly, staring down into his phone, its screen angled enough I couldn't see what he was looking at. He'd lost interest in talking to me shortly after I described the hand, and he had since been reading news articles and scouring social media for more information to fuel his gory imagination.

I parked where we could see Dolly standing inside the glass doors, talking to another woman from the congregation. Matt Morbina stood outside, hands folded in front of him as his flock departed. He looked somewhat like the physically comical cutup I remembered, towering and gawky with a high forehead, but time had added meat to his cheeks and waist. He was glad-handing and grinning, his teeth too small for his red gums, as Timothy and I made our way toward him.

"Benny," he said. He regarded me with a forced jollity, and Timothy fell behind me as he seized my hand. "To what do I owe the honor? I guess I had to reel in Dolly to get you over here, huh?"

"Just here to see my wife," I said, doing my best to look confident in my marriage, not dwarfed and cornered into playing nice with someone I despised. I held my old classmate's gaze and said, "Kind of a weird day and night. Found another hand this morning."

Matt puckered his lips into the little circle he used to make ironically when a teacher threatened him with detention. "I heard about that. Gruesome stuff! You catch the perp?"

I absorbed his mockery without a change in affect. "Unfortunately, no," I said, "which is why I wanted to check in with Dolly. You know our son Timothy?"

"You didn't have to worry about Dolly, not here," Matt said, laying on the greasy bravado. He leaned past me and groped for Timothy's hand, losing his smile when my son recoiled. "I don't believe we've met, Timmy."

Timothy wrinkled his nose and glanced toward the darkness beside us, as if by looking away he could escape this imposing stranger.

"He's been sick," I said. "I think it's contagious."

Matt Morbina frowned, then pulled back his hand and recovered his composure. "Sorry to hear that, Timmy," he said. "I hope it's okay if we don't shake." He bared his little teeth and gave a false laugh.

Dolly was stationed inside the main doors, in the hallway outside the brightly lit chapel, which was the typical setup of pews facing a crucifix. As usual, Jesus's eyes were open, and I wondered if he was supposed to be dead or alive. Dolly's cheeks were red with what I recognized as anger, but she was nervous, too, I thought, because she had no good reason to be annoyed. She was dressed up like she never got anymore, not even for dates or parties, and she had put effort into her makeup. She raised her face and closed her eyes, allowing me to kiss her hello. She'd broken out her old perfume.

"What are you doing here?" she said. "Is everything okay?"

I studied her face, looking for signs that she felt differently about us. She noticed my examination and blushed more deeply, but she held my gaze. There was something defiant in her stare, a kind of statement I could not read.

"Yeah, everything's fine," I said. "Kind of a weird day at work, and then this tribute, so I thought Timothy and I would come out."

"That's not really like you," she noted, accurately—I had no interest in religion or my dead former teacher—and then she sighed. Her eyes moved to Timothy. "You missed it, anyway. You came all this way for nothing."

"Why don't we make something of it?" I said, trying to think of someplace we could go. There were only restaurants, diners mostly, and Dolly would be irritated we had not eaten the lasagna. At the same time, I felt I had to try. "Let's go get a drink. Timothy can have ice cream."

Timothy gave me the side-eye. "Oh, goody," he said. "Hey, Mom. You know the serial killer struck again?"

She put her hand on his shoulder and stroked it, as if to comfort him. "I know. I heard. It's horrible. It makes me want to pray." She lifted sad and stoic eyes to mine and said, "I can't. I have to help here. I'll be home later."

I was searching for something else to say when Matt Morbina appeared with an armload of flowers and passed us, and Dolly hurried over to assist him. She took a few bunches of lilies and roses and followed him down the corridor, and when they were almost to a door at the end of the hall, she burst out laughing at something he'd said.

Something poked my arm. It was Timothy, his eyebrows raised, as if he were looking at a crazy person. "Dad, come on?" he said. "Let's go?"

. . . .

BY NOW THE RAIN had stopped, and cold clear night had replaced the day's cloud cover. I dropped Timothy at home and drove around the city until I arrived at the motel where a colleague had told me he'd seen Dolly with Matt. It was a two-story building with a parking lot that went all the way around, and after circling a couple of times, I concluded they weren't there, after which I found a spot in a throng of cars near enough to the entrance that I could see who came in without being conspicuous from the road.

My situation was bleak, lose-lose. There was no guarantee they'd come back to the motel, and if they did, I would know Dolly was cheating. If they didn't appear, I would remain just as uncertain. I sat in the darkness thinking about what I'd done or failed to do. Maybe I hadn't been romantic enough. Maybe I was too much of a religious agnostic. I went on making excuses for her. It was easier than admitting she might have stopped loving me. Once that crossed my mind, I lost control momentarily and smashed my fist into the dashboard, at which point I acknowledged two things, the more obvious being that damaging the car would only make things ever-so-slightly worse, the more interesting being that I was always controlling something.

This whole time, Gimzer was texting me about the severed hands case. That was typical of him. Most likely, he was somewhere drinking, searching his dating app for women to screw. I read through his messages. He wanted me to know about some occult group in the northern part of the state that rangers had caught in the woods performing rituals with dead animals.

Could be connected, he texted. *What do U think?*

When I didn't respond, he wrote again.

Wut's up? I can see U received it.

Sorry, I wrote back perfunctorily. A pickup drove into the lot, and I studied its driver and passenger as they shot under the parking lot's lamps.

So what U think?

U there?

What do I think about what, I texted.

U think there's a connexion?

I don't know.

I've got a bad feeling.

I burst out laughing. It felt good to ridicule my partner's stupidity, now that he couldn't see me. If he knew how asinine I thought he was, he would have been outraged. *Ditto*, I texted.

U want to meet?

Normally I would have said no, but normally I would not have been sitting in a parking lot waiting to see if my wife showed up with her high school ex-boyfriend in search of a motel room where they would feel safe to be their secret selves.

Where?

His reply came in a fraction of a second after Dolly's small sport utility pulled in and drove past. I saw her unmistakable profile, and Matt Morbina's beside it. My colleague had told me they'd been here in two separate cars, and I wondered now if they thought coming in the same one would be more discreet. They drove around to the back lot, and I got out and walked to the corner of the building, looking down the rows of parked vehicles. At first I couldn't see them, and then Matt Morbina's head popped up above the cars. Dolly emerged on the driver's side, and they met behind the SUV, took each other's hands, and walked briskly toward the motel.

That was enough for me. I turned and walked away. I wasn't the sort of man to seek out confrontation, and the fact that I had my service weapon back in my car never left my mind. Any kind of overreaction— from any one of us—could lead to unforeseen consequences. I could lose my job in addition to my marriage, which I now supposed, with a sickened feeling, had been over for some time.

I got in and sat behind the wheel and let out a sob and said some unintelligible things. After a while I noticed my phone's screen had been lighting up on the passenger seat.

. . . .

GIMZER WAS IN a dive bar not far from the beach. He had a booth in the back with a blonde woman I recognized as the reporter who'd given me her card that morning. They looked hammered, sitting with a half-dozen empty beer bottles and as many shot glasses between them.

The place was crowded, and I moved through the dimness with the feeling of liberated anonymity a good bar supplied. Jukebox rock played loudly, and the air stank of old beer. My partner got up clumsily and pulled me into his embrace.

"Hey, brother," he said. "Thanks for coming out. We got to get the real work done. Detective's job never ends."

"Okay," I said, patting him quickly to make him let go.

He lowered his mouth to my ear. "Where were you?"

"What do you mean?"

"I went by your house," he said. "I know you were out. You got a lead? What aren't you telling me?"

Mentally, I rolled my eyes. "Nothing to do with work," I said, though he appeared unpersuaded.

The reporter stood and brushed off the front of her jeans. She shook my hand and reminded me of her name. "Your partner called me earlier," she said. "You wanted to meet?"

I looked at Gimzer in surprise.

"Just doing my part for the foundation," he said with a wink. "Let me get a round. You need to catch up."

Soon I was sitting beside the reporter and across from Gimzer, a beer in my hand and three shots shifting around in my stomach. My wife was having sex with our high school class clown, but this knowledge grew more abstract the more I drank, and I let it drift to the margin of my thoughts in the moment's incoherence.

The reporter was telling me her own theory of the crime. She thought the owners of the hands might be alive somewhere, imprisoned in a basement or some abandoned industrial facility. "Do you know how many unused buildings remain from the days when this was a bustling port?" she said, referring to the warehouse district that was a veritable ghost town. "If the man who's been doing this—"

"Man?" Gimzer cut in. "How do you know it's a man?"

The reporter frowned and held up one hand and said, "Statistics? Obviousness?"

Gimzer shook his head. "You believe this?" he asked me.

I nodded at the reporter. "As you were saying."

She smiled, feeling vindicated. "If *he* is there, in those buildings, he could be in hundreds of different rooms. You might never find him."

Gimzer folded his arms on the table, visibly troubled. He looked at me. "Benny's been suspiciously quiet."

I shrugged and glanced at my phone to check the time. There was a text from the colleague who'd alerted me to Dolly's affair.

Cypress Motor Inn, room 39.

I quickly pressed the button to darken the screen.

"What's that?" Gimzer said. "What's that say?"

The reporter put down her beer and peered over my arm as I turned my phone screen down.

"Nothing," I said.

"I saw it," Gimzer said. "What's at Cypress Motor Inn?"

"I don't know," I said, supposing that was the truth. I was no longer there and could not say what the motel room contained. "Just a message."

Gimzer was growing angry. "I saw who sent it, Benny. Now tell me, what's in the room?"

For an instant, I imagined Matt Morbina cutting off the left hands of a series of nondescript men. Imagined him throwing them into the sea. I thought of the killer in my dream, the man without any hair, not even eyelashes, and I laughed at the absurdity of it. I was drunk, and I saw that the reporter was watching me cautiously. "I'm not hiding anything."

"Don't bullshit me," Gimzer said. "I'm not a dummy, brother."

The reporter appeared alarmed, looking back and forth between us, but then she grabbed her beer and took a drink, sinking back against the wall.

"It's not what you think," I said.

"Tell me," said Gimzer, "or I'm going over there."

"Fine," I said, my pulse pounding in my ears. "Dolly's having an affair."

Gimzer studied me for several seconds. He pressed his lips together and said, "You expect me to believe that?" He got up and walked toward the door.

"It's true," I called after him, but he kept going.

"What's true?" the reporter said, blinking a few times. She raised a fist to cover a small burp.

I shook my head, wondering if Gimzer had left me with the reporter by design. More likely he'd set up a rendezvous with yet another woman from his dating app. It occurred to me he might go to the motel, to room 39, but I had no proof of that, and even if I had, what made me think I could stop Gimzer? What made me think I should try? I put my phone away and smiled at the reporter. "I could use another drink."

She weighed her bottle in her fingers and smiled. "That makes two of us."

. . . .

I RAN INTO my old partner the following summer, not long after the scandal at the city medical examiner's office. An employee confessed to amputating the left hands of dead homeless men and dumping them into the sea as a kind of prank, though he claimed at first that it was an experiment. He'd been caught by the medical examiner, who covered it up to avoid an uproar. They'd managed to keep the matter under wraps until a wealthy elderly couple showed up after an open-casket funeral, asking why their dead son, who happened to be a veteran, was missing a hand.

By then Gimzer was no longer on the force, and the case had been transferred to a pair of younger detectives, who ultimately made the arrests, though nothing would come of the charges beyond the two culprits losing their jobs and being fined and put on probation. The arrests made me think of Gimzer, naturally, and I supposed it probably made him think about me, too, and so it seems likely that we were, in a way, looking for each other on the afternoon I stopped into my bank to make a deposit.

He was back in uniform, this time as an armed guard, creeping up behind me while I stood in line and murmuring, "Forging a check is crime, you know."

I saw who it was and laughed with exaggerated good cheer. We shook hands vigorously, and I stepped out of the line. We talked for a while about our health and how the baseball team everyone rooted for was having their best season in years. We didn't mention the case of the severed hands, or how Gimzer had burst into the motel room at the Cypress Motor Inn the previous fall, gun drawn, scaring my then wife and her then lover out their wits. How they might have all walked away with their secrets intact, had not Gimzer, drunkenly thinking he was about to break the case open, called for backup before going in, so that a bunch of other cops were present to witness the misunderstanding. After that, it all came out—Morbina and Dolly with their confessions, the stories of Gimzer's intoxication on the job and leveraging his position of authority to get laid.

It all felt like history to me by then, prelude to a present in which Dolly and Morbina were married, running White Sands Church as a couple. Occasionally Timothy told me how crazy his mother had grown, but for the most part he and I avoided the subject of her. He was all grown up now and more or less fine. Our family had collapsed in a typically sad way, but we'd all escaped largely unscathed. Over time, I'd come to think of us as lucky.

Gimzer was another story. He'd been through a lot—the charges, internal review, a couple of newspaper articles. He mentioned none of this now. The past year had been painful for us both, and there, in the natural light of the bank, neither he nor I was eager to revisit what had happened. Still, I saw his wounded eyes and knew he blamed me.

"How are you doing?" he said. "I mean, *really*, how are you?"

"I'm fine," I said, which was the truth. I had the dating app now, like him, but mainly I was content to do my job and then go home to the house where I slept and ate and occasionally cleaned. "You still playing the field?"

He chuckled. "Just bagged two thirty-one. Things slowed down after I got fired, but they picked back up."

I shook my head, thinking about the number. It occurred to me he might know more about people in our city than anyone. "Great to see you," I said.

"Yeah," he said, losing his smile. "You should give me a call. We could catch up."

"I'll do that," I assured him, though as far as I was concerned, we were out of things to say.

I went to the back of the line, and he returned to his place by the bright window, where he could watch everything. I faced forward the whole fifteen minutes it took to get a teller. I felt a slight panic when I was done, then turned and found he'd disappeared. Hurrying to my car, I vowed to use a different branch from now on. He appeared in my rearview as I left, stepping out from the entrance, squinting like he was trying to memorize the description of a getaway car—color, make, license plate. As if he'd seen something suspicious, or had some crime to report. As if anyone would listen to him now, anyway.

FIRST
RESPONDER

MARSHALL REPLACED the gas pump slowly, afraid to look at the stranger asking for help. He couldn't say why he was so ashamed. Going back as far as he could remember, part of him had been chicken-shit. This man wasn't even much of a hitchhiker, had no visible scars or prison tats, just a big graceless body with a bland baby face and a meek way of standing with his hands in the pockets of his extra-large black fleece. The low-top hiking shoes and time-eaten backpack suggested his hard-luck story was true: that a bear had sniffed out his campsite while he was washing in a stream, and though he'd scared it off with an emergency whistle (he pulled down his shirt collar to show the instrument hanging on a cord around his neck), he'd been too late to save his tent and food. After renting a series of motel rooms, he now lacked the cash to get home. He could have made phone calls, but his mom was in poor health, and worrying strained her heart. Nor did he wish to trouble men who'd put their lives on hold to come get him—surely, Marshall understood.

"Take your time, please. I'm in no rush." The man had a thin, high-pitched voice and took his moist little hands from his pockets to show them to Marshall, as if to prove he wasn't hiding a weapon. The impression he made was disconcerting, incongruous, as though he were the lost child of some pale, gigantic, nearsighted species. "I'll understand if it's no."

Marshall felt a grinding in his bowels. *No*, he wished to say, to banish this stranger back into the bright pine woods from which he'd materialized while Marshall was stuck refueling the car. In his head, though, he heard what others—guys he knew—would say: the man was only some poor bastard who needed his help. He imagined his father blushing, refusing to look Marshall in the eye. This stranger seemed to read his mind, showing the faint beginning of a smile, as if he knew Marshall would turn coward and say no, could see that's the kind of person Marshall was, selfish and afraid, and he was only asking because he'd have been stupid not to try.

"Where, again?" Marshall looked up the empty road, longing to be already on his way. "What's your town called?"

Sighing, the man repeated a place name a fourth time, pronouncing it slowly, like he was on a phone with a bad connection. A hamlet in the upper part of the state. He'd shrugged before when Marshall said he'd never heard of it, as if to convey most people hadn't, adding he could afford a bus ticket if Marshall got him to the coast. "Like I said, no pressure."

Yeah, sure, Marshall thought. Pressure was behind all words, men's words especially, and he saw in his mind how the hitchhiker would look at guys he knew, had any been present—with a slight grimace that conveyed, *I don't know why I try; just look at this kid*—leaving Marshall to wonder once more what was so detectably wrong with him. It wasn't his body. He was a little taller than average and in excellent shape and girls often called him cute or complimented his stomach muscles before they turned against him, just as initially friendly guys grew bored with him after a hangout or two. It must have been how he carried himself, right? A confidence thing? He watched the hitchhiker pass the backpack hand to hand and considered revealing he was twenty hours deep in a cross-country drive to the beach, where men he'd only emailed and spoken to on the phone were waiting to make him an ocean lifeguard, a job that was not for the faint of heart or the physically weak. He would be like some plainclothes cop producing a badge, or a volunteer soldier reporting to boot camp, letting a casual gesture make the hitchhiker rethink any criminal plans.

It was then that he saw helping this poor son of a bitch would make the first great story of his lifeguard summer, one of many he'd tell the people who would inevitably, maybe unconsciously, test his character. And maybe this act, as nervous as it made him, would steel him for the discomfort ahead, for moments in which the life or death of a total stranger depended on his ability to plunge into the thrashing sea. Nor would dropping this guy off on the way keep him from his goal of reaching his destination around nightfall and calling his parents, who'd vowed to wait up. He found the dark eyes behind the crooked glasses and pointed to the passenger door, twitching at the prospect of riding with this dirtball for the next nine hours.

"Get in," he said. "I'll take you as far as I'm headed."

. . . .

THE HITCHHIKER introduced himself as Eric, offering no last name. The hairs creeping from his nostrils and sprouting along the rims of his red ears suggested he was north of thirty. Eric looked around the small front seat they shared with an air of vague disapproval, asking Marshall questions about himself and shrugging at the answers, adding bored and disappointed noises that suggested he'd met people like Marshall before. He wrung his damp hands on his lap and only looked at Marshall with darting glances.

Classic defense mechanisms, Marshall thought, steering through interstate traffic. Eric probably felt threatened and embarrassed, begging a ride from a twenty-year-old kid. In a few short months, Marshall would laugh about this with people back home. *Guy was a loser*, he'd scoff, *and it goes without saying he smelled like shit*. They'd hang on his words, everybody impressed by Marshall's newfound gravitas. "Never thought I'd do surf rescue," he said, pleased this time to see the hitchhiker shrug. He felt sure Eric had never been a first responder. "I surprised myself with how quickly I improved in the certification programs."

The hitchhiker exhaled heavily through his nose, as if it pained him to think about this subject. "Lifeguarding, wow." He gazed at the passing spring landscape, the blossoming trees and thin waterfalls spilling down the mountainsides. "Great summer job."

Marshall accelerated, reminding himself Eric was a grown man who'd gotten himself stranded in a rural area hundreds of miles from home. This was not a competent person, not someone who deserved his respect. "After I graduate, I'll get a real job, obviously. Either that or do law school." He smiled, doubting Eric had a real job, let alone a JD. "I could do anything, if you think about it."

The hitchhiker wiped his red, bitten mouth with the back of his sleeve. "I tried college. Wasn't for me."

Marshall imagined Eric a college freshman, one of those sluggish rubes who vanished by the first snowfall. "What didn't you like? Couldn't find the right major?"

"I hated listening to the talk. All those words and ideas. I couldn't keep my thoughts straight."

Marshall decided this was the point of college. He would often lie in bed after a day of class, unable to sleep because his thoughts were racing. He glanced at the large, child-faced man. "That's what's supposed to happen," he said, considering this a checkmate-level remark. "Obviously."

The hitchhiker stared ahead. "I'm not interested in being brainwashed. I can think for myself, thank you very much."

Oh, Marshall thought, a slight shock running down his arms to his fingertips. I've picked up a crazy person. "I guess I'm not afraid of new paradigms."

Putting his hands into his fleece pockets, Eric grunted. "Tell yourself whatever you need to."

. . . .

HE DECIDED TO get off the interstate in the next mountain town. He had to use the bathroom, and he was hungry and wouldn't lose much time if he grabbed something from a gas station mart. Most of all, though, he wanted to rid himself of Eric. Marshall was tired of having him in the car, tired of his heavy breathing and his obnoxious defense mechanisms, tired of the oniony smell wafting off of Eric's oily skin and probably embedding itself in the upholstery. At the same time, Marshall was reluctant to suggest they part ways while speeding along at eighty miles an hour. He could see Eric expected this news. It was clear in the way the hitchhiker pouted and stared through each veil of fog they entered, as if he were counting the minutes until Marshall gave him a chance to say, *I knew it all along*.

Well, that wasn't going to happen. Marshall refused to give Eric that satisfaction. No, it would be better to trick the hitchhiker and drive off while he was in the bathroom, to humiliate the older, softer, less intelligent man on all fronts. It would make a good story: how charitable he'd been until realizing his passenger was a psychopath. How he'd made his clever escape. He'd describe the bad breath, recount the strange remarks, the obviously made-up account involving the bear. He would speculate about what Eric had really been doing where they'd met, and guys he knew would shake their heads in slow disbelief and ask what Marshall had been thinking, letting such a stranger into his car, and he would shrug as though to say, Sometimes you take risks in this life. He'd even tell his parents someday, when he was older and had proven beyond a doubt that he knew what he was doing.

He parked at a gas station in the foggy pines. "Looks like an outdoor bathroom," he said. "Probably a single. I've got to go pretty bad, if you don't mind my going first. I need to get some food, too."

Eric turned to regard the small, decrepit-looking station and the battered brown men's room door in its outer wall. Lowering his head, he sniffed back a jet of snot, resting in the posture of large, sad stuffed animal. He gave no indication of getting up.

Marshall smiled apologetically. "I don't mean to be rude, but I'd appreciate it if you got out and waited. We don't know each other, and I'd like to lock up my things." The more he said, the stronger he felt. "If want to pick up some things for lunch, I'll buy," he said. "You must be hungry."

Eric sighed raggedly and climbed out. Standing next to the car in the cool mountain air, he squinted up at the hazy circle of the sun. He stayed like that while Marshall locked the vehicle and bolted himself inside the foul little bathroom, and he was still there, gazing upward, apparently unconcerned with damaging his eyes, when Marshall came out, drying his clean hands on the fabric of his shorts.

Marshall unlocked the driver's side door, then hesitated. "You have to go?"

In response, the hitchhiker turned and put his hand on the door handle.

Marshall got in and closed his door. His heart began to pound as he shoved the key into the ignition. Eric's disgusting backpack was still on the floorboard. He supposed he could dump it down the road, within the hitchhiker's sight. Still, it was risky. He might run over the man's foot as he pulled out, or Eric might hold on and get dragged. What would Marshall tell the police? That he'd picked up a hitchhiker against his better judgement and then injured him with reckless driving? Eric bent and peered through the window, baring his teeth in something like a smile, taking a long moment to look into Marshall's eyes—acknowledging that he knew what Marshall was thinking—before he gestured toward the door lock.

"Whoops," Marshall said, mouthing the words conspicuously as he reached across. "My bad."

Eric said nothing as he strapped himself in. Paradoxically, his sharp smell seemed intensified by the fresh mountain air.

Marshall's face burned as he drove out of the lot, both ashamed and resentful of the responsibility he'd taken on. He focused on the fact that soon he'd never have to worry about Eric again. And he supposed guys he knew would at least respect his good deed. Maybe that's the kind of man Marshall was deep down, a standup guy people could trust. It wasn't especially interesting, but he could live with having a reputation for being dependable. Women would like that, he felt. Every boring, dependable guy he knew was in a long-term relationship.

As they were getting back on the interstate, Eric looked over. "I thought you were getting food."

Marshall blushed. "Oh yeah. I guess I forgot," he said. "I forget to eat sometimes."

The hitchhiker made a huffing sound, almost like a laugh, and turned to stare at a dead buck bloating on the roadside.

. . . .

THEY WERE HIGHER in the mountains when they came to where traffic was stopped. The road was steep and winding, paved up to the edges of sheer drop-offs that stole Marshall's breath when he looked out over them. He'd always been afraid—irrationally, he figured—of highways like this, and seeing all the slow-climbing semis with flashing hazard lights and the runaway truck ramps leading up rocky slopes filled him with anxiety. Beside him, Eric was biting and eating his fingernails and fleshy cuticles. He looked content.

They were stopped completely on an ascent, a yard or two behind a minivan. A number of cars and trucks ahead had turned off their engines, and people were getting out and stretching, peering into phones and then lifting them into mist before bringing them back down to eye level. Marshall took his own phone from the center console, hoping to be lucky and find information about how long the delay would last.

"Cell phones don't work up here," the hitchhiker said, shaking his large head like people would never learn. Just as he finished his sentence, the NO SERVICE message flashed on Marshall's screen.

"They've been doing construction on this road for years," Eric continued, impassively watching the drivers of separate vehicles consulting one another.

"Is it usually this bad?" Marshall asked. It was late afternoon, and at this rate he was unlikely to get to the beach before it started getting late. He would have to call his parents when he got service back and give them an update. He craned his neck, trying to see past the cars and people who crowded the bend ahead.

"There's a fireroad about a half mile up that goes around," the hitchhiker said. He shrugged. "A bit off the beaten path, but it links up to the state routes. It's probably faster."

Marshall wondered if the man knew what he was talking about. They'd passed numerous service roads up here, and they all seemed indistinguishable from each other. "You know this road?"

The hitchhiker nodded, gazing ahead dully. "Just saying. I'm not in a rush. Could be a while, though."

Marshall swallowed dryly, his every instinct telling him that getting off the interstate and taking Eric's shortcut would be a mistake. But the hitchhiker, who was digging in his ear with one of the fingers he'd just chewed raw, seemed casually resigned to getting where he was going either way. Why not? he thought. Even if they got lost, they'd find their way eventually, and then there would be no question which of them was smarter. If the shortcut worked, he imagined Eric would respect him for taking a chance. It was win-win, and it would make for a great story—his impromptu adventure in the mountains with an unhygienic stranger. He would take a selfie with Eric when all of this was over, post it on social media. *Don't ask*, the caption would read. Hell, maybe they'd end up parting on friendly terms, and years from now he'd think of Eric and laugh, wondering briefly what had become of the hapless wanderer he'd helped when he was young and on his way to the success he'd have achieved by then.

"Okay," he said, and he followed the hitchhiker's directions, changing lanes and pulling onto the shoulder and driving past the stopped cars while the people inside turned and stared.

. . . .

IT WAS DUSK when his car finally ran out of gas and died rolling. He steered onto the unpaved lane's narrow shoulder and looked around. He'd never been so far up in this range, where patches of snow lay along the sides of what could barely be termed roads, and veins of ice split the rock faces that climbed into the darkening sky. Long shadows thickened where the setting sun didn't reach, and the air in the car was growing cold quickly. Marshall could see his breath. He lowered his head, unable look at Eric. He didn't have words to express how furious and disgusted and afraid he felt, and even if they formed in his head, he had no energy to say them.

The hitchhiker had grown more confident, more comfortable, the farther they got from the interstate. Now he was looking around actively, as if he'd woken from an invigorating nap. He took off his glasses and blinked at Marshall as he wiped the lenses on his thigh and slipped them into his fleece's breast pocket. "There's a gas station up where this meets a county road," he said, his rotten breath drifting across the front seat. "Not too far. We can borrow us a gas can."

Marshall studied at the wide face beside his. He couldn't say if its expression mocked him. "Why don't you go?" he said. "You know this area."

Eric's large head nodded slowly. "We could do it that way. But I'd need some money or a credit card. If you don't mind giving it to me, I'll be sure to bring it back."

Of course, Marshall thought bitterly. And leave me up here, totally broke. He could see how that would play with people back home, what a sucker he'd look like. Then of course there'd be the humiliation of needing his parents to come rescue him. "No, it's fine. Let's go."

They walked a mile or so along the ridge. Marshall, having taken extra clothes from his bag, was wearing sweatpants over his shorts and three shirts under his hooded sweatshirt, and he was shivering anyway. A few paces ahead, Eric carried his backpack, seeming refreshed and apparently warm enough in his fleece and jeans.

Marshall stumbled once in the growing dark and realized he was ravenous. The road appeared to be getting narrower, tapering down to a skinny, potholed groove. "How much farther?"

"Just a little." Eric stopped and pointed into the bare trees beside them. A path, thin but visible, led up the mountainside and over the next rise. "I actually know this trail. We can probably cut off an hour."

An hour? Marshall thought. Hadn't Eric said the gas station was just up the road? He didn't believe him. At the same time, he had to admit, it was possible he was overreacting. Eric had walked all the way over these mountains to get to where they'd met. Maybe the guy had a distinct sense of distance and time. Maybe that explained his strangeness. Maybe Marshall was just dealing with a different kind of person. He looked at the large figure who stood shadowed by the trees and twilight, trying to make sense of the face that betrayed no inner feeling at all. "You sure that's not a deer track?"

The hitchhiker gestured at a tree trunk, where someone had chipped away a few inches of bark with a hatchet or knife. "It's a local trail," he said. "I'm going this way. You go on up the road. I'll see you at the gas station."

Some sense of self-preservation kicked in, and Marshall found himself nodding. He drew the line at walking into strange woods at night. "I think we should just say goodbye now," he stated, bracing himself for Eric's response.

A sad smile formed on the hitchhiker's face. "I understand how you feel, and if that's how you want it, fine. But I'll still need a ride." He chewed his lip, and when he spoke again, he sounded disappointed, as if they'd come to the verge of completing something, and Marshall had let him down. "It's up to you, but I'll be honest. I'd appreciate it if you could get me back to the interstate. It could take me a day or two to catch a new ride out here."

Marshall felt his jaw drop, then closed his mouth. The gall, he thought, incipient fear replaced by indignation. Eric genuinely felt in no way to blame for their predicament, was now acting like Marshall was inconveniencing *him*. He understood now how someone like Eric could end up begging for rides hundreds of miles from home. Such a person would never take responsibility for himself, and it was up to those like Marshall to do the work in this world. This was more than a lesson; it was a watershed, something guys he knew would understand, a truth his dad would appreciate, scowling bitterly as he told his tale. Half of this rotten species consisted off freeloaders and takers, and it fell to the respectable and accountable to stay the course and see things through, no matter how unpleasant it was. He tried to communicate this with a hard stare, even as he knew Eric and men like him were invulnerable to shaming. It occurred to him then how awful it would be if he were to walk to the gas station along the fireroad and find Eric waiting, arms crossed, filthy hands tucked into his armpits. The hitchhiker would smile widely, as if to say I told you so. Marshall gritted his teeth. "All right," he said. "Lead the way."

· · · ·

IT WAS much later and very cold and dark when they came to a point where the land flattened out. Marshall could not have said how far they had come or how long they had been walking, or even whether they were on a plateau or down in a valley. The trail had climbed and dropped until he'd lost all sense of altitude, whether the air was thin or simply freezing cold. His mouth was dry, and his breath made rough little sawing sounds. His stomach was cramped with hunger.

The full moon and its complement of stars had slid down over the mountains, throwing faint light on this patch of level earth. Eric was far ahead, gradually shrinking as Marshall struggled to keep up with his moving shadow. The hitchhiker had stopped responding to questions and shouts a while ago, and Marshall only went on following him for fear of being left out here alone.

Coming through a stand of pines, he saw they had reached a meadow. A large fire burned in the distance, and Eric was hurrying toward it, shouting men's names. Beyond the flames were structures, small and boxy, like prefabricated steel sheds.

Several figures silhouetted by the firelight came to the edge of the darkness, heeding Eric's call. Marshall realized this was where they had been bound all along. There was no question about it. Guys he knew were no longer laughing at him, no longer jeering, but crying out for him to turn and run. He stumbled on, scorning them, hungry and thirsty, longing for sleep. Up ahead, the hitchhiker was talking to the men at the fire, and they had turned face to him. They were waiting, and whatever lay ahead would make a kind of story, though he doubted he would tell it.

THE DOCUMENTARY

SO, KODAK, you're not actually from here.

The boy is right. She's not from this fishing town on the Gulf. She grew up in northern Michigan, not far from Sleeping Bear Dunes. But she moved to Los Angeles after high school. Had this pint-sized apartment in Hollywood.

The boy smirks when he uses her moniker, *Kodak*. He's technically not a boy—must be thirty, same as the camerawoman wife, a bone-skinny thing with a bird's voice and sunglasses she's lifted to watch the camera display, recording this dialogue taking place at the dinner table. The couple is old enough to own a house, and they might, judging by the Mercedes outside. Still, when she sees them, Kodak's brain thinks *kids*, making her feel ancient. And there's the way they study the furnishings—this secondhand table bearing someone else's scratches, the mismatched china cabinet she dragged off a curb—which offset the framed blown-up photographs on the walls. She can almost see them thinking, Seascapes are fine (yawn), but who eats alone among portraits of oil-stained birds?

The boy and the girl are from some Brooklyn place, one of the neighborhoods that starts with B. She's tempted to ask, Who brought you to these woods and left you?

So why L.A.? the boy asks, as if it's a chore. His eyes convey his expectation that she'll now waste time talking about herself. Were you doing movies? TV?

Kodak shakes her head. She won't say big brother came home from Beirut and ate a gun, or that her folks went quiet after that. These two—filmmakers, they call themselves, and she guesses that's right, despite the digital—don't care about the endlessness of the pines or the vast and lonesome lake. They don't care about kids on four-wheelers in the forest, searching for something they couldn't name if they tried. It's a story, and it's Kodak's, but it's not the one her visitors want. The story they want has little to do with her, and she's mostly in the way. I wanted to learn to surf, she says. That whole thing.

Right, says the boy. Jeff is his name. Sure. How'd you find this place?

She smiles at this impossible question. There are too many answers she won't give. I was forty-six and broke. I'd figured out the camera. I was lonely. Three, count them, three DUIs. I'd become overfamiliar with the neurochemistry of narcotics. Plus, it's the American story, isn't it? Seizing what's there for the taking? This was my once chance.

I didn't have anything going on, she says finally. There were these poor animals in the news, seabirds and turtles just coated with oil. You could see the people trying to save them were worn down. Figured I'd try to do some good for once.

And did you? Jeff asks, his eyes dark and intent, drilling her suddenly. Do you feel like you made a difference?

Kodak's no dummy. She's not going to bring up the photos *National Geographic* bought or the one that made it into *Time*. She'd like to go on living here after the thing they're making comes out. I helped, you know, she says, getting flustered, ensuring she'll look stupid in the final cut. I did some volunteering with the animal washing, but I didn't have the stomach. With the pelicans, you had to restrain them and hold their mouths open so someone could reach in with a brush and scrub. They have these giant tongues, you know. I worried I'd hurt one. In the end, I did a lot of patrolling—looking for animals, dead or alive. Other stuff, too, like taking people food. Nothing heroic. The whole thing was a collective effort.

What about Captain Ray? Jeff asks. Was he a hero?

Kodak's surprised, but quick enough to say, I didn't know him well. He did more than I did, I can tell you that much. Much more than I did.

. . . .

AFTERWARD, SHE WATCHES them pack up. The skinny wife puts the camcorder and sound equipment into the trunk, and Jeff stands over the windshield on the driver's side, using a plastic card from his wallet to chip away the hard white scum left by lovebugs they've smashed. The insects swarm this time of year, mating in the air, and even now the wife is shooing away a bunch of them with her hand, combing a couple out of her hair with her fingers, her expression pure disgust. Kodak recollects the interview and decides she hasn't said anything too bold or revealing, but she can't stop her hands from trembling, and she puts on the teakettle, thinking she'll drink something calming and take a walk, maybe snap pictures of mushrooms or trees or anything else that catches her eye. She doesn't have to work until this evening.

She feels better once the black car is gone. She listens to the water race and thinks of photographing Ray in the sea, leading a group of men and women walking an injured bottlenose dolphin to shore so people could wash it. She hasn't thought about that day in years, she realizes, surprised because she used to talk about it all the time. Of course, she sees things differently now, but still, those dolphins. There was a whole pod out there, and Ray helped save more than twelve, a tall man in soaking-wet clothes, thin but big-jointed and strong, calmly striding back and forth between the land and the distressed animals thrashing in the oil-patched shallows. He took each sea mammal under his long hands, talking the way one might talk to a dog, surprising tenderness in his craggy face.

Though she'd heard people talk about Ray and his fleet, Kodak hadn't seen him before that morning, and for a few short hours, she fell in love. She shudders to recall. And yet something in the afternoon, even the light, graced everyone present with a saintly glow. She was captivated, shooting picture after picture of Ray and the others, convinced she was witnessing something transcendent, a communion between different kinds of sea creatures, and it was one of these photos that carried her name into the world, though it didn't go anywhere.

Two years later, Ray was dead from lung cancer. By then, the whole country had forgotten the oil spill that gripped its attention for a few angry weeks, and plenty of locals had, too, unless it was to blame the oil company for the economy, but even that comment could start a fight. Yes, the fisheries were still damaged from all the poison on the ocean floor, but that only made the oil company name mean *good jobs* more than ever, and, truth was, everybody wanted to forget. That was the kind of place it was; you didn't touch what was buried. The volunteers were long gone, moved on to the next tragedy. She'd watched them go, three or four or five at a time until their number dwindled away. The last few had worried for her, asking what Kodak would do on her own, but she'd shrugged them off, unwilling to leave as quickly as she'd come. She wasn't like these people, these wanderers of various ages and backgrounds who went disaster to disaster, looking for a cause. She only wanted to be at peace, and she'd achieved it here, in this quiet town with a harbor filled with fishing boats. The place had no need for an art photographer, and so she'd adapted, taking shifts at a seafood restaurant and later the bar where she worked now. It was difficult but manageable, and when Captain Ray died, Kodak had seen an opportunity to resurrect her professional career.

She'd gone to the service with her smallest camera in a back pocket, thinking it unseemly to appear with her Canon slung around her neck, and in the chapel where Ray's family and friends prayed and spoke of their memories, she'd been moved by the changes that came over their red, raw-looking faces. They remained the fishing folk she'd gotten to know—no bath or hairdressing could wash away that wear and tear, but they looked dignified all the same, the men shaved and brushed, the women with their braids pinned up, their faces proudly painted. The children were children, naturally beautiful in Sunday clothes. She followed the procession to the graveyard, where the sun broke through the clouds over the trench they'd dug, and people wept openly and embraced, willing to tolerate her standing at the edge, camera snapping softly.

. . . .

SMALL CROWD tonight. Kodak draws pitchers and pours shots for familiar fishermen, Coast Guard, oil workers. The weather is muggy and still, the window units humming beneath the usual conversations and jukebox songs. Moving back and forth under the various mounted trophy fish—mahi, sailfish, a few impressive sharks—she cleans the counter with a rag and waits for a customer to signal.

Jeff and his wife are here, sitting with three shrimpers they've imposed themselves on. The filmmaker sits at the head of the table, cheeks flushed and talking loudly over his sloshing beer, one hand on the back of chair where his wife leans back, sending a message on her phone with her thumbs. The shrimpers appear somewhere between annoyed and amused, listening with their battered arms crossed. They trade looks and drink their beers, and occasionally one says something and the others laugh. They are lifers, these men in their forties and fifties who've worked these waters since high school, white men made brown and red by the sun. Kodak went to bed with one of them a few times in the months after the spill. Everybody was pairing off randomly in those days, outsiders and locals, drinking and getting stoned and hooking up to forget the dead oil-soaked animals and the reddish-brown slicks floating in the water. Kodak remembers sleeping with this man, that it was fine, fun even, until they both lost interest. It wasn't until Ray died that she learned who this fisherman was in this place and regretted ever touching him.

She squirms now at the thought of his hands on her. She feels someone looking from the far end of the bar, and it's Thaddeus, the local postmaster, calm and smiling with his air of perpetual surprise, his gentleness charming in a man his size. He's sitting with two other Black men down there, one of whom is a city employee. She asks if he wants another pint.

You seeing this? Thaddeus's eyes flit toward Jeff and his wife. His eyebrows go up, and he laughs nervously. The men with him glance at Kodak, then look back at their drinks.

They're making a documentary, she says. They came by and interviewed me about the cleanup. Just a few questions.

Right, questions, Thaddeus says. They're asking lots of questions. For their movie.

The city employee frowns tightly and gazes past Kodak, pretending to watch the muted baseball game. The other friend, a regular who rarely speaks, smiles ironically, conveying without words that the foolishness of outsiders is unfortunate but cannot be helped.

Kodak looks back at Thaddeus, slowly understanding what the men are telling her. That Jeff and his wife know what she figured out only after Ray's funeral, where everyone had been white.

She noticed things after that, the occasional graffiti she'd assumed was the doing of asshole kids, the way white people in the bar smiled pointedly at her after they saw her talking with Black and Latino customers, something closed off behind their eyes. How business dropped off a cliff for a week when someone hung a noose on a tree outside the high school. She might have thought it was all in her head if people hadn't start confiding things, white and Black people alike, low voices that came from nowhere and went nowhere, saying stuff about Ray and some of the other white men around town, how they'd *made trouble* or *done some things* or *had old ways*. She now knew Black men and boys avoided certain neighborhoods and parts of town, especially after nightfall. She'd decided against selling the photos from Ray's funeral, and she destroyed the ones she'd developed. For weeks, she worried someone would ask about them and whether they would appear somewhere, but no one did, and she'd gradually come to understand that the memory of her taking them was buried.

She looks up to see Jeff walking out the door into the thick night. He carries himself with the arrogance she recognizes, and the wife follows, putting away her phone and digging in her big purse. The fishermen at the table are looking past one another. One of them tilts his beer glass back until it's empty. Another puts out his cigarette and stands. The others get up, and together they follow the strangers outside.

Thaddeus smiles down and places his empty glass on the bar.

Kodak takes it, eyeing the residue clinging to its insides before she drops it into the tub on the floor, where it crashes more loudly than she expected. There's a loud voice outside, and she looks up. People are going to the door to watch. She won't call the police until someone says to. Some of the others in here, she knows, are also in on it. She takes a glass from the dishwasher—still warm—and starts to pour Thaddeus a fresh ale. She feels the old impulse to walk to her car and drive away, to light out for someplace new until a vision of innocence presents itself. But she's had her share of disappointment, and instead she watches the amber-colored beer fill the glass to the brim.

EVERYTHING IS GOING TO BE OKAY

AT THE SOUND of my uncle's name, the car rental clerk stopped typing and put on her glasses. I held still while she gave me a second look, waiting for the moment she saw me for what I was, a onetime local who'd spent a decade behind bars. No matter I'd shaved and changed in the station, or that I looked more Clark Kent than generic Hollywood thug. My personal history felt written on my face.

"You're related to Dan Strayer?" She was squinting.

I couldn't place her, but she was around fifty, enough older that I'd have been a random kid when she was in the youthful business of deciding who it was important to know around here. She had one of those kind faces that had learned distrust, possibly from years of renting cars to poor hillbillies too broke to afford their own rides. "Guilty," I said.

She laughed—a sharp *ha!* that conveyed her opinion of my dead mom's brother—then went back to her keyboard, loosened up now. "I know Dan. He's a deacon at Willow Creek. Wasn't aware he had any people left. That's nice," she said, drawing out the last word.

Willow Creek. I'd passed the megachurch on the bus. You couldn't miss the place—a cluster of white buildings with Spanish tile roofs, a parking lot fit for a shopping mall, and a thirty-foot Jesus commanding a retention pond's dark waves. It looked bizarre in the fields, like maybe Luke Skywalker and his robots lived there. "Big church by the interstate, right? Real nice statue?"

"Civilization's last stand." She said it quietly, then focused on something out the window. "Is your wife cold? She want to bring the baby inside?"

I turned, worried Wendy was acting crazy, maybe tossing Gracie in the air like she had outside a diner last week, sending some grandpa to the verge of cardiac arrest. Some hours earlier, she'd scored pills at a travel center, turning pale white and daffy once she'd eaten them, and she was still shaking the effects outside, hiding her delirium as best she could in the pink parka that reached her boots and was too heavy for the mid-forties. Looked odd, but people give a new momma wide latitude, and from the counter she looked like any young woman telling her baby about the saplings reclaiming the land across the road. All I could see of Gracie was the pink cotton hat and a patch of forehead. I swiveled back to the clerk. "She doesn't like being inside. She's into fresh air. For the kid, you know."

The lady gave a snort and smiled to herself. "Okay then. I can see she's a very good mommy."

Sure you can, I thought. People here never missed a chance to judge. That hadn't changed. I grinned wide, pulling myself back into the family man act. "You say deacon? That a big deal?"

The clerk shrugged, clearly unimpressed with Uncle Dan. That seemed about right, both from what I could see of her and what I knew of him. Now I was the one scrutinizing, noting how much healthier this woman was than the bedraggled locals I'd glimpsed in town. Her hands were soft, her red fingernails recently manicured, and her wedding and engagement rings sparkled when she held up my license. I suspected she owned the place, and the gas station next door, as well. There were HAMBY FOR PRESIDENT signs in the windows of both. "Deacon's an honorary title," she explained with strained politeness. "I think it's safe to say he's made some donations."

That worried me, but I kept smiling. "Really? Anything significant?"

"His name might be on a brick. Nothing flashy. He's very . . . involved. Wanted to head the youth ministry when he first joined."

Of course, I thought. The disease he had, you didn't get over. "How'd that work out?" Wendy was bouncing on her heels out there. I felt rushed.

"Didn't." The woman heaved a little sigh and raised her eyebrows. "Dan wasn't the man for the job."

I had a visceral memory of him getting off me, long ago. My face went hot and my mouth dried up. I was sweating, feeling old defilements I worried would reverberate until I died. "I'd guess he wasn't."

She put the keys on the counter and tilted her head affably. "There's room for all in His kingdom. Tell your uncle Misty says hi."

. . . .

NOW THAT I was free of the halfway house, I was back to robbing. I'd ripped off about a dozen men, soft white traveling business types too drunk to stand up straight or see clearly, let alone remember who stole from them or might have. I'd strike between midnight and last call, while there were still crowds and disappearing was easy, follow some fool who broke off from the herd and get in his face on a side street. Or I'd pocket what a dummy left out on a table or bar. I was quick to leave afterward, first the scene and larger neighborhood, then the city. I knew to learn the public transit routes and stay on the go, and to never, ever return to the scene of a crime. It wasn't terribly lucrative, but I'd scrounged up a couple of grand in cash and maybe another few thousand in jewelry and watches.

I'd never felt like a thief. The label didn't stick in my head or heart. The men I robbed were sales types, financial advisors, consultants, guys out taking all they could, money and women and pleasure, and I had no word for someone who takes from takers. I'm not trying to get deep here. The point is I felt no shame. This infuriated judges and prosecutors who demanded to know what I had to say for myself. I just looked back at them, feeling neither guilt nor defiance, until they finished saying whatever they were going to say no matter what. Not that I couldn't have justified my actions. Anybody who's made sixth grade can mash together that argument.

All the same, I had to stop. Not because I wanted to. I hadn't experienced a moral awakening. I was forty-two and scared of another stint in lockup. I dreaded the volatile crowds, the cellmate lottery, the vast inner world of threats and dispiriting smells. If I kept knocking over corporate assholes, I'd get busted eventually. I was good at taking what wasn't mine—like most grownups, I'd made an art of my vocation—but I couldn't control all the variables. Lately, when I flipped through some chump's billfold, smelling the cash and sometimes leather or residue of smoke, I felt a reckless rush, like I'd ripped out a stranger's pulsating heart. It took me back to former days, before I got snatched. If I could pull off this final hit, I told myself, I could move on, start over, get normal before it was too late.

. . . .

WE WOUND up in a red hatchback with Arizona plates and smudged windows. It smelled of ashtray but was cleaner than the bus. Wendy grimaced when I told her to strap Gracie into the baby seat. "If a cop sees you with her up here, he'll stop us." Stubbornly mad, she fiddled with buckles and clips, letting out pissy little sighs until I lurched back and did it for her. The blue-eyed doll stared back while I tightened the harness. It was uncannily convincing, like some fresh little human corpse.

Through the plate glass, Misty smiled and waved, giving us the sendoff a sweet little family deserved.

"Nosy bitch," Wendy said as I pulled out of the lot. Her pink coat swallowed her up to her chin. She only removed it in motel rooms to shower and change the sweatshirts and jeans she rotated underneath. She might have been a knockout in some parallel timeline. In this one, she was underfed and strung out, her greasy black bangs uneven from where she'd scissored them in Louisville.

I concentrated on driving. I hadn't been at the wheel in a month plus and felt too big for the vehicle, like it was a go-cart or bumper car. I kept catching myself speeding. "I'm just glad she didn't come out to see the baby."

Wendy blinked. "If she tried to touch Grace, I'd kill her."

"Totally normal response."

"Fuck you, Aaron." She turned and looked back, the way a new parent might check on a baby's breathing. This was her typical game, mothering the hyper-realistic doll like it was alive. Only now and then would she suddenly drop the act, flick the hollow head or toss the thing on the ground and give a sick giggle. Whatever her issue was—whether the doll was therapeutic or symptomatic—she wasn't telling people. She'd made that clear to a nun two buses ago, screaming until the woman relocated to a seat in the back.

"Change of story," I said as she stared ahead once more, eyes ticking over Illinois flatness. "We're from Phoenix and on vacation. Seeing the whole country, Grand Canyon to the Statue of Liberty."

I knew Wendy didn't care. Her style was to say as little as possible in all situations, and there was a good chance she wouldn't speak to my uncle at all, just stand there with Gracie until he let us in, at which point I'd make him hand over the money and do whatever else needed to be done. Her role was minimal, which was for the best. She had a hair trigger, but we'd established a reliable peace. She knew I wouldn't mess with her, not just because I respected boundaries, but because I didn't have sex. When it came to touching others that way, some inner brake locked down. Wendy had sensed this from the beginning, possibly because she had the same issue. I adjusted the rearview mirror so I could see the empty road and the doll's brilliantly solemn stare.

Shoulders drooping, Wendy propped a filthy black boot on the dashboard, scattering gravel and bits of mud across the vinyl. She was half asleep now, worn out from the truck stop pills. "This uncle have anything to eat?"

It was impossible to know what she meant exactly, whether he had something she liked, or any food at all. "Yes."

Right answer. She fiddled with the seat and soon had it reclined. After a few minutes, she lay sunk in her heavy pink coat, snoring softly over the collar.

. . . .

WENDY WASN'T A homeless person. On this point, she was adamant. At the same time, she bragged about having no permanent address. She'd grinned when I mentioned the contradiction, then gave a light shrug, as if paradox were some charming quirk of her personality. When I met her at a bus depot in Tennessee, she was on her way to Chicago, supposedly to stay with a cousin. She'd made vague references to having left bad circumstances in Tampa. I had no way of knowing if any of it was true, including whether her name was Wendy. Nor did I worry about those matters. Point was, we had an understanding. She'd help me get into my uncle's house, and I'd put her up in motels, cover her meals, and drive her to wherever she wanted.

At the bus depot, she'd been sitting on her crushed and fouled-up green rollaboard. Staring straight ahead, she held the doll in arms while a guy in a black trench coat paced around her, rambling in a rough voice. It was after three in the morning, and my bus was leaving at seven. Taking them to be young parents fighting, I looked for a quiet bench away from the drama. There was a cop making periodic appearances, a bored-looking thirty-something more interested in his phone than crazy people in the station, and he eventually disappeared. I was nodding off when the young guy started shrieking, his voice laced with enough aggression that I opened my eyes and turned around.

Over the years, I'd grown sensitive to the vocal ranges of the mentally unwell. Now I saw the situation behind me differently. The boy stood over Wendy, arms wide, trying to make her look at him. His eyes bulged, and the cords in his neck stood out. "If I get it right, will you talk?" he said. "Mabel, Mavis? Maybelline? Marietta? Fucking Rumplemintz?" He burst into hysterical laughter.

Wendy stared into the lower half of the creep's black coat, as if she could see through it to the darkened counters across the room. She was breathing through her slightly opened mouth, and her hands were shaking. It was clear she was hoping if she didn't react, he would eventually go away.

"I don't know who you think you are," the young guy was telling her. "You're nothing special, you know. Just another little slit."

I got up and walked over slowly, thinking my presence would change the equation. I'd swelled to two forty in prison, having nothing to do but lift weights, read, and avoid conflicts with fellow prisoners. This kid was small, anxious, charged with the twitchy mania I associated with males who'd taken too many ass-whippings and went around hunting for revenge. He wasn't likely to have a weapon, save maybe some old, chipped pocketknife, and he looked too tightly wound to have the presence of mind to do much with it. Point is, I could beat his ass if I had to.

I came within a few yards and said, "Excuse me, miss. You know this guy?"

He was five seven, tipping the scale at one fifty, tops. Immediately, he started making appeals. "Look at her, man. She thinks she can just come in here and ignore people."

It was dawning that I hadn't heard a peep from the baby, and I began to think something was seriously wrong. I raised my hand, and the little guy flinched away. "Hey, buddy. Why don't you take it easy?" I tried to sound calm, but years around men who'd slice you with a folded can lid if the impulse struck had sharpened my voice. "Go on now. Leave her alone."

He was shaking, mouth working as he looked at Wendy with a longing that was disturbing to see. He'd convinced himself he'd get somewhere with her, and even with no sign of encouragement, he was reluctant to give up. I got a step closer, where I could clock him if need be. Trembling, he held his ground for a moment longer, then spun and ran out of the station, like he wasn't even there for a bus in the first place.

After a minute of watching the empty doorway, I blew a tentative sigh. Wendy remained off in her own world, and I figured I'd better leave her alone. I didn't know what to make of the silent baby, but I was exhausted and grateful to be rid of the threat of violence. If she wanted my help, she could ask. I nodded as if we had some agreement and went back to my stuff.

It was hard to sleep at first, as each time I closed my eyes I saw the little guy sneaking up with a broken bottle, but I positioned myself to face the doors and pulled my hat down, and at some point my mind went dark.

PA announcements woke me. It was getting light outside, and the station had been filling with people who were all visibly facing some hardship. Feeling at home among them, I got up and stretched. The girl with the baby was nowhere to be seen, and I took my bag and went in search of my bus. Finding a window seat, I started thinking about my uncle and my plan to get his money. I didn't see how I could do it without drawing attention from the authorities. I was lost in thought when someone small sat beside me.

Wendy. She studied me with her strange blue eyes and gradually breaking into a smile. Then she tipped the baby toward me, and with a jolt I saw eyes the same hue as hers, but lifeless, peering out from fake fat cheeks. The doll seemed so real—even to the thin light-brown hair plugs that could have been human, and the way its lower lip stuck out a little, like it was dribbling—I couldn't make sense of what I was seeing. Though the flushed skin looked like it would be warm to the touch, the unnatural stillness gave the opposite impression. My own flesh crawled at the mixed message.

Wendy read my reaction and grinned in delight. She danced the swaddled doll in front of my nose. "This is Gracie. Say hi."

. . . .

SHE SLEPT HARD, drool collecting in one corner of her open mouth. The radio was a novelty after all the bus travel, even if the only stations that came in were conservative talk, come-to-Jesus, and top forty. I went with top forty, mumbling refrains as I learned them and taking in the sights. The countryside was as stark as I remembered, an endless field split by a road and occasionally interrupted by little woods, houses, or lonely radio towers. Once I'd raced around this land without thinking about where I was or where I was bound. Most of the houses and barns looked familiar, if noticeably older from twenty years of midwestern weather. HAMBY FOR PRESIDENT signs stood in most front yards, grimly identical dark blue rectangles with red letters and white trim. That was different. As a boy, I'd viewed my town and the farmers and hicks who populated it as stuffy and uptight, but never especially political. This year they thought something big was underway, and this Hamby guy was the force behind it all.

My uncle's two-story Greek Revival stood at the end of his long gravel driveway, the old black rooster-shaped weathervane on its roof still pointing back the way I'd come, like an admonition to turn around. The ancient barn my grandfather had used rose up behind it, its roof caved in, and beyond that lay the fields my uncle had sold off when he inherited the property. The house looked smaller than I recalled, but the sight of the tall dark windows in the pale facade that tilted like an averted face made my heart crumple in my chest. I willed myself to drive up the long gravel run, snorting back tears and focusing so hard on breathing that I almost didn't see my uncle had a Hamby sign, too.

The front door whipped open, and the old fucker charged out and came limping down the concrete steps. He'd hardly changed, remained a stocky, cleanshaven man with a shiny bald head, his face oddly young-looking. His gut stretched the front of an old green Army sweater, the same kind he'd worn when I was a kid. He'd never been one to attract much company, yet he greeted visitors with hostility, as if he were the most sought-after man in town and needed a break. He was still up to that chest-puffing, I saw, watching him scowl at me, this intruder who'd appeared out of the blue. His expression changed when he'd had a look at my face. His mouth fell open and his nostrils flared, and he started to back away, like he might bolt for the field.

I was prepared for this. I got out smiling, as if I'd never imagined running him down and beating his face into the cold dirt. I glanced at Wendy—her head lolled to one side—and looked back at him, waving my hand over my head, doing my best to appear happy to see the face of the man who'd raped me more times than I could count. Memories welled up, a mulched recollection of being torn and of blood in my underwear, but it all felt different now. Years had passed. I was taller and whole despite what he'd done to me, not to mention a hundred pounds heavier than the last time we'd met. It was clear to me that I could do as I pleased in the limited context of the here and now.

"Uncle Dan, it's me, Aaron," I called, trying to sound enthusiastic, like a sitcom father with a sitcom family. I thought my voice sounded a little unhinged, but I kept smiling and waving. All I needed was to get inside that house. I took a deep breath. "I just came up from Arizona. Got my wife and little girl here. Thought I'd show them where I come from."

My uncle received these words like they were an incantation in a language he didn't understand. He was speechless for a moment, studying me and then trying to see into the car, where Wendy was cranking her seat into an upright position. The glare on the windshield kept her from being visible, I realized, and I told Wendy to come on out and say hi, which she did, still blinking off sleep, pulling the big pink coat around her and gesturing vaguely with one hand before making it into a visor to shield her from the sun.

The presence of a young woman in his driveway did the trick. My uncle exhaled and let his shoulders down, then stumbled forward a few steps, to say hello or stop or both. He stared at Wendy, mouth open, trying to get a look at her face. You could tell by the cheekbones she'd be pretty, and he'd always been shamelessly horny. He looked at me abruptly, eyes bright with fear and something like laughter. "Jesus, Aaron," he said. "I wish you'd have called ahead and warned me."

I bet you do, I thought. But I went on grinning like I'd won a small fortune through the state lottery. "Unexpected turn of events. We're on vacation and it occurred to me that you were here and never met Wendy. Baby, this my Uncle Dan. Uncle Dan, this is my Wendy."

Wendy yawned and nodded. It wasn't clear she understood where we were. "Hi, Uncle Dan," she said, her eyes half shut. "Can I go back to sleep now?"

I laughed like that was the kind of thing my charming young wife could be relied on to say—*Isn't she funny?* my hiccuping yuk said—and my uncle smiled uncertainly, which I found oddly gratifying. I liked the idea he might think she was snobby.

"Nice to meet you," he called, hands awkwardly on his hips.

I went to him, closing the distance quickly, holding out my hand as he hesitated and squirmed. I loomed over him, grinning down into his finely wrinkled face and wide, startled eyes, the bald head and jowls that were, to me, the very picture of sexual corruption. He smelled like beer and onions. I fought my urge to recoil from the sensation of his warm hand in mine.

He was trembling slightly, but a light crept into his expression, some serpent mixture of curiosity and contempt. "Great to see you. Can't stay, can you?"

I laughed at how easily I could read him. I had a feeling like I could predict his every move, and I could see in his shifty eyes that he felt it, too. This was a good feeling, one I could get drunk on. "Just passing through, stopping for lunch or something. Then I got to talking to some lady. Misty? Says she knows you from church. Anyway, she got me thinking about the importance of family, and I thought I'd see if you wanted to maybe put us up for the night."

The car rental woman's name hit him like a slap in the face. After a moment, he broke into a grin, and nodding his big head stupidly. His mouth worked before he recovered his ability to talk. "Yes, of course. You're always welcome here, nephew. You know that."

. . . .

I DON'T REMEMBER the first time my uncle told me about the widow's money. I must have been eleven. It was toward the end, when I was hitting puberty but still too small to make him think twice about trying to corner me. He thought he could do anything to me, a little boy without a protector. My dad had been gone from the beginning, and my mom came to him regularly for loans. She was in bad shape, closing in on the terminal alcoholism that would kill her my senior year, and my uncle saw his wrecked little sister wouldn't ask what went on behind her back, no matter what signs of damage showed up on her kid. Feeling superior, he came to see himself as a kind of patriarch, and when he was through with me, he would boast about the cash, trying to impress me and secure my silence.

He kept the money in a strongbox on a shelf up in his bedroom closet. Made of heavy steel, the makeshift safe resembled an enormous gray lunchbox with a lock on the top, the key to which he wore on a chain around his neck. I used to fantasize about stealing it, slipping it off him when he slept, and I was always looking for it, spotting the fine links whenever they slipped up the freckled skin above his t-shirt collar. In the privacy of his room, while I lay recovering on the floor or bed, he would take down the box, remove the key from his neck in an almost ceremonial gesture, and open the safe on the rumpled bedclothes, dumping out stacks of bundled bills. He let me count it when I was especially upset, and I knew there was more than seventy thousand dollars in there. He would give me twenty bucks, usually, telling me as he handed it over that he knew he could trust me. Though it makes me ashamed to say so, that amount seemed large enough that I began to value these bribes, and I hoarded the money in a shoebox in my own bedroom closet.

He'd taken it from an old lady years earlier, when he was tending bar in St. Louis. A lonely bachelor in that city, he'd drawn her attention by mixing her drinks each afternoon. She'd been in her seventies and was partially disabled, getting around with the assistance of a steel cane, and when she asked him to repair some furniture in her home, he'd agreed in the hope of picking up an extra paycheck and any potentially valuable possessions she might be eager to part with. Much to his surprise, what she'd wanted was for him to sit in the room she called *her parlor* with her and drink brandy, and he developed a habit of asking to borrow money, small sums and then larger ones, always citing some new cost. One day he would tell her was short on rent, another that he needed groceries, and sometimes he dared ask for more, like when he said he wished to buy a car.

"She always said no at first," my uncle would recall, stroking the cash with his fingertips in the dimness of his bedroom. "All that meant was that I had to wait. There was always something more she wanted. The main thing was never to stick it in her. I knew once I stuck it in her, the money would stop."

I never inquired in these moments about his logic, so intent was I on willing away the physical pain and self-disgust and getting my hands on a *fresh portrait of Andrew Jackson*, as my mom's brother called the note of legal tender he bestowed on me with an absurdly priestly air. Only later would it occur to me that he was paying me off in much the same way the older woman had paid him off, at which point I would wonder if he ever made the connection.

I don't think that he did. He liked to recall how the woman's sons had come after him when she could no longer care for herself and they'd stuck her in a home. "They threatened me with lawyers and said they'd call the police, the IRS." He laughed. "I was too smart for them. I hadn't put any of it in the bank or left a paper trail. What did they think would happen? That G-men would raid my apartment? Hell, I'd done them a favor, taking her off their hands. And they had their own secrets anyhow. Eventually they gave up and went away."

He might have been describing me. A few years later I was mature enough to see how he'd used me and to hate him for it, but shame and silence drove me to avoid him, and before long, I had a semi-adult life of my own, girlfriends I didn't know what to do with and boys I imagined to be my enemies, and when my mom died and it made sense to leave, I headed south, for places like Atlanta and Tampa, where I got into real trouble and saw the insides of many horrible rooms and then jail cells and then prison, all of which was almost enough to make me forget the uncle who'd hurt me when I was young. Almost, but not quite.

. . . .

I KNEW I should drop the family man act and take the money and leave, but I was having fun tormenting my uncle, watching him react to everything I said and did in a way meant to appease the violence he sensed I held in check. He feared taking his eyes off me, and once he did, he became afraid of looking back, and I took special delight in drawing his attention to little changes on the property. Where did that big sycamore go? Tell me about the satellite dish on the roof. He answered, hardly glancing at Wendy and ignoring the doll, staring down as he held the door, letting us into the foul front hallway, where dust bunnies clung to the scarred hardwood floor that ran all the way to murky kitchen. The place reeked of dust and unwashed dishes.

My uncle hustled past us and charged up the filthy stairs, gesturing for us to follow. Wendy looked at me, as if to ask whether she should, and I nodded for her to go ahead up the creaking steps.

Cobwebs hung from the ceiling of the upstairs hall, and the lights were out. The dust on the floor up there was thicker, as if my uncle hadn't come up in months or longer. He scurried into one of the old bedrooms, his rambling voice going on about how he'd have cleaned up if he'd known we were coming.

Wendy appeared unperturbed by the gloomy corridor in which we stood. "Are we going to, like, stay?" she asked, wearing a hangdog expression and holding Gracie to her chest like a stuffed animal. "Because I wouldn't mind finishing my nap."

I was unsure, feeling jumpy now that we were inside and he was so much weaker than I remembered. I would have to see how things went. "Maybe," I said quietly, and went ahead, gesturing for her to follow.

I remembered the bedroom. It had been used for storage even when I was growing up. It had custard-yellow walls and big cracks in its plaster ceiling. It smelled like the rest of the house, full of a mustiness that made me want to retch. I stood in the doorway, watching my uncle clear old boxes off a bed nobody had slept in for longer than I could say. He was concentrating on stacking them along the wall, doing his best to avoid looking at me. I saw he'd aged more than I first noticed, become stooped in the back and loose in the skin of his neck, frail under the old meat, unlikely to come through a fall down the steps without lasting damage. The thin chain on which he wore his safe key peeked above his collar.

That was a relief. He hadn't given the church all his money, after all.

"Hamby, huh?" I said. "Never knew you were into politics."

He looked up like a stunned deer, eyebrows raised, eager to please. "Oh, sure, Hamby," he said. "Absolutely. You can't trust that other one. The woman? Forget about it. She'll sell the country out from under us."

It pleased me that he believed he could win my respect by stating the right opinion. He'd always been a coward with other men, kowtowing for their approval and then talking shit behind their backs. Now I was a man, and he was debasing himself in my presence, surely thinking terrible things about me and wishing I would leave. The longer I stood in his presence, the more dominant I felt. There was no need to rush the money grab.

"You think you can trust Hamby?" I watched him seize on every word I said. "Even after those wild claims on the campaign trail? How he could do anything and they wouldn't touch him?"

My uncle hesitated. He glanced at Wendy, who stood behind me with Gracie, then looked at me with a comical expression of terror. "You two aren't . . . Is she . . . ?"

I laughed genuinely. I didn't care about politics, which I understood to be what people talked about to block out what was happening in front of them. Nor, from what I could tell, did Wendy have any awareness of what went on outside her experience of the here and now. "Neither of us really follows that stuff," I said. "Too busy. What with the new baby and all."

"Phew, for a second there I was worried you might have gone liberal on me." My mother's brother guffawed, then glanced away, taking shelter in the scene out the window. "I used to feel the way you do. Then I heard Hamby talk and thought, 'My God, finally someone who cuts through all the BS. We got to protect what's ours. Stand up to the people who've been screwing us and take back our dignity."

The irony of him saying these last words to me appeared lost on him, and he started moving more boxes off the bed, exciting a cloud of dust.

"You ought to go a rally sometime," he said. "See what it's all about."

. . . .

WHEN MY UNCLE had excused himself—seeing nothing more to do, he ducked his head, said, *I'll leave you two alone*, and marched out— Wendy climbed into the springy old bed, coat and boots still on, set Gracie beside her, and dragged the covers over herself. She lay staring up at the cracked ceiling, the skin around her eyes puffy.

"Would you get me something to eat?" she said faintly. Her eyelids fluttered, and she appeared to be drifting off to sleep. "I'm so hungry, Aaron."

I wasn't sure if she was telling the truth or trying to get me out of there so she could raid the medicine cabinet in the bathroom. What she did was up to her, but the attention of a 911 call would only lead to trouble. "I'll see what he's got. If you go into the bathroom, make sure you read any labels. It's all bound to be ancient."

Slinging her arm around the doll, she turned away, let out a sigh, and the tension went rattling out of her in a series of shudders. After a moment, she was breathing long, regular breaths.

I stepped into the empty hall, listening for a clue as to where my uncle had gone. I wasn't fully convinced he wouldn't try to get his hands on a gun. He'd owned rifles years ago and probably still had them. I didn't want to give him any chance to take the upper hand. I didn't think he'd shoot me, not when it would bring police and questions about what was going on here, but he was enough of a screwup that I could see him pulling a trigger by accident as he tried to scare me out of his space.

From the top of the stairs came the sound of the man clearing his throat below. Hearing him cough and swallow made me feel sick, and I took a few breaths, then realized he was talking to someone.

I padded to the banister and peered down, but he was out of my sightline. At first, I worried he was on the phone, maybe with some local cop friend. But I hadn't done more than street robberies, and I had no cause to think anyone was looking for me. I concentrated. There was something too incoherent and prolonged in my uncle's muttering for his audience to be anyone but his own half-attentive self. I descended steadily, remembering how creaky the steps were. He was in the living room just off the front hall, seated at a table pushed up against the wall, gazing into a desktop computer next to a window with a view of the driveway. Five or six empty beer bottles stood in a cluster at the edge of the table, and his current drink rested near his left hand.

On the screen were photos of some girl, a teenager with long blonde hair. In one she posed in a dress at a formal dance. In another, she stood on a haybale wearing a stars-and-stripes bikini, a semiautomatic cradled in her tanned arms. She was maybe old enough to drive. "Little whore," my uncle said to himself before sitting up abruptly. He minimized the pictures and turned his chair to face me, his expression both vulnerable and surprised. He grabbed his beer bottle. "How's the room? Is Wendy comfortable? She or the baby need anything?"

I pretended not to notice his familiar tone, as if he were friendly with Wendy, and as if the doll were a living baby he'd held in his arms or even asked to see. I wondered what kind of deceptive crap he tried to pull at the church. "She's sleeping," I said. "She's real tired."

"That baby's quiet," he said. "Sure is cute, though. You two got a good one."

I suppressed a laugh and let my chin fall agreeably. "Gracie doesn't make a lot of noise."

He tipped his head to one side and grimaced, as if tasting something painfully sweet. "We've got some cute babies at Willow Creek," he said, "but little Gracie just takes the cake. You ever think about maybe putting her up to model?"

What was he talking about? Child models? Probably something he'd picked up in the megachurch, where he would have found himself among wealthier suburbanites. I imagined him standing at the fringe of some after-church group, trying to keep up with their banter, embarrassing himself each time he opened his mouth.

"Hadn't occurred to me," I said, thinking of how the doll was wrapped in Wendy's arms when I'd left her just now. "Her mother wouldn't go for that, I don't think."

My uncle turned to the kitchen. "You thirsty?" he said quickly, at a loss for what to offer me. "Want a beer? You're old enough now."

I said nothing about his newfound appreciation for age restrictions. Coming closer to his soft little body, I ignored how he closed his eyes and waited me to hit him. As he ducked his head, he once more exposed the gold chain on his neck. I could have reached down and unclipped it. I was confident he wouldn't have fought me. Gesturing at the computer screen, I said, "What's on the computer?"

His head snapped up, and he looked at the screen, laughing nervously. "Oh, it's just Cul-de-Sac," he said. "Social media. Everybody from my church is on it. Are you . . . I mean, I guess you weren't allowed . . ."

So he did know. For how long? I wondered. It was no secret, but he'd never contacted me. No doubt he'd felt great relief, knowing I was in a cage in another state. "I had a couple accounts before I got in trouble," I said. "Not Cul-de-Sac. Everybody was using different ones back then."

He took a swallow of beer and chuckled. "That doesn't surprise me. You were always more hands-on."

I smiled in disgust. It was tempting to ask why he never wrote, if he knew where I was, just to see what kind of bullshit he'd spit out. But now I had a new way to needle him. "I bet that lady from the gas station is on here," I said. "What was her name? Misty?"

A change came over his face then, his eyes bulging, his lips puckering in something like excitement. "Oh yeah, Misty's a big deal over there." He typed and brought up her profile. There she was, the woman who rented me the car. Her headshot accentuated her finer qualities, made her look more attractive and happier than the person I'd met. The picture must have been taken on a vacation, because it showed a tropical beach backdrop. The words HAMBY FOR PRESIDENT made a circle around the edges. The post had three hundred and forty-four thumbs-ups.

Uncle Dan blasted a sigh through his nose. "God, she's good at this stuff."

He started clicking through her other photos, which included her and her smiling husband and their smiling son in a big, clean-looking subdivision house with an inground swimming pool. There was the son, shirtless, shooting hoops in the driveway, his hightops-clad feet hovering inches above the concrete. My uncle groaned. "You wouldn't believe the numbers her posts get. A hundred, minimum. I'm lucky if I get two or three."

I saw his profile pic up in the corner of the computer screen, a shadowy shot of him in a baseball cap, his face backlit by a window, his eyes reduced to dull glints. It took an older single man, already a suspicious sort of person, and transformed him into a disturbing figure.

"That you?" I said.

"Yeah."

With a click, he enlarged what I now saw was an awkward selfie. He'd actually given himself a third chin. It had one thumbs up, from another man.

My uncle looked at me over his shoulder. "How'd you and Misty get to talking about me, anyway?"

I thought about what I'd told him, that I was selling cars in Phoenix and we were on vacation. "We were there to gas up, and she saw the Arizona plates," I said. "Just struck up a conversation, and I mentioned my uncle lived out here."

"And she said she knew who I was?" he said, the most animated I'd seen him since we arrived. "Just like that, huh?"

I studied him for a moment, realizing just how lonely and wretched he'd become. "She knows who you are, sure," I said. "Mentioned you've been quite generous to the church. I got the feeling she thinks highly of you."

He sat up. "She said that?" His eyes widened again, then he turned back to the computer, where Misty returned his stare. "I think she overstated the case. I don't have the deep pockets some of them do. But that was very nice of her to say."

"Seemed like a standup lady," I said, ignoring his course correction.

He winced a little, then hurried to agree, as if he were afraid she'd somehow find out he'd contradicted her. "Oh, yeah. Great lady. You kidding me?"

. . . .

THE AFTERNOON PASSED slowly while Wendy slept, my uncle sitting glued to his computer and pictures of other people's lives, doing his best to ignore my presence, though I suspected it was what he would be doing if he'd been alone. I kept tabs on him by listening while conducting a light inspection of the downstairs rooms, passing off my little forays as trips to the bathroom. He drank his way through most of the many beers in the refrigerator, getting so intoxicated he started to weave in his chair. Eventually darkness fell, and he hoisted himself and shambled into the kitchen, where I was at the table, looking over the pension statements he'd left lying around. Making no connection between the folded pages and me sitting a foot away from them, he reached into the fridge and withdrew a stewpot with a blackened bottom. He tilted this to show me it held a chili with a thick orange scum of fat on the surface. He placed this on the old stove and cranked up the electric burner. "It's my old recipe," he said. "You remember? You used to love it."

The thought of eating anything his hands had touched turned my stomach, but I nodded. I'd calculated that he was officially worth a few hundred grand, between the value of the house and his bank accounts. The cash in his safe was far more than he needed, and that must have been why he gave whatever money he could bear to part with to the megachurch, trying to buy the admiration of people who would always look down on him because looking down on people like him formed the basis of their self-esteem. And probably he'd will it all away to them when he died, anyway. I accepted a beer from him and sat with it open beside me, untouched.

Wendy appeared in the kitchen doorway, sleepy-eyed in her big coat, holding Gracie cradled in one arm. She slipped behind me, taking the chair farthest from the one my uncle now occupied. She didn't appear to be messed up, and I guessed there were no pills to swallow upstairs.

"You hungry still?" I said.

She shrugged under her coat, back to staring into nothingness. "Not so much anymore," she said. "It went away after a while."

My uncle was watching her. An uneasy light appeared in his eyes, and his happy expression was slipping away. He'd either gotten a good look at Gracie or noticed the doll's stillness, or maybe it was that Wendy was still wearing the pink coat. It could have been her dirty hair or the hollows under her eyes, or the sum of all these things. Whatever he'd noticed, this moment had always been coming, and I waited for him buckle under the pressure and face me and ask what really needed to be asked.

"I'm not especially hungry," I said, louder than necessary in the silent kitchen. I raised my hands and cracked my knuckles slowly, watching him cringe each time one popped. It felt good to be seen. "Wendy says she's not hungry anymore, but you might give her a bowl, in case she changes her mind."

He looked at me, his eyes wet with tears. He huffed a phlegmy breath and nodded, too shaken to form the question. With unsteady hands he took down two ceramic soup bowls with cracks in their sides, and as he ladled chili into them with an old coffee mug, I realized the large white bowls had belonged to my mom, that I had eaten from them many times as a boy. It made sense that he would have them, but for some reason the fact enraged me. I found myself staring at them as he brought them to the table, his eyes lowered as he approached Wendy cautiously and placed the steaming stew in front of her. No doubt he imagined a hundred acts of violence he knew better than to attempt. He put his own bowl across the table and returned to the fridge for another beer, which he opened on the countertop, pressing down on the cap with a soft grunt.

Beside me, Wendy gazed down into the chili's typical mixture of ground beef and beans. Then she lifted Gracie and plonked the doll onto the table, an arm's length from the bowl and where my uncle could clearly see the lifeless eyes reflecting the ceiling light. She picked up her spoon and began to shovel bites into her mouth. She didn't bother to chew, only swallowed and reached for more.

Slanting a sideways glance at the doll, Uncle Dan said nothing, but a series of understandings flitted through his dismal eyes. He knew his place in the hierarchy we'd formed, just as he knew his place at Willow Creek, and how a scandal involving the police would play out among the people he wished to impress there. He could say, of course, that his felon of a nephew showed up one day with a fake wife and child to steal his money—but such an outlandish tale would only lead to questions he didn't want to answer. He had a sickness, and a past. There were other people who knew things.

Still, he did try. "Any chance," he said, "you three could come out to the church tomorrow night? Some of the folks there remember you, Aaron. They sure would like to see you again. I'm know Misty would, too."

I smiled slightly. How stupid and fucked up or both did he think I was? "Unfortunately, I don't think we can stay that long, Uncle Dan."

Wendy dropped her spoon in her empty bowl and shoved it across the wood, her eyes locking fiercely with his. "More," she said, chili smeared around her mouth. "Get me more."

. . . .

AN HOUR LATER, he could barely stand or speak coherently. His face was red from ear to ear, his eyes glassy and dark as he rambled about his church and Hamby and sometimes my mom. He said he thought my mom would have liked Willow Creek. That she would have admired Hamby. He said she would have been proud of the man I had become. None of these things were true, but this self-abasement was my uncle's way of making a confession, of telling me he was sorry and asking me to go away and leave his grubby half-world intact. He wanted me to see him as someone helpless and weak who ought to be left alone. Another part of his strategy was convincing Wendy to drink, as if that would work to his advantage, but of course she was simply a piece of stage-craft, and she'd held up her end of our deal. She could get as drunk as she wanted. They'd finished all the beer and opened a bottle of cheap American whiskey from under the sink.

"I haven't drunk with a girl who can put it away like this in years," my uncle said, smiling so wide his eyes almost disappeared. "If the people at Willow Creek could see me now, they'd be in for a surprise. I'm not the little old man they think."

Wendy was cradling the doll below her breast, as though she were about to feed it. She flicked her hand at her empty shot glass. "Give me another one."

Uncle Dan moved to oblige, planting his belly on the table as he stretched over the ruined old wood to splash amber-colored fluid over the glass. He didn't seem to notice the spill. "I'm right, though, aren't I?" He looked at me and giggled drunkenly. "They can't just ignore me. I've made donations. I can have a drink with a pretty young girl. I've got stuff going on they can't imagine."

Wendy gulped the shot and put down the glass, then burst into harsh laughter. It was unclear whether she thought something was funny or simply wanted to share in the merriment. Outside, it had started to rain, the droplets tapping on the windowpanes like insistent little fingers.

It occurred to me that anyone looking in through the window right then would see three adults who seemed to be having a good time. It was strange how the appearance couldn't be further from the truth. At this thought, I began to feel sorry for all of us, aware as I was that none of us had ever wished to become the people we were. That was when I had the idea. "Maybe we could take a picture," I said. "The four of us. Post it on Cul-de-Sac. That'll show them."

Uncle Dan gaped at me, not understanding at first. He glanced at the doll in Wendy's arms, then looked back at me, breaking into a high-pitched laugh. A beat later, he went silent, serious. "Okay," he said. "Let's do it."

. . . .

THE THUMBS UPS came more slowly after ten, but even at eleven they were still trickling in. My uncle continued to drink steadily, licking his lips after each swallow, then dragging his forearm across his wet mouth. He'd turned in his chair to avoid looking at me, and gazed into his phone, examining the photo we'd uploaded and using his index finger to scroll back and forth over the comments from people in his church.

It was a picture of us all—Gracie included—standing back against his kitchen counter, me between him and Wendy, my hands on the ledge behind them because I could not bring myself to touch him and because I knew Wendy would not wish to be touched. You couldn't tell this from the image, though, in which I appeared to have my arms around my smaller, aging uncle and my tiny wife, who held our sleeping daughter. I looked successful enough, normal enough. Everyone was smiling, and there were no bottles to suggest the flushed cheeks were the result of anything but loving joy.

The post had drawn a response, my uncle reported, not only from church members but from others in town, even some who'd moved away—people he hadn't heard from in years. They commented on how I'd changed, he said, how good I looked, how great it was to see me happy. Nobody mentioned my incarcerations. They pronounced Gracie a gift from God and said that he, Dan Strayer, was blessed. At first my uncle pretended to think this was funny, a joke we were playing on these people, but then he gave in and let himself be excited by their attention and good will, the marks of approval he'd always wanted. He read aloud every comment praising him and Wendy and Gracie and me, visibly moved but unable to cry or smile or laugh—just staring, stunned, into that little screen.

Now it was late. Wendy had staggered upstairs a while ago, Gracie tucked under one arm like a football. My uncle and I were alone.

"What's happening now?" I said.

"No more thumbs up." My uncle set his teeth and hissed. "I guess they're asleep. Or they want everyone to think so. Everybody's got church in the morning."

That meant him, too. He raised his head, thinking the same thing. He was drunk and exhausted, longing for his bed, yet delaying, sensing what would happen when he stood to go. His eyes searched the room, and then his arm shot out suddenly, reaching for the nearly empty bottle on the table. "One more," he said, his tongue thick with spit. "A nightcap."

"Not for me." I sat straighter, getting my spine to pop, aware as I did how still he became. "I've got to drive."

He could barely hold the bottle, let alone keep it steady, and the whiskey shook out in messy spurts until his glass was full. I recalled him hovering behind me years ago as I tried to pour a glass of milk, snarling in my ears I'd better not spill a drop. Now he raised the trembling glass, getting only a little into his open mouth, then opened his eyes to stare in confusion at the dark spots on his shirt.

"I guess I'm done," he said. "You know your way upstairs, I take it."

Forcing himself to stand, he staggered past me and through the doorway. He was looking at his phone again, the screen lighting the hallway like a candle. I rose and followed on his heels almost immediately. I waited for him to acknowledge me, remaining quiet even when he'd reached his closed bedroom and was struggling with the old doorknob. I watched him jiggle it hard, pitying the slope of his fallen shoulders, his panting frustration, and finally I reached out, letting the weight of my hand rest on his soiled shirt.

"Two hundred and ten thumbs ups," he said, his voice filled with wonder, like a child's. "I've never had numbers like that."

I cleared my throat, and he jerked his head up, as if he'd forgotten I was there. "You'll get more in the morning."

He remained still. "You're going to take it all."

"Yes."

I tightened my grip on his shoulder. In the moment before his phone's screen went dark, I saw his eyes were shut tight.

He reached up to remove the chain from his neck. When he handed it to me, he clasped my hand, as if seeking comfort. Then, with a wheezing sigh, he said, "Everything is going to be okay, isn't it?"

· · · ·

IT WAS EARLY morning when I let Wendy out in a South Chicago neighborhood of small brick apartment buildings. I'd followed her directions off the highway and down surface streets, finally stopping in front of a two-story that looked identical to the others on the street. The rain had stopped, leaving colorful leaves strewn all over the place. The city was oddly quiet and deserted-seeming, and I remembered it was Sunday.

Next to me, breathing whiskey breath and waking up, she looked at this place she obviously knew, then glanced at me. "I guess this is it," she said, stroking Gracie's hair as if trying to calm the baby. "All that shit with your uncle. You know, you might be more messed up than me."

I made a noncommittal sound, aware I'd miss her at some point but also eager to move on. It had been a profitable deal for both of us. I reached into my pocket and took out the wad of cash I'd decided to give her while she was sleeping, a little more than four thousand dollars. I tried not to think of how she'd use it.

She looked at the money for a moment, nodding as if she were agreeing to my terms, though this was beyond what I'd promised. She took the cash, peeled off a few bills, and shoved them into her coat pocket. Then she held Gracie firmly under her forearm and pulled on the doll's chin. The head came off with a loud popping sound, and she tucked the bulk of the money inside, where it looked like there was plenty more.

I shook my head, impressed.

She jammed the doll's head back into place and blinked at me. "I knew you were one of the good ones," she said. "I guess I'll see you."

Slipping between parked cars, she went up a narrow concrete path to a caged front door, then pressed the bell and waited, holding Gracie by the heel. She glanced around but never looked back, and when the door opened, the woman inside quickly unlocked the cage and ushered Wendy in.

All that was left was returning the rental car, which I hadn't arranged to drop off anywhere. It was another four hours back the way I'd come. I could have simply ditched the thing, but then Misty would probably approach my uncle, and I didn't trust him to hold up under any kind of scrutiny, especially from a prominent busybody at his church. One admission could only lead to others, and the fewer questions about my visit, I felt, the better. I'd decided to return the car as agreed in the rental contract, even though it meant going back to the scene of a crime.

It was early afternoon when I pulled up. The wind was gaining force, rolling off the fields in big cold waves. In the distance, the bus station loomed, its steel roof shining in the sun.

The rental agency was closed, but in the gas station next door, Misty's son was working the counter. He wore a HAMBY FOR PRESIDENT hat and a shirt that read *My other girlfriend is an AR-15*. An angry male voice spewed out of the nearby radio.

"Just leave the keys," the kid said with no interest. "I'll deal with it later."

When I walked out, he was on his phone, scrolling with one finger, and he didn't look up as I hefted the suitcase stuffed with cash and started up the highway on foot. A tractor trailer blew past, whipping up gravel and honking the horn, and raising my eyes, I glimpsed a grinning face in the passenger-side mirror. I thought of the two strangers in that cab who were laughing at the poor son of a bitch walking the highway to the bus station. After a few seconds, I started laughing at him, too.

STORY HOUR

SHE'D FIRST NOTICED Dawn the morning the girl and her mom crashed Story Hour thirty minutes late. Somewhere in the thick of *Where the Wild Things Are*, Alice heard a rush of coats and voices and turned with her audience of children and various adults to find a breathless young woman telling her tiny daughter *Be quiet* and *Sit to the side where we won't be in the way*, all the while grinning and tugging her own jacket's zipper.

Alice shut the book and took stock. The girl, who was about five, with tangled red hair and smudges on her cheeks, was gazing back steadily, smiling like they were old friends. Alice blinked slowly, acknowledging the formidable little stranger. So you're one of the special ones, she thought. Hello.

The mom finally had her coat off, panting. She must have run some distance to be in this warm little room. "Sorry, jeez!" she said, gathering her daughter into skinny arms. "Shh, shh. My gosh, I'm so sorry!"

Noting how worked up the younger woman was, Alice imbued her smile with as much warmth as possible. The daughter laughed into her hands, and Alice allowed herself another moment of delicious eye contact.

The rest of story hour passed normally. Alice read *Harold and the Purple Crayon* before leading the group in singing the songs she'd chosen while curating the morning's picture book displays. Throughout, she was aware of holding the attention of each child and some of the adults, of leading them from one word or lyric to the next. You always lost grownups at some point, to the distraction of the room's fairy-tale murals or another parent's attractive features, or to the temptation of a phone, but this was not the case with the new mom, who spent the duration gawking at Alice, in utter emotional thrall.

Strange, she thought, but nice for a change, a parent as into being there as the child.

Afterward, the new mom came up to apologize and shake hands. Her name was Holly Benson. She spoke in an educated and casual way, and her old army-green jacket and sharp lavender smell reminded Alice of the politically outspoken moms who'd been turning up lately, eager to share information about organic and local foods and natural skin care products and to express their passionate support for the library. Alice appreciated the appearance of these new allies, despite being unprepared for the enthusiasm they often unleashed on her. "I am so embarrassed," Holly Benson said, brushing back long dark hair with one hand. "I could have died. We won't be late again."

Alice wasn't sure what to say. *This is your library,* she wanted to reply, *not work or school. You should feel at home here.* But you couldn't talk like that, or people might misunderstand and think you were inviting them to disregard the rules.

Holly Benson held her daughter like she might a younger kid, hugging the girl around the waist against one shoulder, so their faces were side by side and visibly similar. "That was so so amazing, Ms. Alice!" she said. "Incredible. I don't know how you did it. I was like immersed."

Alice bowed her head. "Thank you." Looking at the girl peering out through messy hair, she felt the same recognition as before, and got the sense the child also saw the mother as a little strange. She felt that peculiar rush of rapport, of kinship, she had come to know but for which she had no name or real justification. "This is my job. That's all," she said to Holly Benson.

"No." Holly took hold of Alice's arm with surprising force. "What you did in there was absolutely fucking"—she paused to cover her mouth and look around, then soldiered on—"magical. That shit was magical."

Alice cleared her throat, uncomfortable with the unabashed praise. "And who is this?" she said, smiling at the kid.

"Say *Hi,* Dawn."

The girl squinted at Alice. "Do you have a daughter?"

"Dawn," said Holly Benson.

"No."

"Why not? Do you have any kids?"

"Dawn, don't be so rude!"

Alice laughed and waved her hand. "There was a problem." She shrugged theatrically, as if she couldn't explain it, getting the child to giggle. She took off her glasses and opened her eyes as wide as she could, making the girl laugh in full. "Nobody told me where to get one."

. . . .

SHE STARTED LOOKING forward to their daily arrival, to seeing Dawn heave open the front door and poke her messy head into the warmth and smell of books. Though she wouldn't have told anyone, the girl made her feel less alone. It was not the first time. Now and then this happened, you met a little one with an intelligence you knew. Usually a girl, in Alice's case, though there had been a few boys over the years. She could not say what it was exactly that she knew so well—if they reminded her of herself at that age, of someone she used to know, of someone she'd always hoped to meet—only that it was deeply familiar, and whenever she found it, she immediately began to dread the day the child who possessed it outgrew Story Hour. Not that it kept her up at night. It wasn't a dramatic fear, but a larger and steadier resignation to the passage of time. She knew she would see the kids again, watch them grow up and come to the library to study with friends and, eventually, significant others. A few were old enough now to bring children of their own. The connection never disappeared entirely—its shadow persisted, and its echo rang out when they called her *Ms. Alice*—but it went without saying that the original bond was gone forever. There was nothing more to say.

As for Holly Benson, the young woman intimidated her. She was kind but unpredictable. Some mornings she was as filled with wonder and awe as she'd been that first day, while on others she seemed worn out, disgruntled, vaguely confused. She could be irritable and gruff, and sometimes she looked as though she hadn't gotten enough sleep or, alarmingly, had been up all night crying. On those occasions she ignored Alice altogether, taking Dawn firmly by the wrist once Story

146

Hour ended and pulling her out of the library despite the girl's objections.

One morning Alice saw an abrupt change in the woman. She had started reading the *Madeline* books that day, and Holly Benson had reacted as though she'd been granted a divine revelation. These moments were not unknown to her, especially with moms and dads who were struggling with the loneliness and boredom of early parenthood, and the reaction intensified if they remembered reading the books in their own youth. Alice was doing her best to appear interested and not show too much attention to Dawn, who was hugging her around one leg and gazing up adoringly. Every minute or two, the girl would let her mother pull her away, only to wait a few seconds and then reattach herself to Alice. Alice had said once that she didn't mind it and wouldn't risk repeating herself. The thought that someone might see how she felt—that having this little girl cling to her was heavenly—frightened her.

Holly Benson seemed too wrapped up in her own experience to notice Alice was feeling anything. "I didn't realize how many memories I have of this book until you started reading." She spread small, neatly manicured hands to show the abundance she'd discovered. "It's like a whole other lifetime."

"Well," said Alice. "It's always here if you need it. We have multiple copies."

Several patrons were watching them. As if aware of this, Holly Benson lowered her voice. "Books are so so amazing. They're like these points of convergence in your life or something. So you end up remembering whole like swaths of space and time around them."

Alice nodded, half-listening and smiling at Dawn's unwashed face pressing against her thigh. She wasn't sure she understood what Holly Benson was talking about, but unhappy young parents were always saying flaky things. This new generation was terribly upset about the state of the world, and they simultaneously wanted to rescue and obliterate it.

"Books have always held a special place for me," she said. "I'm probably the last person in the world who needs convincing that they matter. You've probably figured that out."

In the time Alice had taken to reply, the young woman had stopped smiling, and the color had drained from her cheeks. She was staring past Alice, looking toward the entrance, where one of the city police officers who worked this beat, a matter-of-fact but friendly enough man named French, had just come in from the cold and was rubbing his hands and peering hopefully in the direction of the circulation desk. He was dating a librarian who worked there—the budding romance was a topic of breakroom gossip, which Alice tried to ignore—but even standing thirty yards away, hitching up his pants, he was having an effect on Holly Benson. She was breathing hard, swallowing, and now she lowered her head sharply and took Dawn by the arm. "Let's go," she said, peeling the girl away from Alice's leg. "We have to get home. Daddy's waiting."

Dawn protested in a whining voice, saying, "I want to stay, Mama," snatching at Alice's skirt. "I want to stay with Ms. Alice."

Alice folded her arms and took a step back, unsure what had Holly Benson so shaken up, but so used to dealing with resistant children that she went on autopilot. "Thanks for coming today, Dawn. See you tomorrow?"

Holly Benson tugged her daughter toward the door, then leaning in to deliver a more private threat as she steered the unhappy girl past the officer and out into the windy day.

French had reached the circulation desk and assumed his usual flirtatious lean, but he turned and watched the mother and child until they dropped out of sight. He was frowning as Alice walked over.

"She always bring her kid in here?" he said to the circulation librarian, who shrugged. "You might keep an eye out if she goes into the bathroom and stays a while. Maybe have someone go check."

Alice faced the large man, studying his wide, wind-reddened face, trying to understand what he could possibly mean. Was he making some kind of joke? He sounded annoyed.

"Really?" the circulation librarian said. "*She's* one of them?"

"Her and her husband both," he said. "Conked out in their car last summer. Kid was playing on the floorboard in back. For a minute I thought we had two bodies on our hands. Who knows how long they were like that." He paused and turned to regard Alice with an expression of resignation. "I guess the court let them keep the kid. Can't do much with these people."

Alice stiffened in indignation. Even if French knew something about Holly Benson's past, the story he was telling had clearly taken place months ago, and it was none of his personal business, particularly if he was using the information to show off in here. Loose talk could affect how people treated the mother, and that could wind up harming Dawn. Not that she was one to get confrontational, especially with a police officer.

"Maybe she's cleaned up her act," the circulation librarian said. "It's been almost a year."

"Husband hasn't," French said with a shrug. "Still hanging around the drug corner by the trailer park. So maybe she's cleaned up. But I doubt it."

. . . .

THERE WAS NO parking lot here, only the gravel driveways beside each modular home. The long boxy structures all dated to the same era, but some were noticeably cleaner than others. All of them had little plots of land than ran up against the woods, and some of these yards had little gardens or playground sets. *Trailer park* was the wrong term for this place, Alice felt. It was something slightly nicer.

She drove her small car past the home with the address she'd found in the library's computer and kept going. There were two vehicles there, a car and a jeep, and the home, with its light blue siding and lawn chairs outside the front door, was neither the nicest nor the saddest in this place. Alice hadn't been able to stop herself from coming out here, but she was leery of Dawn's dad. She'd looked up his name online and found three mugshots of the unshaven, scowling redhaired man, who was perceptibly thinner and more haggard in the most recent. She had only looked at the images for a few seconds before closing the browser, fearful he would somehow know she'd seen them. She wasn't eager to encounter Holly Benson, either. The woman had tried to make a certain impression at the library, and she might resent being unmasked in the place she lived. Alice didn't want to think of her friendly exuberance turning to anger.

Parking at the end of the road—a dead end where the already over-grown grass was littered with scraps of food and cigarette packag-ing—Alice sat in the car, trying to decide whether to go ahead with her plan. The presence of the jeep, suggesting the father was home, gave her pause. Thinking of Dawn, she gathered her nerve and got out, walking back in the direction of the house. Under one arm, she car-ried a selection of the Story Hour books they'd missed these past few weeks, having taken the liberty of checking them out in the mother's name. She thought both mother and daughter would want to borrow them, though mainly she hoped to get a look at Dawn and confirm the child was okay. She wasn't so naïve as to think a look would tell her what the girl was going through, but she would be able to rule out worst-case scenarios. And maybe leaving the books would bring them back at least once, which might be enough to convince Holly Benson the library was safe.

She reached the driveway and proceeded to the front door. Taking a deep breath, she rapped on the light metal and waited, listening. The place sounded completely still inside, and for a moment she imagined something terrible had happened, that she had come too late. As she was envisioning the bodies, she heard footsteps approaching slowly.

He was smaller than she'd expected, a slight man who looked far less dangerous than in his mugshots. He wore an old t-shirt and soft sweats, and the hair on his long bare feet was as fiery an orange as the tangle of curls on his head. He was not fierce, like she'd thought, but held himself gingerly, as if he'd been hurt and was nursing the wound. He blinked muddy brown eyes, confused by her presence.

"Can I help you?"

She felt at a loss to explain herself. "Is Holly Benson here?"

"She's asleep. What can we do for you?"

It was almost noon on a Tuesday. Alice saw now that he himself was just waking up, taking in her glasses and wool cardigan and long skirt, and she sensed he would be quick to form suspicions if she said the wrong thing. She didn't dare ask about the girl. "It's nothing," she said. "Maybe you could tell her Ms. Alice from the library stopped by. We miss her and Dawn."

He was looking at the books. He reached out. "Those for Holly?"

She froze, tightening her grip. She couldn't give them up, not without seeing Dawn. "No," she said. "No, they're for someone else."

He furrowed his brow. "So just the message then," he said, clearly not believing her. "That's it?"

"That's it."

She was shaking as she walked away, feeling silly, but also expecting that at any moment Holly Benson would charge out and berate her for showing up where she wasn't invited. Sometimes her imagination got the best of her, and she couldn't stop anticipating screams from inside the house, a gunshot, some other telltale signal of tragedy. She wondered where Dawn was and hated herself for being too weak to demand to know. Did they have the girl drugged in there? Locked up? Scared into playing in silence? She listened for doors and footsteps as she walked back to her car but heard only birds and the branches of old trees creaking in the wind.

She was passing the last of the homes when she heard someone call out. It was a small voice, but it broke in among her thoughts like a dream, and it wasn't until the child repeated herself a third time that Alice realized the voice was getting closer, shouting her name. She stopped and turned to see Dawn coming out of the woods at the edge of a yard she'd passed, her face dirty and her hair mussed, her forearms and little blue jeans smeared with soil and bark. Emerging from the young ferns and dead undergrowth, the girl hesitated, then ran to Alice, smiling with a child's easy joy. Alice barely had time to smile back before Dawn crashed into her leg and hugged her around the waist.

She reached down and patted the girl's back, then looked up the road for the parent she knew must be coming to collect Dawn, not because it was time for the girl to go home, but because she, Alice, had intruded and shattered whatever rhythm this place created for itself. There was no one, though, only blocky homes with dark windows.

"Come on," Dawn said, unmistakably thrilled to see her. "Come with me. Hurry! Come to the library!"

"We can't go to the library." She hesitated. A car appeared in the distance and pulled into a driveway. She imagined herself driving,

Dawn on the seat beside her, ducking as they passed her home and then, later, rolling down the window to let the wind blow through her red hair. She shook her head. "Won't your mom be looking for you?"

Dawn took Alice's free wrist in both hands and pulled her back into someone's yard. "Not that library," she said. "My library."

"Oh." She smiled, relieved Dawn didn't seem offended or upset. The girl was tugging her in direction of the woods. Alice supposed it was harmless enough—and wasn't this what she'd come for? To see that Dawn was all right? Looking into the girl's little face, she felt re-assured. When she nodded, the girl turned and raced for the tree line.

Alice followed, trying to keep an eye on the tiny figure as well as the nearby houses, worried some adult would see her and call the parents or, worse, the police. Coming to the edge of the woods, she stepped in and almost immediately slipped and fell. Her knee hurt slightly when she righted herself, but she was okay, and she laughed it off. Soon she found it easier going, following a faint but perceptible trail, and reached out without thinking to part some branches.

Dawn waited in a clearing, standing by an old white tree stump tinged with moss and rot. She smiled at Alice, as if she'd put hours of work into preparing the spot for the librarian's arrival. The grass here was trampled down, and a dozen or so plastic dolls and stuffed animals sat in a circle, facing the stump. A few old picture books, deeply rain damaged and coming apart, lay among the roots. The familiar config-uration brought a tightness to her throat.

"Read to us," Dawn said, gesturing for her to sit. "Read to us, Ms. Alice."

Alice carefully made her way to the place that had been prepared for her. The flat surface of the stump was dry and cracked. She turned and sat, facing the girl she had missed so much. Dawn smiled back without hesitation or doubt, infinitely patient, as if they had all the time they could possibly want. As if the other librarians would not notice Alice's empty desk, as if Holly Benson would never come walking up the road, strung out and exhausted, shouting her daughter's name. As if Alice's visit could somehow go unnoticed, though she'd knocked on the par-ents' door. There was a chance, she knew, that she would not see Dawn again soon, not tomorrow or next week or next year—that by the time the girl could make it to the library on her own, Dawn would be too old for Story Hour or Alice. But all that was in the future, far away and uncertain. Now there was only this, the two of them in the clearing, the spring wind, the birds scattered in the trees, the ring of silent watchful toys. Alice felt no regret or sorrow as she opened the first of the books she had brought, pronouncing its title and its author's name clearly over the gentle sea of outdoor sounds. She always relished the feeling at the start of a book, the sense that something was about to happen, even if you'd read it dozens of times before.

THE SECRET SELF

WHO KNOWS WHY Anthony Haug set out to make me an accomplice in murder. Only he could say, and if I were to find him and ask, he would surely reject the question. My wife Monica has a theory: Haug was lost in the world and getting more lost, that he'd been heading in this direction for years. First had come the attacks, then the career-ending injury and trying to survive on disability payments. Then came the humiliating move home and the acceptance of a job—school security guard—that mocked his former occupation. He was single, he was sad, he was getting older. He had nobody to impress or care for. More than anything, he longed for the approval of another man.

"Maybe," I say. "I'm not so sure."

"That's all he wanted, Thurston Savage the Third." Monica's eyes laugh up at me. "That and for you to bestow it. In his mind, you weren't just a man. You were The Man. You had archetype status, baby."

On this matter, too, I am agnostic. It is true I performed a variety of masculine roles in our former town, being, as I was, its most widely employed bartender. I worked everywhere, the beer bar, the townie bar, the wine bar, the whiskey bar. I poured drinks in the hotel, pulled taps at the concert hall, and it was I who dressed cocktails with paper umbrellas at the place with the Michelin star. I turned up at the Elks and VFW and even at St. Vito's, mixing rum or Jim Beam with various kinds of soda. In each venue, I made myself into a different character, shifting my shape to flatter the crowd I served. For the beer bar, I wore old rock shirts with torn-off sleeves that showed my tattoos. For the hotel, I shaved my cheeks to a glow, brushed back my profuse black hair, and knotted my tie. If it was the Elks, I dusted off the POW/MIA hat I'd found in the flea market. Et cetera, et cetera. To each look I added changes in manner and speech. Such adjustments come easily to a failed actor and onetime model.

Had I become the town mascot? I know was immensely popular. I can't say why, but I was more beloved there than I had or have ever been in any of the many locales I've tried to make my home. Men and women both sought my attention, and though they went about it in slightly different ways, I knew the appeal had in part to do with what I considered my wasted magnetism: a fashion model's generic facial symmetry, a lantern jaw capable of sprouting a beard in forty-eight hours, and blue eyes as clear and pure as the lagoons of your island dreams. From the neck down, I am as lanky and lean as a company dancer, with long hands that drunken women snatch and admire in crassly suggestive terms. I am a head taller than the majority of men, too, and most people appear childlike next to me. But the fascination reached beyond my looks and size. Because I served them, locals treated me with a spirit of jealous ownership. Wherever I went, they smiled and said my name—Thirsty, they called me, thinking themselves funny—and asked if I had a new gig lined up. When I inevitably said no, they smiled, reassured by my failure, and told me that my agent would probably call soon. Then, often as not, they told me what to fetch them.

This took place in the late teens, in a rapidly gentrifying town situated in the hills overlooking the Hudson River. Monica, Matty, and I had moved to this former port a few years earlier, fleeing the rental traps of upscale Brooklyn in hopes of buying a house on a tree-shaded block and calling it home. That idea had yet to take shape (and because of what was to happen, never would), but I was plugging along behind the town's bars, pouring and mixing beverages with the faith that one day all the cash in the tip jars plus Monica's measly earnings as an adjunct professor of philosophy would somehow enable us to move out of our rented townhouse with peeling siding and a ceiling that leaked when it rained.

Each morning I woke and, while my loved ones slept, jogged the hilly streets—rain or shine, snowy winter or muggy summer—to the local high school, where I performed isometric exercises and pumped iron with the few other adults who trained there in the hours before the teenagers began to appear, keeping my body toned and steeling myself for the long dull hours of listening to whatever it was my customers wanted to say. The real work of a bartender is not the physical labor but the surrendering of attention, hearing people out, laughing at their jokes, and saying a few words of commiseration when the moment calls for it. It may sound easy, but over the years the constant affability wears a person down.

. . . .

HAUG APPROACHED ME at the high school one morning in midautumn. It was dark as night out, the last week of daylight savings, and I'd come huffing up to the yellow light of the school's athletic entrance, striding through the dim halls past trophy cases and various bulletin boards to the weight room, which smelled of must and the emanations of countless adult and adolescent bodies. The retired Korean War veteran who worked as the attendant didn't look up from his newspaper while I signed in a few lines below where I'd signed in the day before. The only other person among the treadmills, resistance contraptions, and free weights was Anthony Haug.

The school security officer sat at his usual pulley machine, baring his teeth under the white sweatband he always wore while he made the stack of plates clink and crash. He was an immense man, nearly as tall as me and much wider, with a large head that narrowed above his thick cheeks. He was both very powerful and very out of shape, sweating through the cutoff gray sweatshirt he wore over a soaked-through tee. He had an ugly face, and I knew people who joked meanly that he had the right last name, not only because of his features, but because of his former life as an NYPD officer. Yet for all this physical beastliness, there remained something boyish about Haug, and his large and earnest eyes were watching me eagerly as I made my way past him.

"Thirsty, I'm glad you're here," he said, breathing hard. He glanced back to make sure the attendant was still reading and gestured for me to come closer. "I want to talk to you about something. It's important, but discretion is a must."

I approached warily, combating the usual unease I felt when Haug had me in his crosshairs. I had seen him drunk many times at the townie bar, Dugan's, and I was well acquainted with his reactionary worldview. He believed, for instance, that the twentysomethings who assembled every Sunday, with signs calling for equality or peace or protesting injustice, were plotting to take over the government in the upcoming election and hike property taxes to redistribute local wealth. He called them *Commies* and claimed they were dangerous, and he insisted they were funded by a rich Central European Jewish financier. A known bully on social media, Haug was as likely to grow enraged over something he saw on his phone as he was over an overheard scrap of a neighboring conversation. Whenever he went off, leaning over the bar to rant, I would stand back and glance toward the off-duty cops who frequented Dugan's, letting those meaty, tired-looking men know the security guard was past the limit. Once they were through enjoying the sight of me twitching with what they must have considered yuppie fear, two or three of them would walk over and talk Haug into staggering home.

The police laughed at Haug and called him harmless, but the security guard had boasted on several occasions that he always carried a gun, including while walking the elementary school grounds, even though it was illegal and could have cost him his job. Staying armed was necessary, he said, because bad guys were everywhere. They could be anybody, he said, average-looking men or women, even boys as young as eleven or twelve. Trust him: I didn't want to know what they were capable of. It was better if I didn't get involved, he said, and let men like him protect what he called *our way of life.*

The fact that this man lurked around Matty's school horrified me, but I was also afraid of crossing him. In the weight room, responding to his summons, I made a point of smiling. "Great to see you, Anthony. What's up?"

"Saw you talking to that Arab yesterday before we opened the doors," he said. "That surprised me. What do you know about him and his operation?"

For a moment I could not reply. There were several reasons. The first was his venomous tone. Then there were the unusual word choices.

Finally, I had no idea what he talking about. Then it hit me. He meant Ranvir Khattri, the Sikh who owned a car wash out by the city limits. Khattri's daughter was in Matty's class, and the two were friends and liked to draw animals together, a sweet thing Khattri and I would discuss to pass time in the mornings while waiting for Haug to open up the school.

I nearly laughed at Haug finding our exchanges suspicious. I stopped myself, though, supposing it would offend this potentially unhinged bigot who spent much of each week in the vicinity of my son. "I don't think he's an Arab," I said, trying to sound diplomatic. "He's a Sikh, isn't he? They're from India, right?"

Not that it should matter, I might have added, had I thought Haug would be sensitive to the implications.

As it was, the information I'd given had no visible effect on his expression. "Towelhead's a towelhead, far as I'm concerned," he said. "I know there's like sixty kinds. You can keep them all straight if you want, but I don't got time to play Hands Across America. I've got lives to protect."

Again I held my grin, breaking into a sweat from the effort. "I'm not sure what you mean by 'his operation.' Do you mean the car wash?"

"That's exactly what I mean," he said. "You know where he gets all the towelheads who work there? This isn't exactly towelhead country. How do we know they're not plotting another attack?"

Faced with such a hopelessly offensive line of questioning, I gazed back in dismay, speechless, wishing the attendant would say something. Behind me, the old man shook open a new section of his paper.

Haug went on: "Where do these guys come from? That car wash could be a front for a madrassa. Is anybody paying attention to this? No, all anybody talks about is development and eating gluten-free. What I want to know is, who's thinking about our safety?"

My skin was flushing from anxiety and shame over my fear of this man. Summoning my courage, I said, "You've got the wrong idea about Ranvir. He's like everybody else around here, trying to make a living. He's a good person. Him and his family."

Haug shook his head pityingly. "Listen, I know you're a nice guy. Too nice. You artsy, acting types don't get it. You weren't there that morning. You didn't see the planes, the fire. You didn't see the people jump. The sky was gone. It was all smoke and ash. Like the end of the goddamn world."

I'd heard this speech before, late nights in Dugan's. Checking my phone, I said, "I'm sorry. I need to head back and get Matty ready. Monica teaches this morning."

Haug accepted this without a word—lack of time is the great unifier in that part of the country—and turned back to his pulleys. As he resumed hoisting the stack of plates, I spotted an odd bulge on the side of his sweatshirt. It was about the size, I thought, of the lump a handgun would make.

. . . .

I SHOULD SAY I never doubted Haug's sincerity or the reality of his trauma. Many older firemen and police in our city told me they respected and even revered him for the role he'd played in responding. Every year on the anniversary, the city holds a ceremony on the hill over the river. There's a small memorial there, and a few local organizations stick tiny paper flags in the grass around the block of granite and twisted steel to honor the memory of the thousands who died. The mayor, police chief, and other local politicians take turns speaking, and in those days Haug was always present, front and center, crying into his gigantic hands while men and women alike patted him on the shoulders and arms and said comforting words. There is something undeniably moving about the event, not only the commemoration, even crowded out as it is by so many tragedies since, but by the sight of people like Haug, for whom time stopped on the day of the disaster. I knew plenty of people, younger and relatively responsibility-free, who rolled their eyes at the patriotic pageantry and Haug's public weeping, but I sympathized with the man—not politically, but as a human being, and also because I was no longer young and knew that I too could one day suffer a shattering loss that warped my sense of the world.

Of course, Haug's grief did not excuse his hostility to Khattri, a perfectly kind and gentle man who'd done nothing to invite the attention of a local conspiracy theorist. Khattri was a businessman, a family man, and he seemed to be a leader in the town's tiny Sikh community.

He employed people, and he treated others with respect, even as he showed little interest in the lives of strangers, minding his business like so many New Yorkers. He was brown man whose traditional head-wear set him apart from other minorities in a largely white community. It was as simple as that—and Haug's imagination had done the rest. The security guard's suspicions were so deeply wrong, so riddled with errors and baseless assumptions, that I grew angrier the more I thought about them. As a result, I entered my house that morning with such force that Monica startled where she sat sipping coffee and said, "What's your freaking problem, Thirsty?"

Her tone brought me back to Earth, and I looked at her, perched at our crummy secondhand table behind a spread of lecture notes. She wore her glasses, and her dark hair was bound in her signature bun somehow held in place by a single pencil, which I'd always found both mysterious and deeply sexy. I held up a finger and checked for signs of Matty.

"He's watching TV," she said, grasping that I was genuinely upset. She let her glasses hang from her neck and came over to where I stood sweating and heaving. "What's going on?"

The thing to understand about Monica is that she is much smarter than I am. She has an academic intelligence, but she knows people, too, and I am incapable of concealing anything from her. I told her everything, from the stuff about Haug's guns to his disgusting theory about Ranvir Khattri. I kept my voice low for fear Matty would overhear, and also to show my wife that I was in control, rational. I watched her face change as she listened, beginning with a creased brow and gradually relaxing as her blue eyes detached from the stare with which I sought her indignation.

Once I'd finished, she stared out the window a few seconds, considering how to say what she had already decided. Most days, her mettle and reserve reassure me, but that morning her poise left me feeling totally alone.

"Like you didn't know the guy's an ass, Thirsty," she said. "They're everywhere. That's not new. This place is crawling with creeps like that. This whole country is. You should ignore him."

Ruffled by her lack of outrage, I threw my hands in the air, the way I might have at the townie bar when the refs on TV made a terrible call. "I never said it was new. I said this is dangerous."

"How long has he been guarding that school?" she argued. "Twelve, fifteen years? He hasn't done anything to get himself fired yet. He's full of hot air. I bet he's always going on about somebody. He's probably got a bunch of charts in his basement. Everybody needs a hobby."

I couldn't believe what I was hearing. "What about carrying a gun at the school?"

She nodded. "I'm sure the district wouldn't like it, but probably more of those guys are armed than you or I could know. Let it go. If they fire him, they'll just hire another asshole like him."

I gawked at this PTA mother who regularly volunteered for school festivals, unwinding wheels of raffle tickets. "That's really what you think?"

Monica frowned, as if offended by my reaction. She dropped her hand from my arm. "Come on, Thirsty. Grow up."

. . . .

AN HOUR later I was back at the school, standing in the crowd of waiting parents and schoolchildren, keeping a distance from Haug that was too great to speak across. I occupied myself by eavesdropping on two young moms who were too fit and fashionably dressed to have lived in town for long. They took turns complaining about the local restaurants, and while some were places I worked, I agreed with their assessments. Hearing them made me miss the city and the chatter on sets while I sat for makeup jobs (I'd been a corpse, a salesman, a junkie, a drive-through customer, a birthday party magician, an intoxicated driver, a happy call-center employee, a farmer, and many other things). I was tempted to break in and join their conversation, but one looked at me and smiled, and I turned away, unwilling to become the married man who might be flirting at his kid's school. Matty stood a few yards off, waving a big stick over yellow leaves and shouting made-up incantations. I envied him his innocence. Ranvir Khattri appeared beside me, letting go of his daughter's hand. The girl, whose black hair was cut short around the ears, ran to join Matty, and her father and I watched the children play.

Presently, I felt Haug's stare. When I peeked, he was glowering at Khattri, as if there were something insulting about this short wiry man standing casually, hands stuck in his jeans pockets, his burgundy turban neatly bound. Khattri himself was oblivious, glancing at his watch, his eyes lined with typical parent fatigue. He smiled up with his usual good cheer.

"Thurston, are you okay?" he said, tilting his head. He'd always called me by my full name. "You look like something's bothering you."

Realizing I was scowling, I shook my head and laughed. I saw myself as everyone there must have—my face, one strangers might recognize vaguely from men's vitamins advertisements and underwear boxes, drawn tight; my bright blue eyes shuttered; my jaw moving methodically as I ground my teeth. I must have looked slightly off my rocker, in other words. "Nothing more than usual," I said. "The collapse of civilization is around the corner, and I'm on five hours of sleep."

Khattri nodded, zipping his windbreaker against the chill. He glanced at his daughter and Matty and then noticed the two young moms, who had moved on to ranking the town's various yoga and Pilates studios. His eyes lingered on them a moment, then he sighed. "I know, the times are never so bad. But really, Thurston, we have it pretty good." He spoke with conviction and satisfaction, unaware of the large, gun-toting menace glaring at him.

Up by the school doors, Haug shifted his eyes to mine, and he dipped his head faintly, as if to remind me of the conversation we'd had earlier. I glanced back toward my son and Khattri's daughter, who were lost in their game, one of thousands played in their perfect childhoods.

"You're right," I muttered. "You're right, you're right, you're right."

. . . .

IT MIGHT HAVE ended there, had I stayed home that day. It is tempting to think so. But later that morning someone called from the wine bar, dangling the offer of a shift, and I got off the couch where I'd been napping and said I'd take it, abandoning my plans to stay in, cook dinner, watch a family movie, and stay up late with my wife. Had I declined, Monica and I would have sipped my THC pen and had one of the postcoital conversations in which she was always pointing out things I hadn't noticed, blowing my mind, and maybe she would have changed my view of Haug, convinced me he was an enormous child who saw monsters everywhere he turned, a fool who would have found a new bogeyman by next week. Maybe I would have laughed him off the next time he and I met.

Instead I jumped at the offer to make a couple hundred more of the dollars we were trying to save, and a little while later I left the house with my hair gelled back and my dry-cleaned, collared shirt pressed and untucked, my dark jeans fitting tight in the crotch, my leather shoes polished to a greasy shine. It was thus attired, halfway between disco dancer and adult film star, that I strolled up Main Street toward the mountain that also bears the name of the small city where we lived, taking in the leafy reds and yellows and oranges that covered the slope above the familiar brick buildings. As usual, I felt hopeful and open to the future, and as the evening wore on, I immersed myself in the elegant atmosphere of the wine bar with its soft electronic music, smiling and hugging and shaking hands with the people who came at me, it seemed, from all directions.

A number of customers that night were parents of kids who attended Matty's school, people in their thirties and forties, transplants from Brooklyn and Manhattan who were doing their utmost to bring NYC standards to this Hudson Valley scene. Tonight they'd come without spouses and partners, having left them at home with the children, and they were juicing what pleasure they could from a night of freedom. I knew them all, from this bar and other bars. I knew who they were sober and who they were drunk, and they all knew me and trusted me to look after them should they do too much self-harm.

A few hours in, I became aware they were talking energetically about something, and I waited, content to stay uninvolved until one of them needed a drink. The reprieve wouldn't last—it never did in that place, where customers often wanted long conversations about wine and geography—and sure enough, my friend Callie made her way over a couple of minutes later, tipsy enough to kiss me hello on the cheek. "Hey Thirsty, what's your take on that dumpy-ass security guard at the elementary?"

I felt heat climbing my neck. Monica wouldn't have mentioned my private fears to any of these people, not without my lead, and so I worried Haug had been running his mouth around town, making us out to be some kind of racist team. Deciding to play the handsome naif, as I'd once done in the pilot that never made it to broadcast, I said, "Haug? What about him?"

"He's been fucking with Tasia on Facebook," Callie said. "Big mistake."

Hearing her name, Tasia met my gaze and took a big gulp of red wine. I knew the woman well. We'd been acquainted since a long-ago cookout, where we'd both drunk too much and shared a potent moment. Though nothing had happened beyond a thrilling staring contest that ended with us saying goodbye awkwardly, she'd acted ever since like she knew everything about me.

"He's fucking crazy," Tasia called over the music and voices. "Says he has enemies. Like, plotting against him. He actually imagines there are people here who think about him."

I could have pointed out that here we were talking about him and therefore we were thinking about him, but it would have annoyed her and everybody with her, so I stayed mum, aware of how the crowd looked at me now, excited by alcohol and the suspicion I was holding good gossip. I felt a flash of hope that they'd heard Haug's racist conspiracy theory, and that I could safely ignore him, leaving someone else to deal with the problem.

I turned back to Callie. "What's he saying, exactly?" I said, slipping into a detective character. It was a role I'd played many times since high school, both on the stage and once on an educational kid's show.

"Oh, you know," she said. "Bunch of shit about liberals and ethnic groups. Everybody's a communist. Everybody hates the president. Well." She laughed. "He's right about the last part."

"Huh," I said. "What's this have to do with Tasia?"

"The fat prick took offense to me standing up to him on Facebook," Tasia said, loud enough that a couple down the bar stopped talking to listen. "Started harassing me with private messages. I could block him, but I won't give him the satisfaction of thinking he can intimidate me. I don't care how many gross memes he sends. Besides, he's not half as edgy as he thinks he is."

One of the dads stepped forward, a guy named Edward Lemmon-Grier, a fellow city transplant with a high faded haircut he dyed purple, green, and blue. He taught painting classes at Monica's college and organized the small political protests that took place on weekends. Holding a tiny glass just beneath his papery lips, he said, "I heard a rumor that he carries a gun at the school. Know if there's any truth to it?"

An alarm went off in me. Something about the man's tone suggested he was too invested. I shook my head, unwilling to take part in a personal vendetta. As much as I wanted to see Haug fired, I worried such a disturbance in the uneasy order of things would end with the psycho doing something rash. It seemed unlikely that he would hurt Matty, but there was collateral damage to consider, and the more I thought about it, the more reluctant I was to say anything against him to this group of angry parents.

"I have no idea," I said, then retreated into my bartender act. "Let me know if I can get you a another."

Tasia danced toward Edward Lemmon-Grier, narrowing her eyes playfully. "Where'd you hear about the gun?" she said. "A word in the right ear, and he'd be gone."

Lemmon-Grier's mouth curved in a knowing smile. "Even without a gun, he's got tremendous potential to get himself fired."

The other moms and dads were laughing now, and I had no idea why. Callie leaned in and confided, "Edward made a fake account to troll him with. He's gotten him to rant a bunch of times. Crazy stuff, racist as hell. Haug deletes them, of course, but we've been saving screenshots to send to the superintendent."

Lemmon-Grier held out his phone so I could see a picture of a Facebook thread. He scrolled through several of these, going too quickly for me to read them, not that I tried. All I saw were tiny faces, lots and lots of words, random emojis, and a number of overused memes. "I just sent him a couple of personal messages. He's going to go ballistic!"

"I see," I said, and looking into the laughing faces around me, I felt deeply nauseated. These people had no idea what they were doing, conspiring against a man who was deeply paranoid. I saw a flicker in my friend Callie's face, and I smiled to reassure her I was on their side, then commented that her glass was getting empty. Could I interest her in a bottle?

. . . .

I GREW UP believing that in America you could be anybody you wanted. I still believed it when all of this was happening. I believe it now, I think. At least, I want to.

"Your problem, Thirsty," Monica says, "is you think everyone will do the right thing, given the chance. Some people are just rotten inside. You expect too much from them, and they let you down again and again."

I shrug. She's the philosopher, and there's no question she'd beat me in an argument. What she says is probably true, too, or mostly true. I'd like to believe all people have good inside them, that their desire to help is stronger than their desire to hurt, but there's so much evidence to the contrary. If anything, I tell myself motivations are complicated, confused, sometimes inscrutable. Though often I don't understand why people end up doing what they do, what I know is that everybody has their reasons.

. . . .

THE NEXT NIGHT Haug came into Dugan's and made straight for the bar. He was wearing a coarse black Carhartt jacket zipped halfway up, and as he bore down on me, he kept his eyes moving, surveying his surroundings for potential threats. He pushed by a couple of municipal workers, ignoring the looks they turned on him as he settled against the polished wood in front of me. He was sober and full of purpose. "You been avoiding me?"

I shouldn't have been surprised at his suspicion. I'd slept in that morning, skipping my workout, and Monica had taken Matty to school. Though I admitted to myself the break from Haug had been a relief, I'd made no special effort to get it, and I'd even succeeded in getting through most of the day without thinking about him. But of course he would draw a paranoid conclusion. "Late night at work," I said. "My wife let me sleep."

"She was talking to your little friend," he said. "Thought you'd want to know. Think he might want her for his harem."

Such a statement did not deserve the dignity of a response, but I attempted to appeal to whatever reason he possessed. "Our kids are in the same class. They're friends."

Haug snorted like I was naïve, then chuckled and leaned in closer. "Anyway, I'm onto something. They've activated the sleeper cell. At the car wash or whatever safe house they use. It's happening."

Hearing these words, I imagined Tasia and Edward Lemmon-Grier looking at their phones and chortling. I put down the glass I'd been drying. "Can I get you a drink or something? You know this is a bar, right?"

Haug seemed to miss my sarcasm. "Something light to settle my nerves," he said. "Staying sharp is a must. I'm going on patrol in case anybody makes a move. With a little luck, they'll see me out there, get spooked and call it off."

I opened a brown bottle and watched him take a quick sip. He appeared to have no idea how absurd he looked and sounded. "What do you think their target is?" I said. "They going to blow up the laundromat?"

He blinked, as if thinking about it. "Honestly, I don't know. This isn't the city. Twenty years ago, I would have said one of the Catholic churches, but nobody goes anymore. Vigilance is key. People around here are living in a dreamworld. But don't worry. I'll save all you bimbos."

I sighed, ready to give up. It was all so far-flung and fanciful. There was more to it, I thought, looking into his creased face. A missing piece, something buried deep in Haug's psyche, but nothing I could access or influence. "How do you know they're activated?" I asked despite myself. "What's your proof?"

He gave me a sidelong glance. "I have my sources. Someone has reached out online. That's all I can say for now. Keep that under your hat, and don't worry about sending your son to school. He'll be safe as long as I'm there. You have my word."

I gave an involuntary grunt, thinking again of Tasia, of Edward Lemmon-Grier's puppet account. Of course, I couldn't tell Haug about the prank he'd fallen for. I could see the fallout easily—how Haug would confront his "enemies," how the police would come, how all the transplants would blame me. Nor could I persuade Edward and Tasia to knock it off without appearing supportive of Haug myself, or worse, inspire them to go to the superintendent with their incriminating screenshots, setting off a series of events that would lead to Haug's termination and whatever terrible thing he'd do in retaliation. I let out a breath and said only, "You can't trust everything you see online."

Haug threw back the rest of the beer and belched. "You forget I was a cop," he said. "I know a credible threat when I see one."

After he'd gone, I got the attention of Lieutenant Connors. The tall, athletic woman was standing at the far end of the bar, withholding laughter as the three patrolmen around her joked and cackled. Seeing me wave, she grabbed her glass of wine and wandered toward me. She was attractive, and out of uniform as she currently was, wearing her long hair down, a person might have taken her for a local business-woman, even an artist. I had the sense that she prided herself on her ability to blend in with the gentrifiers she claimed to loathe.

"What's going on, Thirsty?" she said as she drew near. "You got something to say to me? That wife of yours out of town?"

I grinned sharply. I hadn't noticed she was this drunk. "Monica's home with Matty," I said. "I was wondering whether you'd seen Anthony Haug out and about? Like patrolling, doing beat cop stuff?"

The lieutenant's smile fell away, telling me she was aware of the security guard's activities. "I do my best to not think about the Haug-ster," she said. "Whatever little game he's playing to keep himself out of trouble, that's his business."

"Absolutely," I said. "But what if he got it in his head that someone was a bad guy? What if he decided to do something about it? Took the law into his own hands?"

She tossed back the last of her wine and shook her head. "I know how he comes off, okay? But he's been part of this place for over a decade." She tapped her glass for a refill. "He's never done anything that couldn't be solved by telling him to go home. He hasn't he told you he intends to do something illegal, has he?"

"No," I admitted.

"Do you have evidence he's done anything wrong?"

Once again, I had to answer in the negative.

She raised her eyebrows. "He's a hero, Thirsty. He has plenty of flaws, but he was brave when it mattered. Let the man be."

I'd annoyed her. It was tempting to tell her about the guns Haug claimed to carry and what he'd said about Khattri, but her expression was closed. I could already hear her responding that Haug was within his rights to say whatever he wanted, and that people lied and exaggerated all the time.

"Sorry," I said. "You're right."

She gave me a once over, sizing me up in my Dugan's outfit—a flannel shirt, slashed jeans, and scuffed Doc Marten's. "Don't call me down here again unless it's to hit on me."

. . . .

AFTER CLOSING AROUND three, I went to my car in the tiny lot in back. The night was clear and quiet, the sky glittering with stars and airplanes and satellites and whatever else we've dumped there. I was worried about Khattri, and I drove out toward his car wash, thinking that if he happened to be working late, I'd knock on the door and warn him about Haug.

As I pulled onto the state route where his business stood out among the strip malls and broken-up empty lots, a large vehicle turned the corner behind me and began to follow closely, turning its headlights to bright and all but blinding me. It was Haug, I knew. Patrolling. Did he know it was me? And if so, did he think I was involved? What was going through his mind as he peered down into my car's interior, where his headlights illuminated my head and shoulders? What weapons did he have, and were they lying on the seat where he could reach them easily?

I wasn't interested in finding out, and I drove along at the speed limit, letting him tail me. I wondered if he believed I wouldn't know it was him, or if he believed he could intimidate me into keeping silent. It occurred to me as I passed the car wash—seemingly empty, its windows dark—that Haug would play innocent if I brought this up at the gym or any other place. The only way to catch him being his secret self was to confront him in the act.

I came to an intersection and turned right. He followed. I came to another intersection and turned right again, this time toward home. I was going to threaten him with going to the school district, I decided. I would tell him I was going to the police. I would tell him I would not be terrorized by some phony cop who excited himself by imagining that people he didn't know were plotting unthinkable crimes. I have never been an especially righteous man, but I have played them onstage, and I can be convincing. I sped through the silent and empty town with Haug's truck riding my bumper, preparing to get out and make a scene that would wake all the neighbors.

Approaching my street, I turned on my blinker and slowed, expecting him to follow, but he seemed to sense the trap I'd tried to set, because he spun behind me, heading back up the road we'd come on, his truck roaring like a giant in some ancient tale.

. . . .

I LAY AWAKE until dawn, my anger turning to dread as the alarm clock marched toward daybreak. Monica had long since rolled away from me, sensing my sleeplessness and wanting nothing to do with it. I looked at her shape, nearly as small as a child's, trying to imagine what she would do if something were to happen to me. Would she and Matty stay? Would she find someone else? Someone who could provide for her better, and who treated them differently, however slightly? Or would she go back to the rural midwestern town where her parents lived, where Matty would learn to ride four-wheelers, chew tobacco, and shoot guns? Haug would be waiting in the gym, I knew, sweating in his place on the pulley machine, ready to interrogate me.

It was tempting to roll over and take Monica in my arms, to close my eyes and try to sleep in that room with her forever, though obviously I would have to emerge eventually and go to work, and I knew if I put off going out until the last possible moment, I would feel trapped in the bar later, the day behind me wasted in wretched fear, and that my righteousness would be tempered when I did confront Haug. I slipped from bed, groggy and stiff in my joints, and began to dress, my heart pounding as I willed myself through each step.

A noise sounded in the doorway, and I turned, startled. Matty stood in the frame, a little human shadow saying nothing, giving no indication of feeling one way or another. He was still half-asleep, I realized, and probably surprised to find me standing there. I whispered for him to go on and get into bed with Mommy, which he did, burrowing under the covers, where she took him easily into her arms. I lingered over the sight of them, telling myself to treasure it, aware of the chance, however slight, that it would be the last time I saw them.

. . . .

IT WAS RAINING slightly, and an unseasonably warm wind was blowing, big and soft. I didn't have it in me to run and trudged along instead, climbing and descending the hills in the darkness, stepping carefully over the familiar places where the sidewalk was broken, glancing at old houses that had recently been renovated or rebuilt and which I was faintly aware of no longer being able to afford. I would make it up later in the day, I told myself, sleep a little in the afternoon and bolster myself for another night of bartending with a pot of coffee and a good sandwich with lots of meat. I would ask Monica if she wanted to go look for a place we could buy, if there was anything left in town. The barest, most rundown shack would do, I thought, provided it was ours.

I came to the block where the school stood and broke into a jog. The athletic complex entrance glowed yellow in the darkness, a rectangle I watched grow closer as I ran. Reaching the lot, I and slowed to catch my breath, letting my arms swing loosely at my sides. I was no longer afraid but ready to look Haug in his small eyes and tell him to leave me alone, and to leave Khattri in peace as well—to use my abundant words to put him in his place and to free myself from the tyranny of his horrible imagination.

He was behind me when he said my name. "What were you doing out by Khattri's?"

I stopped and stood very still, my shirt billowing a little. Something was different in his voice, and all the speeches I had been planning to give to him dissolved at once into a blankness as impenetrable as the dark morning sky. I turned, squinting through the misting rain. Haug stood some ten feet away, in the shadow between two cars where he'd been kneeling in wait. His hair and clothes were soaked. He was holding a small handgun down by one thigh.

I didn't move or take my eyes off the gun. "I was worried you had done something."

"Why would you worry about that?" He cocked his head. "I'm the one trying to protect everybody."

I might have laughed if I hadn't been so afraid. Haug was the only threat for miles. Two dozen Canadian geese flew over in a V, honking as they went. Far out in the sky, a passing airplane winked against the approaching storm's low ceiling. "You have to leave people alone," I said. "You're making it all up. You know that, don't you?"

He came toward me, his head lowered now, as if he were looking at my midsection and nothing else, a posture which was strange enough to concern me. "Turn to your left and start walking," he said. "You'll see a large pickup truck. It's got a peeing Calvin on the rear windshield."

This was surreal. I knew his big stupid truck. Everyone did. Was he unaware of this?

"Walk slowly. No funny moves."

. . . .

I FOUND MYSELF wedged into the narrow backseat of his cab, my wrists and ankles bound with zip ties. Haug drove silently, refusing to meet my gaze in the rearview mirror. He had gotten beyond self-questioning, I saw, could not risk the possibility he might be wrong. For the first time, I entertained the thought that a man could kill me, and there was nothing I could say or do that would affect his choice. The weight of this realization was crushing.

Khattri and many of the other Sikh families in our town lived in a neighborhood built on the side of a small mountain. The houses there sat back from the road. The rain was stopping, first light spilling over the mountaintop and changing the sky as Haug drove down one block of well-kept two-story homes, then turned around down the street and pulled off to the side to keep watch. He focused on a big green double ranch with a new deck and a trampoline in the yard. Four vehicles in the driveway. This was Khattri's house, I supposed.

The security guard's breathing filled the truck's cabin. On the armrest, his hand was wrapped around the gun. After a while he spoke. "I'm taking you both in, in case you were wondering. This is a citizen's arrest."

"For what?" I said.

"Criminal conspiracy," he said. "Suspected terrorism. I've been in touch with the FBI."

I thought of Edward Lemmon-Grier then and wondered how far he'd taken his deception, supposing he and Tasia might have put many stoned, laughter-filled hours into constructing an alternate reality for this dangerous buffoon who'd tied me up, but it all seemed too strange to try to explain. Besides, Haug would refuse to believe he had been tricked, especially if I were the one telling him so. He'd come to view me as an enemy, unwitting at best, and I understood it would be foolish to say anything that contradicted his account of what was going on. I kept my mouth shut as he studied the house and waited.

The road and driveways were dark and wet. I tried to imagine Khattri, walking his daughter out the door, only to be confronted by the large bigot who usually guarded the school, bearing down on him with a weapon. What would he think, say, do? It was easy to see envision how things could go wrong, how his daughter might stand witness to her father's murder. I thought of Matty seeing me die, and tears sprang to my eyes. It was too painful to contemplate, even as I knew countless children had lived that experience.

I cleared my throat, terrified of what I was about to do, yet unable to produce an acceptable alternative. "This isn't the way to get him," I said. "It's not safe here for you."

Haug's face appeared in the rearview mirror, his eyes homing in on me. They were wary but excited, begging me to say more. "What do you mean?"

"He's armed," I said. "He's always armed. They all are."

He took a breath. "Who's they?"

"The jihadi cell," I said. "You know, the guys who work at the car-wash. They all live in the house, sleep in one room. It's their safehouse. You think they haven't seen you snooping around?"

Haug was staring at me in the glass, trying to figure out if I was lying. He wanted to believe me, though, and when he spoke, his voice was full of both suspicion and something like longing. "How do I know you haven't already alerted him?"

"I don't want to die." It was the one true thing I'd said so far. The rest of it was coming from a script I'd read for a cable show about a bunch of terrorists lying low in California, planning to attack Disneyland. I'd been called back for that one, but in the end they went with someone younger. My agent said I brought too much nuance to the role. Now I was playing this part for Haug. That was all this poor son of a bitch wanted, to be part of a story that made sense to him.

"Listen to me, Haug. They're more armed in there than a SEALs unit. And they know you're here. They know every vehicle that comes into this neighborhood. Right now, they're waiting for you to make a move that'll allow them to shoot you legally. Better let the police do this. You've got me. That's all the collateral you'll need."

Haug's eyes bulged. "Bullshit."

"Do you think for an instant that Ranvir fucking Khattri will leave his property if he sees you?" I said, as if the car wash owner were an international fugitive. "We're talking about a man who took the time to build up a respected business and make himself a pillar of the community. You think he won't wait you out for a day, a week? He'll sit tight until you come onto his property with your gun, and then someone in one of those upstairs windows will take you out."

Haug looked at the house, studying the curtained windows. "I don't know," he said. "You could be lying."

The part I'd wanted had been that of a profoundly disaffected American who joins a terrorist cell, and before auditioning I'd learned multiple Arabic phrases, mostly for the sake of pronunciation. Now I opened my mouth and began to say them randomly, making my voice guttural and leaning into the consonance of each *kh-* sound.

"Motasharefatun bema'refatek," I shouted. *Pleased to meet you.* "Allahu akhbar!"

In the mirror, Haug's tiny eyes grew huge with excitement and terror. "What the fuck did you just say?"

"Ayn al-hammam?" I said. *Where is the bathroom?* "Kul 'aam wa antum bekheir!" *Happy birthday!* "Allahu Akhbar!"

His lips were quivering now. "Who are you?" he said, his voice rising in fear. "Who the fuck are you?"

"Hilūl as-sanah al-jadīdah!" I shouted. *Happy New Year!* "Allahu Akhbar!"

"Holy shit!" Haug cried out. He put the truck into gear, slammed on the gas, and raced out of there.

. . . .

THE ADMITTING OFFICER was relatively new to the force. He knew me from Dugan's and all the other bars where I worked, and like all the police in town, he was familiar with Haug. Having buzzed us into the station, he stared hard, his brow wrinkled in confusion over everything about us, from our physical appearances to the time of our entry. "Everything all right, you two?"

Haug had put away his gun to walk me up to the precinct, holding the back of my shirt bunched in his fist. "This guy's not who says he is," he informed the cop. "Thirsty might not even be his real name. We've got a safehouse situation on the north side of town. We're going to need to raid it; we're going to need backup; you know, I think you might want call in SWAT. There's at least one child in the house."

The officer's face screwed up as if he thought this might be a joke, though he stopped smiling when he saw how I was looking at him. "Just a moment," he said. He got up and went into the back.

He was gone for maybe a minute, and I stood there with Haug. I could just see the slightly out of breath security guard from the corner of my eye, standing with his shoulders and his head back, his eyes fixed on some invisible point in front of him. Though he affected this proud stance, he seemed oddly vulnerable, caught between believing he was a hero and seeing he'd made an enormous mistake. Despite everything, I pitied him.

Three officers came out with the young guy, everyone smiling weirdly.

They fanned out around us, talking to Haug in soothing voices, like they were trying to distract a panicked dog. Haug immediately recognized what was happening and moved his hands from side to side as if to roll out a piece of pizza dough. "Listen to me," he said. "Just hold on, just hold on. There's a safehouse."

"Do you have any weapons on you now?" the officer behind him said.

"Hear me out," Haug said. "It isn't what it looks like."

I closed my eyes against the sounds of the security guard protesting and starting to hyperventilate, though I made a point of raising my voice when I said, "He's got a gun. There's probably more in the truck." I was almost crying when I spoke these words, my throat raw with relief. It was as though I'd never uttered language before, and I kept talking, fascinated by the sounds I was making. "He was going to kill us. I think he was going to shoot us both. He's out of his mind. He's a menace to everyone in this town."

Haug yelled in protest when they went to handcuff him, and when he resisted, one of the officers tased him. I didn't see it, but I heard the shock, and then I smelled it, and Haug fell behind me like a bag of sand and started to sob. It was pathetic, but the police who'd subdued him were fired up now, giving loud orders. One of them crashed against me, almost knocking me to the floor. He quickly apologized, then made me hold still while he cut the zip ties from my wrists.

. . . .

IN THE WEEK or so that followed, the story made its rounds, and I did my best to say nothing about how it happened that I was with Anthony Haug when the city police booked him for false arrest and illegal possession of firearms. People were horrified, though plenty laughed and gossiped, and the moms and dads at the wine bar and the twentysomethings at the beer bar all begged me for details and boasted in concerned-sounding voices that they'd seen it coming, how they'd known all along what a threat the fucked-up former cop posed to what they called *our little community*, though they never said who belonged and who didn't.

Eventually, the interest faded. Everyone seemed to become self-conscious of talking about a person they'd always been embarrassed to admit thinking about. People stopped asking about it, and life moved on as it had before.

But life there would not go on as it once had for my family. Some balance had been upset. My first intimation of this new state of affairs was when Dugan himself called to say he was letting me go. A Vietnam vet who was in recovery and spent all his time in Florida, he had a smoker's shredded voice and coughed his way through a brief explanation. "I don't think the clientele appreciates your presence anymore," he said. "Sorry, Thirst."

I was stunned. A little hurt, too, though I was able to shake off the wounded feeling that night at the wine bar, where I joked with my fellow transplants. I didn't need the love and affection of the old-timers, anyway, not when I had the support of the people who were making the city the place it was becoming. It wasn't until an officer came in and ticketed the establishment for failing to card an undercover cop—something that had never before happened—that I began to see things here would be difficult for me from now on.

We held out for a few months, but in the end, we had to go. Strange men in pickups started following Monica, and there were mornings I came outside to find someone had keyed our car. One night we were awakened five or six times by what sounded like gunshots out front, and the police, when they showed up, told me there was nothing they do to help us. The officer who said this flashed us a big smile, standing on our front porch with his arms crossed.

Nor were the moms and dads who hated Haug on our side. Some took offense I'd withheld what I knew, like my friend Callie, who couldn't talk to me without reminding me I'd hurt her feelings with my silence. Others became upset when I refused to go into detail about what had happened that morning. On Facebook, Edward Lemmon-Grier and Tasia suggested I was responsible for what they called Haug's *nervous breakdown*, claiming *this all could have been avoided if people who knew certain things had been forthcoming*. Regulars stopped coming in during my shifts, a pattern my remaining employers were quick to notice. People who'd begged me to attend lame house parties and cookouts now ignored me on the street or made for the crosswalk when they saw me. The last straw came when the house was heavily egged while were out of town, and the landlord threatened to hike our rent to cover the cleaning costs.

By then, leaving felt like the logical thing to do.

The last morning, once we'd packed up the moving truck, I took our car to get it washed and cleaned inside, thinking Monica would have an easier time returning to the Midwest in a vehicle that wasn't trashed inside. I wound up making small talk with Ranvir Khattri while his guys drove the car through.

He was surprised to learn we were moving. "Why are you going? For work?"

I smiled as cheerfully as I could. "I don't think we're really welcome here anymore."

He narrowed his eyes, not understanding.

"You know, because of everything that happened with Haug."

He looked even more confused. "Why does that name ring a bell? Who is he again?"

I was stunned. No one had told him he'd been in danger, not the even the police, who'd charged the former security guard with the crimes he had committed, but nothing with relation to the one he'd been planning. "You know, from the school?" I said. "Big guy? Kind of menacing?"

He nodded. "Yes, that's right. A detective came and asked me about him. Whether he'd ever threatened me. It was strange. He was only here a few times. A very rude man. I heard he held someone hostage?"

I laughed. "That was me!"

Khattri's eyes bulged, and his mouth formed a circle of perfect astonishment. "That was you? What happened? What for?"

I regarded the man in amazement, but I supposed the explanation was simple. On the one hand, many people in town treated him like an outsider, and on the other, he was absorbed in his own business and family life. He probably dealt with casual racism all the time, and Haug's belligerence might have simply blended in. After an awkward moment, I shook my head. "He's got lot of problems. Who knows, really?"

Of course, that was true enough of everyone, and what else could be said? Khattri nodded, clearly sad this was goodbye for us, and because he was feeling sad, I became that way, too. We stood at the register inside the store and watched the big window in the wall as my car came through, its keyed-up finish foaming.

"Where will you go?"

"We'll stay with my wife's parents for a bit," I said. "Then go on to the next thing. Maybe we'll head to the mountains out west. Maybe the coast."

He frowned and squinted, as if he could see snowcapped peaks in the distance and the vast blue sky stretching above them. "It's a great big country," he told me. "I've been out there. It's very beautiful."

"Ugly, too," I said.

"And ugly," he conceded. "And beautiful and ugly."

My car was finished now, and his Sikh employees were drying it off energetically. I was impressed by the job they had done, hardly recognized the dirty station wagon I'd brought in. I laughed and turned to Khattri and shook his hand.

He tilted his head toward the open door. Outside, my car sat dripping, its heavily scratched finish shining in the pale pre-noon light, ready to carry us all to our next life.

MODERN
WONDERS

Vor seinem Tode sammeln sich in seinem Kopfe alle Erfahrungen der ganzen
Zeit zu einer Frage, die er bisher an den Türhüter noch nicht gestellt hat.

—KAFKA, "VOR DEM GESETZ"

NOW THAT DAVE has reached the end, he would like to access his
memory once more. There's something unrealized there, he thinks,
some insight floating out along the edges, unsayable yet possessing
undeniable substance.

The Tomorrow interface prompts him: *I can perform this function.
Would you like me to proceed*?

"I have instructions," Dave says, or feels like he does. He hears his
voice, though he understands his ears are plugged, encased in the machine along with the rest of his head, and that he does not move his
mouth to speak. It's easy to forget that he's imagining all this, or that
only his eyes move, surrounded by the interface's dark screen. Of course,
it's supposed to be easy. That's what he's paying for. "I want to put this
into words, and then I'd like to send it, as a message. Just in case."

The interface replies in an electronic voice represented by a squiggly
pink light flashing across the visual surround. *I can perform this function. To whom would you like to send a message*?

Dave hesitates. The unhappy truth is his ex knows him best, but
Leslie is also wired into this life-extension network, and a message

from him would get lost in the background of whatever virtual experience they're having. Besides, she was at pains to hear him out in even the best of times. Maurice is observant, he knows, and would listen closely, but his son, no longer young, would let the words sink to wherever he stores things he'll never repeat or revisit. There is Delia, the intuitive choice, though Dave worries she's light years beyond any insight he might muster. His daughter has always been far smarter, but he supposes there's a chance experience has taught him something she doesn't know.

"Beggars can't be choosers," he says. "Send it to Delia."

I can perform this function, the interface responds. *Would you like me to proceed?*

. . . .

HE KNEELS IN the flowerbed in front of his house, the first he ever bought, pulling weeds impatiently. He's been alive thirty-four years and had many formative experiences. He's grown up, seen both parents die, married a woman and reproduced with her (Maurice is six at this point), and assumed ownership of an expensive and demanding suburban half-acre. Tall and quiet with floppy blonde hair he brushes back from a gentle-looking face, he has a good job in the local refinery and drives a powerful car. He's attractive to many women and men, and he's long used his appeal as a license to be casual and easygoing.

This is the moment the red fly bites him. He has committed himself to uprooting little knots of crab grass and is coated with sweat and dirt. His tolerance for the presence of an insect on his grimy arm—even one he's never seen, a bug that looks like a blue bottle fly, only with crimson iridescence along its brief abdomen—has expanded a few seconds. The instant before he moves to brush it off, the insect lowers its maxillae and tears loose a tiny piece of flesh, firing a lightning bolt of pain down through his fingertips and then back up his arm.

It hurts so much he hops up, swearing inarticulately. The fly is gone, having left a small pink wound just above his elbow. It generates an extraordinary agony, unbelievable, nearly funny. Dave becomes aware he is cursing loudly enough to disturb neighbors, and he bites his lip hard enough to leave teethmarks. In the ensuing peace, he hears the sprinkler three yards down spattering water across the pavement. He decides to take this melodrama inside, pinching the damaged skin until he can hold it under the running faucet. He waits and waits for the stabbing, shooting pain to subside. Instead, the bite and the area around it grow more and more inflamed, and finally he goes to the medicine cabinet and smears cream on the burning pink dot. He pops a couple of yellow tablets and stands in the bathroom, the only lighted room in the house, waiting for the drug to take effect. A headache is forming. Outside, he senses, it has clouded over. The day has shifted. He will not return to gardening.

. . . .

THE DOCTOR PRESCRIBES an antibiotic he's never heard of. It takes him a few attempts to pronounce its name correctly. She gives him the pharmacy slip and takes another look, her eyebrows suggesting a mixture of wonder and concern. The skin surrounding the bite has risen to a purple lump. The whole thing looks like a ripe miniature plum with a piece missing. She frowns and exhales through her nose.

"No alcohol with this medicine," she says. "No prolonged direct sunlight. You might have insomnia and some diarrhea."

"For a whole month? It's just a fly bite."

"If this doesn't go away, or if you develop splotches, we'll break out the big guns."

Dave doesn't want to think about what *the big guns* might entail. "This some new disease?" He tries to block out the horror stories he's read online. "Should I be worried?"

The doctor watches him with inscrutable blue eyes. She is small, unconventionally beautiful, and relentlessly solemn. "It's cause for vigilance. But it's not new. It should clear up in a month. The odds are in your favor."

The odds? He thinks, with a sense of disbelief. "What'd the deal with the fly? I've never seen a red one like that before."

She shrugs. "They've always been here."

Ah, he thinks, disappointment mingling with relief. That explains it. He's the outsider, the one who comes from another state.

. . . .

IT'S THE YEAR an October hurricane rides unseasonably warm waters a hundred miles upriver, flooding towns, washing out railroad tracks and destroying crops. Several people drown, and a larger number die when the resulting power outages and traffic jams prevent them from receiving the medical attention they require. Dave and Leslie's house is significantly damaged, the windows blasted out, the flowerbed annihilated, the furniture waterlogged, though they are fortunate enough to get an insurance payout that lets them raze the wreckage and build another.

They are also fortunate enough to be relatively far away when the storm hits. Way out on Interstate 80 in western Pennsylvania, they inch forward, surrounded by miserable-looking families in cars and SUVs and trucks and minivans. They are bound for the Chicago suburbs, where they'll stay with Leslie's parents until the authorities deem it safe to return. The storm is bigger than any Dave has seen. It covers the sky even here, and they only emerged from the outermost belt of rain half an hour ago.

Leslie is driving. It makes sense that someone with both arms would do it, especially in an emergency. She insisted, just as she insisted Dave remove his robotic arm to keep it from being damaged in the torrential rains they faced at home. They have good insurance, but the device still incurred heavy out-of-pocket costs, and though its most sensitive electronics are protected by waterproof seals, it's best not to take chances. He's wearing his rubber prosthetic—an unwieldy but comforting extension of the nub medical professionals call his *residual limb*—for the appearance of normalcy, or at least that's what he tells himself. Leslie isn't fooled for a second, and Maurice accepted the change in his father's body as if amputations were common. He looks at the man driving the minivan beside them, a little ashamed to be sitting shotgun. He knows this probably makes him a sexist, though that amuses him a little in light of everything else he's become. He is happy with his current medication. It leaves him drowsy, but he hasn't had an inflammation attack since the last adjustment, and he can't help but feel like he has his health back. Of course, it's all relative.

He's gotten good with his remaining hand. He uses his phone to tune in to news from New York City, which describes the destruction in their north Jersey suburb. The anchor interviews a scientist who studies hurricanes and other oceanic storms.

"This is new," the anchor says. "I've been living here my whole life, and, well, I don't want to age myself, but let's just say this hasn't happened in almost half a century."

"That's not accurate," the scientist replies in his needly voice. "Just seven years ago Hurricane Bernard struck the city as a tropical depression and flooded the valley to the north."

"Wait a second," the anchor cuts in peevishly. "That was a splash in the face next to this."

Is the anchor doing a bit or being candid? Dave looks over at his wife for her reaction, but her chin sags like she might vomit. She squeezes the steering wheel and inhales mightily.

"Perhaps that's true," the scientist says quickly, "but there was a far more damaging hurricane in the region in 1912. And there were other such storms throughout the nineteenth century. We like to think of this region as unlikely to be affected by hurricanes, but it's simply not the case."

"Well, I guess you learn something every day," the anchor says in a satisfied-sounding voice. "It's easy to get caught up in the present and lose sight of the big picture. We could all use a history lesson now and then."

The segment ends.

Leslie glares at the radio. "What the shit was that?"

He wants to do something, to say words that make all this better. Looking over his shoulder, he finds Maurice engrossed in his tablet's touchscreen game. Normally the sight of the addictive device makes Dave anxious, but now he's glad it's there. He guesses every generation of parents has a love-hate relationship with some new technology.

A weather map shows the hurricane has moved north of their town, and on social media he sees pictures of the flooding. There are no streets; the yards are gone. In one image he can just make out a roof. He is able to stop himself from crying until he shows Leslie and she bursts into tears.

"It's the end of the world, isn't it?" she says.

"It only feels that way." He runs a finger down the prosthetic arm, thinking of flood stories in the Bible and mythology. "There are people in the world who face this on a regular basis. We're just like them."

Leslie looks at him fiercely. "Fuck that," she says. "You sound like the jackass on the radio."

Dave blushes, angry and hurt. He's said the wrong thing, and Leslie resents him for it. Worse, he resents her for resenting him. She is a shallow person, he thinks. These words have been floating into his head more and more often. He tries to recall when it started, but he can't be sure. Maybe it began with his medical issues. Then again, maybe it was always there. She has long regarded him as a little slow. The difference is she used to think it was cute.

But that's all beside the point. When the fighting started doesn't matter. What matters is that it's happening. It matters because they love each other and have responsibilities. It matters because of Maurice. It matters because Leslie is pregnant with their second child, a daughter whose name they disagree on.

. . . .

DAVE FINDS HIMSELF looking into the dark field of the Tomorrow interface. "What's going on?" he says. "Why are we stopping? We're not there yet."

Safety protocol, the interface says. *Would you like me to proceed? I can perform this function.*

. . . .

AFTER THE delivery, the hospital sends Delia to the NICU. Something is wrong with her heart, and the doctors are doing everything they can to get the little organ to cooperate, but it will never function like a healthy one.

"It's congenital," the pediatric cardiologist says. She has the kindest face Dave thinks he's ever seen. An occupational necessity? he wonders. "Let me be clear. It's not something you could have prevented."

Dave nods at this news, but Leslie refuses to accept it. She stares at the doctor hollowly, groggy with postpartum exhaustion. The birth was difficult, and she's swollen and tender. Strands of her dark hair are pasted to her face.

"There is no history of heart defects in my family," she says with fury that scares Dave a little. He has never seen her like this. "Not in my husband's family, either. Someone must have made a mistake along the line. Someone or something. Maybe it was my husband's disease. They amputated too late. He almost died. I know it's in your charts. He still gets sick sometimes."

The doctor's smile is infinitely wise and sad. "There's no known linkage. I'm very sorry. Neither of you is to blame."

Leslie shakes her head slowly. "I know how to do research," she says. "I've read the studies. There's a lot that needs to be explored. There are vaccines, food additives, pesticides. There are contaminants in the water. We're walking through a literal maze of poisons. A fucking thicket."

"The world can be terrifying," the woman says softly. She is first person Leslie has allowed to hold her hand since the revelations about Delia's heart. "You have my utmost sympathy. The unfairness is crushing."

It's a heavy day. For once, Dave is glad that Maurice has joined the Scouts. This new organization is a bit macho for his taste, a bit nationalistic, a bit promilitary. It's his imagination, most likely, but Dave gets the feeling that the Scout sergeant and the older boys look at him with contempt and might even joke privately about his prosthetic. He gets the feeling they think he's somehow inferior, and he worries the Scout sergeant imposes a frightening politics on his "troops." But what is he supposed to do? Bring Maurice into these impossible discussions about Delia's health? The boy loves camp, the archery and the outdoor challenges. It's good for him to be in the woods, learning to cooperate with others. Besides, wasn't Dave exposed to all kinds of toxic masculinity when he was growing up? His uncles and cousins are racist joke machines, yet he turned out fine.

They take the baby out of the hospital. The city rises around them, thunderous with street noise. Leslie holds the swaddled baby close, refusing to look him in the eye. Staring at the robotic arm, she tells him to bring around the van they left in the parking garage.

Dave knows she dislikes it here, on the crowded sidewalks, among sounds that go on forever, and he looks down the block. A homeless man stands on the corner, shouting aggressively at passing cars. "Are you going to be okay alone?" he says. "Are you sure?"

Now she meets his gaze as she might the eyes of a stranger in a supermarket. "I was okay all those years before I met you, wasn't I?"

. . . .

HE FINDS HIMSELF in the dark. "Why are we stopping?"

Your pain index exceeds the default threshold, the interface tells him. *This is an automatic message.*

"There's more," he says. "Keep going."

I can perform this function.

. . . .

IT IS NOT EASY dating again. He's no longer young, and he struggles to parse the current trends. The women he meets are eager and happy to spend time with him, at least at first, but they are plainly racked with guilt and hangups of their own. He sees how they look at the robotic arm, hears the anxiety behind their questions about his medication. It's not the prosthesis or the pills that rattles them, he thinks, but the specter of old age and infirmity, the reminder of mortality just as they are trying to start over. Naturally, there remains the question of romantic chemistry.

One woman he falls in love with right away. It's torture, gazing across the table as she smiles sadly and plots her escape. She is sorry, her wonderful face tells him, but she is not ready for this. She waves over a waiter and orders a second margarita.

"Might as well make a night of it," she says, her hair falling over her eyes. "Tell me about your ex and your kids. Give me the whole fucking rundown."

He laughs. This is freedom, he supposes, with a horrible sense of having wasted decades. He takes a huge drink of his own margarita— he uses the robotic arm, winking as he does, which makes her laugh— and tells her Leslie left him years ago, after becoming convinced government scientists were to blame for Delia's heart condition. How she met Lou, a chiropractor with similar beliefs, and how they now live in rural Florida, in a concrete house with its own electrical grid and water supply. They regard themselves as having left society, though they still go out for groceries, gas, and, of course, ammunition. Maurice lives with them most of the year. It's the boy's choice. He owns an assortment of guns and altered American flags, and he participates in maneuvers with a militia group in the surrounding swamplands.

"Wow," the woman tells him, resting her chin on her hand. "I don't get a right-wing vibe off of you at all."

Dave grins. "I hope not. That's my son and his mother. I'm not sure what happened there. I guess you can live with people and not really know who they are. That's an old story, right?"

"What about your daughter?"

He hesitates. He rarely gets personal right away and never talks about the person he loves most, but he can sense he's going to tell this woman about Delia, even though they'll only spend this one night together. He knows he'll boast about his brilliant eleven-year-old, the science whiz who lives with him and likes to look at the night sky through her high-powered telescope with her adorable nerdy friends. He'll tell her about his child's heart condition and her internal pacemaker, how he and Delia joke that they are two cyborgs living together in the twenty-first century, a pair of regular Jetsons, and that these jokes are a secret source of reassurance and happiness. He takes a drink and holds the liquor on his tongue until the tastebuds cloud over, aware that after he confides these things, this woman will never call him again, leaving him feeling he's betrayed the most important person in the world.

· · · ·

WHEN HE FINDS himself in the darkness again, he's ready. "Keep going, yes. Yes, I would like you to perform this function."

· · · ·

ALL THIS TIME the weather has been getting hotter. Maurice knows it as well as anyone. The man works along the border, armed with a high-powered rifle and driving a government vehicle. His job is to round up undocumented border-crossers and take them to a holding facility. Now and then he sends a photograph from his phone to prove to Dave and Leslie just what dangerous people these are. It's his way of pushing back against what he calls *the liberal agenda*, *the globalist narrative*, and *the great hoax*, by which he means the countless news reports and footage of the concentration camps along the border where families are being held in squalid and sometimes deadly conditions.

He sends an image of three filthy young men in t-shirts and jeans. They sit on a dusty roadside in the desert, handcuffed and looking unhappily away from the photographer, whom Dave supposes is his son. Out in the road, beyond their reach, a uniformed officer stands guard over the small heap of firearms, ammunition, and pouches of drugs these youths were transporting. The officer's face is red and slick with sweat.

Leslie's text response is almost immediate. THUGS! THANK YOU FOR PROTECTING OUR BORDERS SON! BLESSINGS!

Maurice does not reply to his mother's texts. He almost never sends anything in writing, only photos of what's going on around him. If pressed to write something, he produces a one-word reply, an internet acronym, or an emoji.

Dave refrains from texting back. He knows this message's recipients were chosen to leave him outnumbered, just as he knows Maurice would deny this and say he's simply letting his "people" know what he is doing, that Delia wouldn't want to hear from him anyway. That he only wants to make Dave and Leslie proud. That he, Maurice—though he wouldn't come out and say it—is the real victim here.

Dave has fallen for this setup in the past, with the predictable outcome that Leslie sends cruel and paranoid messages for the next hour, calling him a Nazi and saying he brainwashed their daughter. It is too painful and stupid to go through again, though he's tempted to point out that the three handcuffed men in the picture are clearly very poor, little more than teenagers, and that they would not stand out on any US street. In comparison to the heavily armed man looming over their seized contraband, they appear frail.

He calls Delia instead. Talking to his daughter always cheers him up. She works in the same state as Maurice, as it happens, though she has nothing to do with her older brother or mother and is reluctant to even discuss them. She is a government scientist who analyzes particles from cosmic rays that reach Earth from distant galaxies. This work is difficult for Dave to comprehend, but Delia does her best to simplify it for him, and he appreciates this. She is single and, he suspects, lonely, but she seems committed to living alone until she finds the perfect mate.

"Your brother sent me another photo."

"Gross," she says. "I'm sorry he tortures you. Mom, too. You could cut them off, you know. Then you wouldn't have to bother me at work. Though I'm starting to think that's why you keep in touch with them. To have excuses to bother me. Which I guess is acceptable. But you don't really need an excuse, Dad."

He sighs, thinking of the young men in the road and the countless others in fenced camps. "Those poor kids in the photo," he says. "I guess they have no choice."

"It's genocide," she says. "It's just beginning. It's going to get much worse."

Dave doubts this. "Things always seem to be getting worse," he says. "The end always seems just around the corner. But it never is."

"The world is disappearing," she says. "It's accelerating. We have the evidence."

He tries to change direction, to keep things lighthearted. "Anything out in the skies? Any new planets for us to move to?"

She groans, hates being patronized. "The problem is that the world we live in, the human world, is largely imaginary," she says. "It's an extremely bad copy of the underlying concreteness, but we don't appreciate that. We treat the bad copy like the thing itself. And almost everything we imagine is based on that bad copy, so what we call our ideas or dreams are even worse copies of the extremely bad copy we're all working from. It's a built-in flaw, and it's fine for living in the woods or what have you. But it lets people believe in fantasies, like the one where we could just pack up Earth and move to some other planet."

Dave is quiet for a moment. He doesn't understand what she's told him, not exactly. Finally he decides to say something he thinks sounds smart. He tells her that every generation believes it is facing the apocalypse.

"Those stories are about the survivors," she says. "I'm talking about something else."

. . . .

ONE DAY THE news is full of reports about extraterrestrials. They've always been here, the newspeople say. Dave thinks this is a big deal, but his coworkers shrug it off, saying they knew as much, deep down. Dave is confused. The evidence remains spotty, a few fuzzy films and photographs, recordings so choked with feedback he can't make sense of them and must rely on transcripts compiled by strangers. He still has no idea what these creatures from outer space are supposed to look or sound like. He has no idea how big they are, or what kinds of technology they possess. Are they, like him, enhanced by machines? Or are the visitors all robot—machine emissaries? He wants to be skeptical but feels he is flirting with paranoia. When he calls Leslie against his better judgment, she laughs.

"Of course there are aliens," she says. "Of course you believe now that it's in the mainstream media. You lemming."

There is no point in talking to Maurice about this, and he fears asking Delia, who's surely thought more about the matter than most people. The fact that she's never mentioned space aliens should tell him all he needs to know. Still, he calls.

She answers, but she's preoccupied with a current project. It's hard to get an answer out of her that isn't tinged with irony. Finally, she says, "Dad, there are so many things you'll never be sure of. Like the existence of God. You've never lost sleep over that, have you?"

"No," he admits. She's right. He has long since made peace with the unknowable. Yet this is different, he thinks. There are news articles. Shouldn't the evidence be clearer?

Delia sighs as if they have been arguing about this for years, a signal she's reached the end of her rope with the topic. "Aren't you the person who told me I shouldn't believe everything I read?"

In the end, he hangs up disappointed. He has gained nothing from his search for the truth, not even a connection with his daughter, and while this isn't the first time she's dismissed him, something about this conversation feels especially defeating.

. . . .

HIS SICKNESS COMES and goes. Some days he can't get out of bed. More and more, he's unable to do what's required at work. He asks for a transfer to a less demanding, lower paying, largely ignored office. The request is granted at once, and at the end of the week he boxes up his supplies and personal effects and carts them to a subterranean cubicle in a room occupied by other aging men and women who sit bent at their machines, typing away. In the flickering fluorescent light, their faces look slightly monstrous, which unnerves him. He wishes he'd known about the fluorescent lighting, which he's always detested. He thinks it the one kind of light that is in fact a disguised type of darkness. But now it is too late to go back. He glimpsed his young replacement moving in when he retrieved his last box. A charismatic woman fresh from one of the good universities, she moved with an excitement he has not felt in years. He knows he could not compete with her. He sits at his desk and recalls how, when he made small talk with her, she blushed and stammered and avoided looking at his robotic arm, eager for him to leave. He vaguely remembers being on the other side of such an encounter long ago, when he was just out of school, remembers the pain he felt on behalf of the old-timer he'd dislodged, and also his resistance to feeling it, which is why the memory is so fragile and murky now. He gets caught on this thought about memory, and he sits at his new desk, face frozen in a grimace, sensing a resonating significance he cannot articulate.

. . . .

SOMETIMES HE THINKS he slipped from one dimension into another. He wonders if other worlds exist, parallel to this one, and whether he's gotten lost among them. He suspects this is possible, even commonplace, and the more he considers it, the more persuasive the explanation becomes, and the less certain of he feels of anything else. But no, his arm is proof that he is anchored in this world. Then again, maybe there exist an infinite number of worlds in which a man named Dave who is basically him has a robotic arm. He can only think about this so long before his thoughts turn to mush. The problem is he's been alive too long. He's had too many thoughts.

"Maybe that's it," he says to himself, watching news coverage of a fire that has engulfed the remaining habitable land in eastern Australia. Here is a woman saying that the people have escaped their homes, but nothing else will survive this unprecedented inferno. "It's not the world that changes. It's just you."

. . . .

"NO," HE TELLS the interface, finding himself back in the darkness. "That's not it. There's more. Go on."

. . . .

HIS STINT IN the subterranean office is short-lived. There comes a morning he cannot walk. His feet and joints are too swollen to rotate or bend, and everything under the skin sears constantly, as if it's burning away. The ambulance comes and carts him to a hospital, where he's moved from floor to floor before being put into a room where the doctors and nurses say they expect him to mount a partial recovery. Delia is there throughout, exhausted but tough, giving directions to apathetic nurses, arguing with specialists, shouting at the people in billing, whom she calls *motherfucking criminals*. She no longer works for the government. She has joined an activist group Dave has always associated with environmental terrorism, though she tells him those characterizations are overblown and he shouldn't believe what people say about things they don't understand.

Maurice arrives with his family. He comes in uniform, wearing his gun. He has grown quite thick, and he treats his body like a force of nature, knocking people out of the way when they don't move for him. He is absolutely unapologetic. His hair cut into a flat top, he and stands over Dave without expression. His two sons stand at his sides. They, too, have flat tops, and they wear shirts that declare their support for the Second Amendment.

"They let you in with a gun?" Delia says.

Maurice stares at the younger sister he knows is far smarter. No dummy himself, he has learned to never engage on her terms. "Some people feel safer with a sworn officer around."

She closes her eyes in exhaustion. "You disgust me."

He blinks and replies immediately. "You disgust me. You and all the people like you. It's you extremists who are ruining this country."

Delia opens her eyes and looks down at Dave. "Sorry, Daddy. I can't be around him. It's just as well. Mom and her crazies are coming tonight, so you can have these freaks all in one dose. The nurses all have my number."

Dave is too tired to speak. He smiles a little for her. He wants her to know he still believes in her. That there is nobody else.

. . . .

LESLIE AND HER second husband arrive with their oldest daughter, a seventeen-year-old girl in camo shorts and a tummy shirt. The first thing she does is locate the remote and to turn on the television high up on the wall. She finds a reality program in which married women wearing lots of makeup drink cocktails and complain about how the world has slighted them. She then looks at Maurice's boys and sighs with boredom, and the boys, who are thirteen and fourteen, look back in a worshipful silence. The three of them leave, the girl first, the two boys a moment later, when they have secured Maurice's stern permission to go.

Dave endures the blaring television while his ex-wife and his son converse with one another's spouses and avoid speaking to each other. Leslie talks exuberantly about how *living off the grid*, as she puts it, has contributed to her health and good figure.

"Look at us," she says to Maurice's meekly nodding wife. Her face and arms are dark and leathery. "Strong as bulls! We don't need any of the poison they have in here. They're making him sicker with drugs when they ought to wheel him out into the daylight and treat him with herbs. You can't trust these people."

Over by the wall, Maurice eavesdrops, smirking faintly. He has always taken a pleasure in observing his mother make a fool of herself, though he stopped commenting on it in high school. He is an emotional black box, laughing only occasionally, and unexpectedly, when nothing seems funny. He leans on the wall, big arms crossed, nodding as his stepfather Lou brags about hunting invasive Nile monitor lizards with a modified semiautomatic and barbecuing the animals with their survivalist friends. Maurice clearly doesn't care what the gray ponytailed man has to say. He understands Leslie is the one in charge here and that she simply expects him, the oldest child, to be present. Of everyone in this room, he is the person Dave understands least.

Leslie eventually tires of talking at Maurice's mute wife. She turns on her heel and addresses Dave, raising her voice unnecessarily.

"I can't tell you how much it kills us all to see you like this. But you brought it on yourself. You should have cashed out years ago. You should have stopped taking all that junk medicine while you had a chance. You should have thrown that arm in the ocean. Now the pharmaceutical companies and quacks have your money, and there's nothing Maurice or I can do about it."

At the sound of his name, Maurice turns to the window overlooking the parking lot, as if to distance himself from his mother's valediction.

"We talked about it, and we all agree. Delia's in the best position to nurse you. She doesn't even have a real job anymore. She doesn't have a husband or boyfriend or, who knows, girlfriend. . . ."

Lou bends over and laughs into his fist.

Leslie grins, pleased with his reaction. "I wouldn't be surprised," she says. "But she's made her bed, and she can sleep in it. I just want you to know we all love you, Dave. Always have and always will."

Dave is having difficulty following this speech, and now he sees, with a sense approaching shock, that his ex-wife, whom he hasn't seen in years and wishes would go away now, is sniffing forcefully, as if to draw up tears from some deep reservoir of feeling for him.

"We came up here to say goodbye," she tells him. "I really wish it could have been different. But this was God's plan."

. . . .

CONTRARY TO WHAT the doctors predict, he does not recover. When his health deteriorates to the point where he must choose, he has his consciousness moved into a computer network. It's what everyone seems to be doing, including people he knows. The program is called To-morrow, and the technology requires keeping his body on life support while the mind engages in what's billed as a practically unlimited num-ber of virtual contexts. It's a big deal, a modern wonder, and even Delia, who tends to roll her eyes at these things, says he might as well try it.

"You could always opt out," she says, using the company's euphe-mistic language, though Dave doesn't blame her. How else is his little girl supposed to talk to her dad about this stuff? She frowns at the slick brochure's page of dense fine print. She's doing her best to be strong, trying to convince herself this isn't the end. "Everybody says it's basically the new retirement, only better. Because you can imag-ine whatever you, you know"—here she wrinkles her nose in discom-fort—"you want."

It's true. It is all of that—a second, virtual life. Through Tomorrow's programming, Dave is finally healed. He has both his arms; he is no longer sick; he is young and stronger than he ever was. He's re-united with people he hasn't thought about in years, and he meets new people in various virtual worlds. On beaches and mountaintops and sumptuous yachts, in castles and night clubs and concert halls and countless bedrooms. He has a wide range of virtual experiences, many of them sexual, especially at first. Through these experiences he learns things about others, and he learns things about his own desires, though none of these discoveries is terribly surprising. After all, he's been alive more than seventy years. He's had many thoughts, and he has rarely been afraid of them. When he hears that Leslie and Lou have joined Tomorrow, too, he's amused. It was only a matter of time, he thinks, but he has nobody to enjoy the moment with. In this world, there's nothing lamer than sharing one's petty resentments. Anyway, it's beside the point. By now, he and other first generation Tomorrow users have moved on from rampant virtual sex in all its possible configurations, and he has no contact with his ex-wife or her husband. He supposes they're probably still conspiracy theorists. The Tomorrow technology has a tendency to bolster, rather than correct, such fantastical frames of mind.

He's well aware of that same community in here. It has captured many he knows, inspiring even strongminded people with a hopeful spirituality. There is talk of going full Tomorrow, freeing consciousness to exist in the machine with no monitoring, no guidance, though some worry about the finitude of the resources that keep the machines going. Someone proposes the idea of further detachment, the concept that the spirit might be freed from hardware altogether. It's at this point that Dave loses interest. These hopes are no different from those of his devoutly religious grandparents.

By and by, he comes to see Tomorrow in a new light. It's a scam, he thinks, a new ploy for bleeding old people of their money. He supposes this should have been obvious to him a while ago. Maybe it would have been, had he not still hungered for experience.

Others he knows are figuring it out more and more. They just disappear. Some say goodbye before dropping out, but many don't bother. He understands. What exactly are you supposed to say? There's always an awkward moment, just before you disconnect.

What Dave does know is he's ready. And he'd like to be out of here before Maurice shows up.

. . . .

HE FINDS HIMSELF back in the interface. There is nothing more to remember, nothing he hasn't revisited so many times it would be boring to see it again now. His blissful yet vague childhood. His aimless adolescence. All the time he wasted, the years of existence he frittered away unthinkingly. Of course, he had no compelling alternative.

He does not weep. He's too bored to be sad. All the same, he is afraid, unsure about what will happen when he dies. That never goes away, though he knows it could be no worse than the oblivion beyond the deepest sleep he can imagine.

"Send a message to Delia," he says. "Let her know I've decided to opt out. I would like you to proceed."

The interface confirms the message has been sent with a whooshing sound.

He waits then, confident she'll respond quickly and come to his bedside. Still, he feels anxious, flustered. He wants to have something to tell her, something wise for her take away. *You were right*, he could say. *The apocalypse is always personal. The end of the world is something else. I missed you.*

A soft bell notifies him a message has arrived. *I'm here, Daddy.*

He hesitates, wondering what emergence will be like. Will he be coherent? Probably, but maybe not. He is aware of the risks. They are always there. Nor can he imagine how things will appear out there, how much Delia will have aged, or what qualities of the current year will prove taken for granted by those who still keep track of time and events. But what is the alternative? To wait longer, knowing nothing will happen, for some eventual *then* that will feel the same as this *now*?

"I would like to log out," he says. "I would like to terminate my account."

Maybe, he thinks, it will be like being born. Like surfacing for air after too long underwater. It's a nice idea. But what comforts him is the presence of this person without whom he cannot rightly imagine his own life. Knowing she feels the same way. The knowledge that they existed, against all odds, and that they do. That's it, the thing he's been trying to think to say.

I can perform this function, the interface tells him. *Would you like me to proceed?*

ACKNOWLEDGMENTS

I want to thank Nicola Mason, without whose eye and exceptional editorial talent this book would not exist: I cannot express my gratitude enough. Thanks also to Ben Sandman, who found merit in the original manuscript, and to everybody at Acre for making this book a thing.

I'm grateful to many friends, colleagues, and peers: Morgan Fritz, Andrew Wollard, Neil Prendergast, Thomas Darwish, Nick Chastain, Michael Ambrose, Damien Schlarb, Keith Tuma, Michael Martone, Josh Russell, Tony Grooms, Ray Levy, Lori Ostlund, Amina Gautier, Greg Gerke, James Hoch, Todd Barnes, Erica Bernheim and way too many others to name: You know who you are.

I miss James Reiss and Nancy Zafris, whose help and encouragement I will never forget.

Thanks also to the editors who published these stories individually: Michael Nye at *Story* ("Rest Area"), Ashley Mayne and Rebecca Wolff at *Fence* ("Amontillado"), Anthony Varallo at *Crazyhorse* ("Demonology, or Gratitude"), and David Lazar and Jenn Tatum at *Hotel Amerika* ("The Help Line," previously "Family Secrets").

Finally, thank you to my family, especially my wife Katie and my daughters, Anna and Naomi. I love you.